What revie
V.

2003 EPPIE finalist for Science Fiction novel!

"...Author Jennifer Macaire is ahead of her time in creating this "possible" world for readers and lovers of the futuristic and sci-fi genres."

—Kari, *Loveromances.com*

"This science fiction mystery has a fascinating premise that readers will find pulls them into the story line almost from the start. The characters are well developed and believable, but the star of *Virtual Murder* is Monkey, a mutant with a human heart and soul, who can operate independently of the net. Jennifer Macaire is a talented writer who has found her niche in futuristic mysteries. One hopes that readers haven't seen the last of Monkey."

—Harriet Klausner, *Bookreview.com*

"An incredible sci-fi tale that kept me glued all night long! It reminded me of the old movie "Total Recall" but this novel took the virtual tour idea even further! If this book was made into a movie or television series it would be an instant hit. Recommended to readers who love to game online especially!"

—Debra Fitch, *Huntress Reviews*

"*Virtual Murder* will appeal to Sci-Fi readers, Net fanatics and gamers alike. The story is science fiction, with a bit mystery and government intrigue."

—Brenda Weeaks, *MyShelf.com*

Loose Id®

ISBN 10: 1-59632-152-0
ISBN 13: 978-1-59632-152-6
VIRTUAL MURDER with bonus story A WORLD BETWEEN
Copyright © 2006 by Jennifer Macaire
Cover Art by April Martinez

This book is an original publication of Loose Id®. *Virtual Murder* was previously published as a single title by Novel Books, Inc. A revised and re-edited version was published as a single title in e-book format only by Loose Id®. Each title contained herein is a work of fiction. Any similarity to actual persons, events or existing locations is entirely coincidental.

Printed in the U.S.A. by
Lightning Source, Inc.
1246 Heil Quaker Blvd
La Vergne TN 37086
www.lightningsource.com

Dedication

For my cousin Tony (Professor Betrus) for his real help on everything virtual.

VIRTUAL MURDER

and

A WORLD BETWEEN

Jennifer Macaire

LooseId®

www.loose-id.com

Contents

VIRTUAL MURDER

Chapter One

Where are you off to, lady? For I see you,
You splash in the water there, yet stay stock still in your room.
—Walt Whitman, *Song of Myself*

He had blond hair, bleached almost white by salt water, and turquoise chips for eyes. Dressed in the Virtual Tours uniform of khaki shorts and a white button-down Oxford shirt with the sleeves rolled up, he also wore a whistle around his neck for no other reason than aesthetics. A red bandana flirted insolently out of his back pocket.

He put one hand over his eyes, shading them from the bright sun. With the other, he motioned to the gangplank, calling in a loud voice, "Welcome to Virtual Tours. I'm Mitch, your tour guide for this leg of the voyage. This way, ladies, please watch your step. The boat will be leaving in five minutes. Take your assigned seats. The number on your ticket corresponds to the seat number, clearly indicated on the front of each chair. Can I help you, ma'am? That's right, third seat on the left. You'll have a magnificent view of the island as we cruise by Redhook."

When all the tourists had boarded, he waved to the captain and jumped into the cabin. He strolled down the aisle, making sure everyone was seated. Pausing in front of a woman wearing a red sundress, he flashed a brilliant smile. "Hello, Rhonda. I saw you in the sending room at the tour headquarters. I hope you have a pleasant trip. If there's anything you need, don't hesitate to ask."

Rhonda blushed and leaned over to the woman next to her. "My, isn't he a nice-looking man?"

The woman smiled at her in a conspiratorial manner. "They're all gorgeous! The Virtual Tours Agency goes out of its way to please their clients—in this case overworked career women, like us."

"I still can't get over it. I feel exactly as if I'm sitting on a boat, speaking to you. I can even smell suntan lotion, sea air, and the diesel fuel from the boat's engines. I'm having a hard time believing it's all an illusion!" Rhonda gave an amazed laugh.

"Okay, I'll prove it. What seat are you in?" the woman asked.

"The first seat on the left, window seat, with plenty of leg room and a superb view. Why do you ask? You're sitting right next to me, in the aisle."

"No, dear. I'm sitting in the first seat on the left, next to the window, and you're sitting on the aisle. We both asked for the same seat, and the Virtual Tours gave it to us."

"Well, I'll be! I'm Rhonda, by the way, from Nashville. You must be a regular virtual-traveler. It's my first trip." She smiled nervously.

"My name's Veronique. I'm from Paris. If you have any questions, don't be afraid to ask. I've been doing these trips for three years now, once every six months."

"That's wonderful." Rhonda settled back in her seat. "Oh, look at that view! The sailboats in the harbor, the sunlight sparkling on the waves and the islands in the distance, it's all so romantic. I can't wait to get to Tortola. I'm staying in the Sea Cow Hotel. Are you staying there too?"

"No, I'm going on to Virgin Gorda, but I've been to the Sea Cow. It's wonderful. Ask for the stuffed grouper; it's divine."

"How do they make everything seem so real?" Rhonda asked.

"Everything is real, in a way. Even this boat, the *Bomba Charger,* is an actual ferryboat making its way from St. Thomas to Virgin Gorda, stopping in Tortola. It's extremely sophisticated from what I gather, which is why virtual tourism costs nearly as much as a real trip does."

"'It's a two-week adventure, with all food and drinks included in the deal!'" quoted Rhonda.

"You're getting everything intravenously, chérie, don't forget. And in reality, it only lasts for two days. On your virtual trip, you won't sleep but a few minutes a 'night,' although you'll feel as if it's been a full eight hours. We won't get stiff either; electrodes take care of stimulating our muscles for us while we sleep."

"I know." Rhonda giggled. "I was nervous when they explained that part to me. I hate thinking of my body lying back at the institute, with all those wires and tubes in it. But I always wanted to go to the Caribbean, and this seemed like the perfect plan."

"It's a great idea. Especially for people like me, who work practically non-stop. You cram two weeks into only two days. I feel so refreshed after these trips. I'm even more relaxed and toned than after a real vacation, believe me. The scenery is unspoiled, no waiting in dreary lines, and we can do anything we want from scuba diving to hang-gliding in total security. Our guides take care of our slightest wish."

"Our slightest wish?" Rhonda felt a spark of interest and twisted in her seat to get a better look at the blond man. "Do we get to ask them out on dates?"

"No!" Veronique shook her head emphatically. "You can't even get near them. I've tried, believe me. But they don't let you touch them; it's against Tour rules. It's frustrating, especially at the beach, when they're strolling around in their bathing suits." She sighed. "But there are other people. I've met a few other tourists and even dated one for a while after I got back from the virtual trip."

"You exchanged names and addresses?"

"Of course."

"And he wasn't, you know, disappointed?" Rhonda asked.

"Why?" Veronique sounded amused. "Don't tell me you've chosen a virtual body for your trip?"

Rhonda nodded, reddening. "I'm not as young as this! When the tour operator asked for a photo of me, I sent them one of me in my twenties. I wanted to feel young again. It's amazing what the brain can do. I feel as if I've gone back in time." She hesitated a moment. "Forgive me if I'm being rude, but…is that your real body?"

Veronique shrugged. "Give or take a few pounds, wrinkles and gray hairs. It's true our brains can imagine us young again, but we can't choose a completely different body. It would be impossible to keep up the illusion. As soon as we saw something that captured our attention, we'd change back to the body our brain was familiar with. That's why the tour guides are all so young and handsome in real life, too." She winked. "You'll meet many people on your virtual trip. The trick is learning which ones are real and which are simply computer-generated images. There's nothing as embarrassing as finding out you're flirting with a figment."

"A figment?"

"That's what people created from a computer program are called. Real people's projections are called virtuals."

Rhonda was dismayed. "How can I tell the difference between a figment and a virtual? I thought everyone was based on a real person!"

"Well, figments usually wear white uniforms. The best way to be sure is to ask, but if you don't want to appear rude, just ask if he's been on many trips before. A figment will reply that he's part of the program."

"I can't thank you enough for your advice," Rhonda said. "Can you touch someone in this, um, world?"

"Of course. Try, touch my arm!" Veronique grinned, patting her arm.

Rhonda reached over and touched her forearm. She could feel everything—the woman's skin, her gold bracelet and even the fine hairs on her arm. "Amazing," she murmured. "How do they do it?"

"Sensor devices, implants. It's all done through the brain, all highly sophisticated. You'll taste the food, feel the sand on the beach, splash in the ocean and burn in the hot sun. The only thing that isn't the same is making love." Veronique lowered her voice. "As you probably have heard, it's a Net prohibition. It's about as exciting as filing your nails."

"Oh, of course I heard. But I didn't come on the vacation for that." Rhonda blushed. "I wanted sight-seeing and relaxation. Look, we're almost there!" Rhonda craned her neck, pointing out the window. "Isn't it beautiful?"

"That's Tortola, a British Virgin Island. Is your passport in order?"

Rhonda drew it out of her purse and flipped it open. "Look, isn't that funny? It even has a picture of my virtual self."

"We're docking now. This is your stop. Have a great time, Rhonda."

"Thank you. I will." Rhonda made her way off the boat, down the gangplank and onto a cement dock. Three other tourists were waiting there, suitcases at their feet. Rhonda had a small duffel bag slung over her shoulder. The sun was scorching, and she was glad she'd brought a wide-brimmed hat.

The handsome tour guide waved to them from the boat. "Go to the end of the docks and pass customs. Your new guide will be waiting on the other side. His name's Arthur and he'll be in charge of you for the rest of your trip."

Rhonda turned to the woman next to her and sighed. "I wish he was staying with us."

The woman picked up her bag. "I'm sure the next one will be just as charming. Shall we go? I'm looking forward to a nice, cold piña colada."

The group made their way to the end of the quay, carrying their luggage, wilting a bit in the blinding heat. Small waves clapped against the sides of the pier. The water was so clear it was like glass. Black, spiky sea urchins and pink snails spotted the seabed, and barnacles encrusted the tall, wooden posts holding up the cement pier. Schools of tiny, silver fish flashed as they darted about. The smell of seawater, fish and the tar that covered the posts was amplified by the hot sun. Rhonda narrowed her eyes against the dazzle. She would have to buy sunglasses in town.

Once past customs, a man wearing the Virtual Tours uniform met the little group. Introducing himself with a bright smile as Arthur, he gallantly took their luggage, leading them to a white Jeep with the words 'Virtual Tours' painted on it in bright pink. He settled the women into the Jeep and climbed in, apologizing for the hot seats.

"There's no shade in the parking lot, but once we get moving the breeze will cool you off."

They drove on the left-hand side, as befitting an ex-British colony. The narrow road wound around the mountainside, climbing higher as they left the docks and headed inland. They drove past a small village where shops flaunted bright dresses, shell necklaces and leather goods. Natives sat in wicker rocking chairs on their porches, fanning themselves and waving in a friendly fashion at the tourists. Goats grazed in the shade between the buildings, and white chickens scratched about in the red dust road. Fuchsia bougainvillea grew in profusion, clambering boisterously over crumbling stone walls and the brightly painted wooden houses. The tin-roofed houses were painted sugar-candy pink, red, yellow or robin's egg blue.

Rhonda was seated in the front, right next to Arthur. As they climbed higher, she had a splendid view of the village nestled cozily in a deep harbor. "What's the name of that town?" she asked, pointing.

"Roadtown. It's the main town here in Tortola. The hotel is on the east end, on Sea Cow Bay. We have a private beach with wonderful snorkeling. If you wish, a bus leaves twice a day to town so you can go sightseeing or shopping." He glanced over his shoulder. "A few words of advice, ladies. All the goods you see in the stores are existing objects, duplicated and delivered to your home after the vacation. Your credit card will be debited for all purchases, so buy only things you want to take home with you." He drove expertly up the steep mountain. The road twisted and climbed so violently at times that Rhonda was obliged to brace her feet against the floorboards and hold tightly to the seat.

"Don't worry." Arthur glanced at her white knuckles and grinned. "I'm used to this road, and there's hardly ever any traffic."

Rhonda nodded thankfully and gazed at the houses, now as tiny as dollhouses, below. The water sparkled in the harbor where sailboats and fishing boats were anchored. Flamboyant trees spread their huge branches covered in scarlet blooms. Flocks of green parakeets flew among the trees, and tamarind trees waved feathery fronds in the nearly constant Trade Winds. Spiky century plants and prickly 'monkey-puzzle' trees grew on the steep slopes. Where the dirt showed through it was bright red, like a raw wound in the earth. Along the seacoast, black volcanic boulders made a striking visual contrast to white coral beaches and peacock-colored water.

The air was torrid. It was noon, and the sun blazed overhead. Rhonda's head nodded and she dozed off; the heat pounding through the canvas roof of the Jeep sapped her energy.

She woke with a jerk to the feel of sweat trickling down her neck, between her breasts, and tickling her skin. She plucked at her shirt, lifting her heavy hair off her neck and sighing in relief as the breeze touched her damp skin. In her virtual body, she felt as if her senses were magnified. Everything seemed brighter and stronger. She blinked and shook her head.

"It'll be cooler by the sea." Arthur nodded towards the blue expanse of water visible between two tall mountaintops. "We'll be there in half an hour."

All at once, no matter how she tried, she couldn't stay awake. She felt her eyelids getting heavy, and although she tried to speak, she couldn't. In an instant, Rhonda fell asleep and her mind slipped away. A minute later, her eyes reopened. She blinked and focused on the man next to her.

His voice was deep and warm, and when he spoke, she had the impression they were alone together. She stole a glance at the man sitting so close to her. She could feel his hand brushing her thigh when he shifted gears, and she wondered if he was doing it on purpose.

He was looking at her from the corner of his eye. She smiled to herself. The body she'd chosen was so ripe, so voluptuous, it was like a heavy fruit just begging to be picked. Her fingers trailed sensually down her chest, tracing the unfamiliar line of bony collarbone and the swell of exquisitely soft breasts. Her breathing quickened. It must be the heat that made her respond like this. It was overwhelming. The air was so hot she could feel it as a constant caress.

She looked at the man again and noticed he was sweating. A bead of perspiration trickled down his temple, over his cheek, down his neck to disappear into his shirt. She wanted to lick it away. Could the feeling growing in her body be love? It felt as if her blood were getting thicker, as if her limbs were too heavy for her. She wanted to lie down, stretch her arms above her head, arch her back, and spread her thighs wide open. A sharp pang in her belly made her moan softly. Was that love? She had never felt as completely real as in this virtual body. She felt her whole attention concentrated on one person, as if her personality suddenly distilled, and the drop of her that was left absorbed into the man right next to her.

Her eyes slid once more in his direction. He was beautiful. His wavy chestnut hair was tousled from the wind, and his bright, hazel eyes were nearly the color of amber. He had a deep, even tan on his muscular arms, and his lashes were very long. She yearned to feel those arms around her and have his lashes tickle her hot skin. He was driving with an expression of fierce concentration on his angular face.

The road twisted and climbed steeply. "What's your name?" she asked, her voice husky.

The man smiled. "Arthur, ma'am."

She whispered his name, her tongue trying it out, letting it slip between her teeth. He glanced at her, and she felt the weight of his look like a hot touch. Amber eyes made his gaze burn. Was she falling in love with his wide shoulders and narrow hips? Was that why her legs longed to wrap themselves around his lithe waist and draw him into her? The thought was so evocative she felt her head spin. She closed her eyes, leaned her head back and opened her mouth wide, drawing in deep gulps of air. Oh God, this heat!

"Are you all right?" Arthur asked her, concern in his deep voice.

She opened her eyes and licked dry lips. "I never thought it would be so hot. I suppose I expected something more, well, lush."

"It's greener during the fall, when the rainy season comes. It's April now. We're heading into the dry season, and the heat leaches the moisture out of the air. Most folks don't know that these islands are truly desert islands, with little or no source of water. Take care when you shower. Wet yourself, turn off the water, lather your skin, and shampoo. Then turn the water back on to rinse. The same goes for brushing teeth and flushing toilets." Arthur raised his voice so that the other tourists could hear him. "In this land of sun and fun, we never flush for number one," he quoted. "I hope you all know what that means?"

"I thought that this was a virtual trip. I mean, we can do as we like, can't we?" a woman, asked, leaning forward.

"We'd like everyone to enjoy themselves exactly as if they were truly traveling," Arthur's voice was laced with a hint of impatience. "If you thought you could do anything, I invite you to try jumping out of the Jeep or off a cliff. Your experience will be quite the same as a real accident. You'll feel pain, and if your limbs break, you'll feel that too. Back in the institute, you'll wake up screaming with a whole team of psychiatrists ready to analyze your antisocial behavior."

"I understand." The woman gave a weak attempt at laughter. "I didn't mean to insult your tour company. You're doing an excellent job."

Arthur looked into his rearview mirror and flashed a charming smile. "I try my best. And that's why I want you all to have the best possible time. Tonight there's going to be a live band at the hotel; I hope you'll all feel rested enough to come and dance the night away. If I can give any advice, it will be to lie down as soon as you reach the hotel and nap for a couple hours. Then go for an evening swim at the beach. The water will be calm, and you'll feel refreshed. Afterwards take a quick shower, put on a light robe, and join us for dinner. It's an Italian buffet tonight."

Arthur pulled around a corner and stopped in front of a low, perfectly kept bungalow. Three men in white uniforms trotted out to collect the suitcases. He stepped out of the Jeep and opened the door with a flourish. "Here we are, ladies!"

* * *

Steel-drum music woke him out of a sound sleep. Arthur stretched, yawned, and glanced at his watch. Almost seven—he'd better get moving or he'd be late for dinner. He sat on the edge of his bed and rubbed his face. His room was spacious, with a screen door leading outside to a thatch-roofed veranda where he had his breakfast. He loved to sip his coffee while watching the sun rise over the ocean. Tonight there was a gorgeous sunset, and the water was deep indigo with a bright, orange swath reflecting the setting sun.

He shrugged out of his shorts and headed towards the bathroom for a quick shower. His head felt a bit muzzy, as it often did after an afternoon nap. He wondered if the computer programmer could correct this. He would have to speak to Digby about that.

He opened the bathroom door and paused. The sound of his doorknob turning made him look back over his shoulder towards his room. No one ever came into his room, except room service in the morning. He grabbed a towel and held it around his hips as the door swung open and a woman entered. He recognized her from the group he'd picked up that day. She'd washed her hair, and it hung in dark ringlets around her narrow face. Her skin was pale, faintly flushed, and her hands were trembling on the doorway. Her eyes were huge in her face, almost terrified.

He opened his mouth, to speak, but she raised her finger to her lips. "Don't say anything. They're listening."

Her face was so pale, her eyes so troubled, that he was caught off balance. "I don't..."

"Hush." She walked towards him across the wooden floor, her bare feet making no sound. A lavender silk sarong swirled like cool water around her long legs. Behind her ear was an exotic scarlet hibiscus, the same color as her full lips. She smiled tremulously. Her lips moved. "Arthur," she breathed.

"I don't think..." He backed away from her but stopped when his legs hit the coffee table in front of his wicker couch. "You're not allowed in here," he said weakly. Her hands were running up and down his bare chest; she hadn't stopped gazing into his eyes. There was something bewitching about her, something troubling. "Who are you?" he whispered, as his towel dropped to the floor.

"Shhh," she begged and laid her head on his shoulder. "Just hold me, please?"

His arms encircled her slender shoulders. Her skin was smooth, satiny, and scented with tuberose. Her hair tickled his neck and chest. His arms tightened. Her body was vibrating, as if an electrical current were running through it. Arthur tried to gather his thoughts, formulate words, but his mouth was dry, and he found himself pulling the woman towards his wide, white bed. A heat of desire was building within him so strongly it was like fingers reaching into his skull. The fingers danced downwards towards the very center of his being and set him afire.

This isn't right, he thought, as his breath grew ragged. *You can't experience arousal on the Net.* He felt as if his head were full of helium. Thoughts came and went, faster and faster as erotic images flashed through his mind. He was so stiff it was painful, and the only thing he wanted was release. He fell backwards onto his bed, harsh groans escaping his lips. Waves of electric, tingling pleasure paralyzed him, and he could only arch his back and shudder.

"Oh... my... Lord..." he gasped and closed his eyes. A frantic pulsing began in his groin. Ecstasy, he was swirling through ecstasy. He rolled over, heaving his body over the woman and thrusting into her. Excitement such as he'd never known seemed to explode in him. His breathing grew faster, his heart pounded, and still a powerful frenzy of sexual stimulation overpowered him. He ejaculated and then hardened again, and it went on and on, never slaking the incredible hunger he felt for his partner. She was a sexual vampire, devouring his entire virtual being, and he was helpless to do anything but thrust and strain towards unattainable fulfillment. Towards ecstasy.

I'm being eaten alive, was his last, incredulous thought.

Chapter Two

All truths wait in all things,
They neither hasten their own delivery nor resist it...
—Walt Whitman, *Song of Myself*

"Hello, Virtual Tours, Sally speaking. Oh, good morning, Ms. Girt. No, I just arrived. What can I do for you?" Sally's hands were free; the phone was simply a wire headset. As she talked she switched on her computer monitor, flipped open her Rolodex, grabbed the morning mail from its tray and started slitting envelopes with a silver letter opener in the shape of a palm tree.

"Sally, listen carefully. We have a problem."

Sally put the letter opener down and leaned over her desk. "What is it?" she asked, conscious that her heart was suddenly beating very hard. "Is it Mitch?"

"Who? No, no dear, it's not your fiancé." Andrea took a deep breath. "It's Arthur. Something very strange has happened, and I want you to contact Jonathon and tell him he has to join the tour. I know it's not ordinary procedure, but we can't leave the tourists without a tour guide."

"What happened to Arthur?"

Andrea seemed to hesitate. "He's dead. I…I can't tell you any more. I don't know all the details. Call Jonathon and get him over to the Virtual Tour sending room right away. I've called the Net Government and the police; I'll let everyone know what happened as soon as I know myself."

Sally sat for a second, stunned, after Andrea disconnected. Then she grabbed her Rolodex and found Jonathon's number, dialing with shaking fingers. He was home and none too thrilled to be called back to work so soon after his last trip. When she told him about Arthur there was a deep silence. Then he said, "And she didn't tell you how he died?"

"No, she said she'd let us know when she found out. I don't think she knew. She sounded so strange, Jon, as if she'd been hit in the stomach."

"All right, I'm leaving right now. Call Digby and tell him I'll be there in three hours. There's a train at nine; I'll be in the city by eleven. Sorry, I can't do any better than that."

Afterwards Sally dialed another number, gnawing on her nails. "Digby? It's Sally. What's going on?"

"Sally! Did Ms. Girt call you? Is Jonathon on his way?"

"He is. He'll be there by noon. Tell me what's happening, Digby, please."

"We're going to have the tourists sleep a bit longer, to cover the guide's disappearance; until then, we have a figment taking over. We'll make up lost time with a nighttime cruise around the island."

"No, I mean, what happened to Arthur?" Sally's composure slipped and her voice rose.

"Take it easy, Sally. I'll tell you what I know." There was a slight pause. "He died of a heart attack. I don't know how it happened. Suddenly the buzzers started ringing. His body was convulsing so we unplugged him, but his heart had stopped beating. We tried everything. The emergency medical team was right there, I swear, Sally, they were right there as they always are, but they couldn't do a thing."

"I don't believe it."

"It's true, I swear. A heart attack. Who'd have believed it? He was so young, only twenty-seven. But do you know what? He died with a huge smile on his face. It was the weirdest thing, and…" His voice trailed off and he cleared his throat.

"And what, Digby?"

"Nothing." Digby sounded nervous. "I've got to go, Sally."

"How's Mitch?" Her voice was strained.

"He's fine. Your fiancé is resting comfortably. Please, don't worry. He'll return tomorrow morning; you'll see him then."

"All these euphemisms! Returning, resting…can't you just say he's in suspended animation and we'll revive him tomorrow?"

"Sally, I really have to go." Digby sounded pained. "I'll talk to you later."

"Yeah, later." Sally hung up and looked bleakly at her desk. "Oh, Arthur," she murmured. "You poor, gorgeous boy."

She should have gotten back to work. There was no reason to leave her desk, but she had to see Mitch for herself. She got up, smoothed her curls, and took the elevator to the first sending room, where the tour guides lay in suspended animation. Inside the glass-paneled office, she saw Digby. He was standing still, his arms waving in the air, his head hidden in a round, black helmet. A thin shunt wire ran from the helmet to the computer console. Digby moved in slow motion, like an underwater conductor, and he was chanting what sounded like a litany. Sally crept closer to listen.

"...Jeep engine starting. Map two. Roadtown in Tortola. Sounds now. Jeep gunning over hill. Goat bleating. No, nothing out of the ordinary. Cut to scene thirteen. View of harbor. Flock of parakeets. Okay, all that seems to be fine." Digby ducked his head a bit. "Cut to scene fifteen. Arrival. Sounds. Door opening. Three figments are activated to carry luggage. Footsteps on gravel..."

Sally tapped his shoulder, making him jump. "What are you doing?"

Digby lifted the helmet just high enough to glare at her. "I told you I'd talk to you later!"

"Digby, please. I need to know more. Can you just tell me if you've found anything?"

Digby sighed and pulled off the helmet. "I'm checking the past three hours in the sequence experienced by our virts and figments. Maybe one of them saw Arthur during that time and I can find out if he was acting strangely."

"Did you notice anything different? Was everything normal in Mitch's part of the tour?"

"Everything is fine, Sally. He's fine. I've got to get back to work." Digby replaced his helmet. All she could see was his mouth, drawn in a frown of concentration.

Sally drifted over to the plate-glass window and watched the three bodies behind it lying motionless on reclining chairs.

Attached to their arms, legs and hands were electrodes for muscle stimulation so that no muscle tone was lost in the two days of enforced sleep. Intravenous lines trailed from their left forearms. Their heads were covered with the same sort of bowling ball helmet that Digby wore, only theirs were even larger and nearly hid their mouths. These were the tour guides.

The empty chair where Arthur had been was the only sign of the drama that had occurred that morning. The guides were plugged into the machine generating their part of the program. The room was white, with a white, tiled floor and silver-plated machinery lining the walls. Behind the far wall were the tourists in another, more colorful, comfortable room. Their surroundings were not as stark—they were on vacation.

Sally studied the man in the end chair: Mitch, her fiancé. She hated coming to this room; seeing him lying so still was like watching him in a coma. He wasn't sleeping, yet nothing except unplugging him from the system could wake him up. He wasn't dead; the glowing green lines on the screen above him rose and fell with his heartbeat and respiration. His brainwaves darted up and down—normal activity—and every once in a while his hands would clench or he'd even laugh. Small, physical signs of what was going on in his brain. He was living a virtual life, right down to the mundane activities of eating and sleeping.

Sally turned away from the window and watched Digby, who hadn't moved. His mouth was halfway open and he held his hands out in front of him like a sleepwalker. Black gloves, connected by electrodes and fine wires to a gleaming console, were his commands to a world that she had never seen. A virtual paradise created by technicians for people too busy to go on a real trip.

There was something obscene about the whole idea. Sally rubbed goose bumps on her arms and took a deep breath. She wasn't usually so negative. In the beginning she'd been enthusiastic, thrilled to get the job as secretary-receptionist for the company. When she'd started working here, Andrea Girt had seemed a visionary, someone whose dream was bigger than life. Now, Sally had to clench her teeth in order to approach the virtuals, or 'virts' as Digby called them, as they lay sleeping.

Another thing that bothered her was all those euphemisms. Sleeping, resting, 'virts,' figments, tripping, and...what did Digby call inanimate objects? Oh yeah, the inams. He was always making up new words. Half the time Sally had no idea what he was talking about. He was probably part mutant, and thinking that, Sally shuddered. Mutants were an urban legend; everyone knew that. The Net Government protested that mutants were in fact a myth, but rumors about their existence still made headlines whenever something went wrong on the Net.

Digby made a funny sound, and Sally frowned at him. A bright, slender thread of drool hung from his open mouth. She sighed. He looked like one of those genius kids you laughed at in cartoons, only Digby was real. He was a bona-fide Virtual Tour computer-programming technician, the very thing Mitch dreamed of being when he wasn't acting the part of a virtual tour guide in paradise. When he wasn't working, in computer class or with her, Mitch hung out with Digby, going over transcripts, writing new programs. They could spend hours talking together about computers, programs or the Net.

Sally grimaced and looked at her watch. It was nearly noon. Jonathon should be here any minute now. She was waiting until he came. Then maybe she'd hear more about what happened to

Arthur. Digby had refused to answer any more of her questions and Andrea was still up in her office on the second floor—with three police officers, a coroner, and a representative from the Net.

* * *

Andrea Girt didn't show the slightest outward manifestation of the seething caldron of nerves beneath her calm exterior. The only hint of her turmoil was the steady tap, tap, tap of her cherry red nail against the serpentine pencil holder.

Typical, that the Net Government would send someone right away. Ms. Andrews had the palest eyes Andrea had ever seen, and her platinum blonde hair was pulled back in a strict bun. She sat in the middle chair in front of the three standing police officers. To the left was the coroner holding a sheaf of papers on his lap. The Net Rep wore an expensive suit, and the ring on her finger was set with a diamond. It was a small, tasteful diamond, but it sparkled with all the icy fire of a perfect gemstone and was doubtless worth a fortune.

Andrea dragged her eyes from the stone and smiled at the occupants of the room. "My expert, Mr. Daniel Glover Brims, will be finished in a few minutes, and he'll make his report directly to the police. I believe you've met him, Ms. Andrews." The Net Rep shifted her pale eyes a fraction but did not reply.

Andrea continued, directing her comment at the coroner. "I certainly appreciate your coming back with the report on Arthur Kenner's death. It was a shock, but knowing that it couldn't have been foreseen or anticipated is a slight consolation." Andrea smiled again but no one smiled back.

Biting the inside of her cheek, she stood, intending to see them all out of her office.

They all left except the Net Rep. When they were alone, the woman said, "You realize, of course, that this is not to be publicized in any way."

Andrea felt a small muscle start to twitch in her jaw. "I don't think you have the authority to give me orders," she said quietly.

"I think I do. You mentioned stopping the tour. I can't let that happen at this time. I represent the Net, and I take orders only from two people: President Megalot and Frank Dinde, chief of security."

"I realize your dilemma, but I want to stop the tour because Mr. Glover Brims doesn't know what happened. It could be a malfunction from within the program!"

Ms. Andrews shook her head. "Impossible. It's no such thing. A heart attack. You heard the coroner." Her voice softened. "Let's talk about your company. I've been fascinated with you ever since I read about you in *Newsweek.* Virtual Tours is a huge success. Can you tell me a bit about the new tour? I haven't had time to go on it."

Andrea nodded. "Usually, in a computer world, the more precise the parameters are the more limited the range of movement can be. Instead of a whole town, for example, you would only have an incredibly complex house. Virtual voyagers go much further. For once, you are entirely submerged in a virtual world, which is so real, so huge, it's nearly impossible to perceive the difference between the real world and the Virtual Tour. On our tours, two days become two weeks. You can taste and feel just as if you were in the real world. My tour is the first of its kind, but I imagine the Net will be developing others."

"They won't be ready for another year or so. There are lists years long of people waiting to go on your Virtual Tour." Ms. Andrews narrowed her pale eyes. "If the tours stop, we'll be set back millions of dollars."

"Arthur was a good friend." Andrea's voice broke for the first time that day.

"I'm sorry." For a split second, Ms. Andrews appeared touched by Andrea's emotional outburst. Then her expression hardened. "Your judgment is clouded. The tours must continue, and there is to be no mention of this in the news or in the next press meeting. These are my orders. You'll do well to follow them." The Net Rep stood up and waited until Andrea finally nodded. Then she strode out of the office, shutting the door quietly behind her.

Andrea collapsed at her desk and buzzed Sally. What she needed was a nice, strong cup of coffee. What she'd get was a rather odd brew made from South American herbs. It was called maté, and it was the newest rage. Maté was refreshing, low calorie, all natural, and supposedly bursting with many vitally important nutrients and vitamins for your health. It was also caffeine free. Andrea wanted lots of caffeine right now.

Sally came up. "Did you need anything?"

"Is there any coffee left in the building?" Andrea pressed a shaking hand to her forehead. She'd give half her fortune for a strong cappuccino with black chocolate shaved over it right now.

Sally shook her head. "Sorry."

"Go to Pierre's Café on the corner and get me a cup of black coffee. Make that two cups. No, you'd better get a thermos full, all right?"

"Of course." Sally hesitated a minute, as if she wanted to ask something. Instead, she gave Andrea a sympathetic smile and left.

Andrea sighed and leaned back into her soft, leather chair. Sally was perfect. With her unassuming manner and efficient ways, she was exactly the right receptionist for the business.

She peered through the window down at the reception room below. To the people waiting, it looked like a huge mosaic representing a churning sea, but it was a clever window, letting Andrea spy on those below. Not that she could hear what they were saying. The window was more for security reasons than for spying. She always let everyone know about it, so there were never more than a couple curious glances upwards. Right now, she saw the police officers speaking to Digby and the coroner talking earnestly to the Net Rep. Sally appeared and everyone followed her with their eyes until she'd disappeared into the hallway.

Andrea's nails tap, tap, tapped against the marble desktop. It was only after Sally had been working for her a month that she'd realized whom she reminded her of: Betty Boop. She had huge, saucer-shaped eyes, so soft they looked like brown velvet, and a sleek cap of glossy curls. Her mouth was always a bit pursed—not with a pout, but more of a pensive expression. She was very curvy and only about five feet tall. But her fingernails were a disaster, chewed to the quick, polish chipping. You could be sure that if Sally did her nails she'd shut her hand in a drawer a moment later.

Andrea gazed at her own impeccable nails. What difference did it make? Sally had a fiancé, and she had no one. Andrea's boyfriends were like flashes of lightning in a stormy sky: bright, dazzling...and fleeting.

Sally and Mitch were engaged, and Sally wore a small diamond band on her left ring finger. A tiny stab of jealousy surprised Andrea. She'd never wanted to get married. Why think of engagements and wedding rings now?

Sally entered, carrying the coffee thermos and a mug on an enameled tray. She set it down on the desk and asked if she needed anything else. When Andrea shook her head, Sally left with a little wave of her hand, the halogen light above the doorway making her diamond ring flash.

Andrea would give her eye-teeth for an engagement ring. Just her eye-teeth, however, not her soul, her company, her wardrobe, or even her King Charles spaniel. The dog had been her mother's, bequeathed to her on her mother's deathbed.

A diamond would look good on my hand, Andrea thought. But men were such fools. All of them were fools. It was no use trying to imagine one not being a total idiot, locked in some futile power struggle with the world. Power struggles with Andrea usually ended up with Andrea the winner and single once more.

Beneath Andrea's desk, in a small, wicker doggy-bed from France, Cocotte, the spaniel, twitched restlessly as she dreamed, her silken ears trailing over the sides of the bed and onto the floor.

* * *

At that moment, Sally raised her eyes toward the magnificent mosaic on the wall. The mosaic was beautiful, but that was not why she stared at it. She was trying to imagine what Andrea was doing at that moment. What was it like to be one of the wealthiest, most powerful women in the country?

Then the telephone rang, interrupting her reverie. She answered mechanically, her eyes still on the brightly colored chips of glass, which formed blue waves breaking over a rocky shore.

"Virtual Tours. Yes, I'll put you through right away." She buzzed Andrea's private phone, wondering why Andrea had her boyfriends call her through reception when she had a private line.

There was much to wonder about in Andrea's life. Her mother had been philanthropic, giving away all her immense fortune and leaving none for her daughter. Andrea had founded Virtual Tours, and now it was the third biggest company on the World Stock Market. The Virtual Tours building took up an entire city block in New York City, and the number of tourists willing to pay between ten and twenty thousand dollars for a Virtual Tour doubled nearly every month. There were hardly enough reclining seats for all the tourists now. Three hundred had grown to five hundred, then a thousand, and now there was talk of opening another center in Texas.

One could never call Andrea Girt beautiful; beauty was too soft a word for Andrea's rangy looks. She was tall, nearly six feet five, and her face was all cheekbones and sharp angles. Her eyes were a deep, smoky gray. Her thick brows arched like black wings across a wide brow. Her hair was a true auburn, so deep it had purple highlights. Her photos appeared in gossip columns as she dated polo players, playboys, helium tycoons, racecar drivers, the son of her lawyer, and lately, a senator from the Net Government. The Net senator was on the phone now, and from the tone of his voice, he hadn't called to ask her out on a date. It was probably about Arthur's death, and Sally wished she could listen in on the conversation. It would be so easy—just push the little button on the console, and she could hear the voices in her headset. Then she would find out exactly what was going on.

The three police officers were easy to explain, and so was the coroner, but why was the representative for the Net Government here so soon? Usually you had to call them weeks in advance, beg them to come, bribe them, practically, and you were lucky if they showed up three hours late. This woman had come right on the heels of the coroner and, most fascinating of all, was sitting in the reception like any other common mortal. Net Reps never sat in waiting rooms. *Ever.* This was an unusual circumstance, and Sally was dying to know about it. She gnawed her fingernails until she realized what she was doing. With an exclamation of annoyance, she slammed her hands on the desk. The coroner and the three police officers jumped. The Net Rep didn't even blink her pale eyes.

"Excuse me." She busied herself on her computer with the list of tourists. As she worked, she muttered angrily to herself, "Stop biting your nails, sit up straight, don't put your elbows on the table, and stop swearing."

There was a sharp buzz from the clock on her desk, and she slapped her keyboard into a drawer, closing it with a bang that made the police officers flinch again.

"Sorry." Sally gave an apologetic smile to the police officers, stood, and shoved her chair under her desk. It was lunchtime.

* * *

It was low tide. The sun and the moon were on opposite sides of the earth, and the resulting pull flattened the great bodies of water at the equator. Waves were tiny kitten licks on the soft, white sand, lapping at the beach. Standing knee-deep in water the color of pure aquamarine gems, Mitch held his silver whistle loosely in one hand, tossing it to the end of its string then catching it. He did it automatically. His thoughts were far away, far from the pristine beach where two of his charges snorkeled over the reef, a hundred feet from shore.

Behind him, two other women lay on lounge chairs gossiping lazily, frosty glasses of strawberry daiquiris in their hands. Occasionally, they would break off and look at Mitch from beneath lowered eyelashes while they pretended to drink. He knew that in their minds they were peeling off his swimming trunks and running their hands over his body. Mitch pretended not to notice. He was immune to the lusty glances women threw his way. They'd been chasing him since he was a teenager, looking at him with cool, calculating eyes and darting the tips of their tongues to their lips. At first he'd been embarrassed, then shocked, then annoyed and finally resigned. It still irritated him, but he'd learned to hide his annoyance behind a wide, beguiling smile. His eyes, very pale blue, could become icy cold, but he could keep his smile warm and inviting.

He thought of Sally, and a smile—one that reached his eyes—tugged the corners of his generous mouth. She excited him as no other woman could ever hope to, and she did it with just a long, languorous look from her velvet eyes. She would gaze at him a certain way, and no matter where he was or what mood he was in, he'd blush and get hard. He'd think of the first time he'd seen her naked, the first time his hands touched her soft skin, and the first time they'd made love, and his head would get light and seem to float off his shoulders.

He was crazy about Sally, and even if he lived to be a hundred years old, he'd still get a hard-on just thinking about her walking naked across his room, her breasts bouncing with each step, hips swaying, her delicate curls beckoning him from the point of her saucy triangle. Even after five years, he still desired her with a fierceness that stunned him sometimes. Not here, however, not in this world. He glanced down at his swimsuit and shook his head wryly. In the virtual world, he was practically numb from the waist to the knees. Everyone was. It was a quirk of the program to keep the Net from becoming a den of virtual iniquity. If people had been able to have virtual sex, absenteeism at work would probably have brought the economy to a crashing halt, Mitch thought with a grin.

"Mitch!" one of his charges called. He turned, a ready smile on his face. "Why don't you come sit down with us?"

"Of course!" Mitch glanced once more at the women snorkeling and then walked across the sand to the cool shade offered by the coconut palm trees. He pulled up a lounge chair and sat by the ladies. "How is everything?" he asked.

"Almost perfect," the blonde woman said.

Mitch raised his eyebrows. "What's the matter, Flora?"

She ran her tongue along her lips. "What I'd really like to do is engage in some virtual sports."

"We have water-skiing, hang-gliding and scuba diving, if you'd..."

"No, silly." Flora interrupted him by putting her hand on his arm. She batted her eyelashes playfully. "Not sport sports...something more romantic. You know what I mean."

Mitch did. Every tour was the same. He had his speech down by heart. "Well, ladies, I know this is going to come as a disappointment, but the Net decided to retain the sexual stimulation restrictions in our Virtual Tour. The Net

Government is a nervous beast with far-reaching arms and eyes everywhere."

"We know that." The other woman spoke up for the first time. "I work for the Washington Post. I can tell you everything about the Net. Its wealth is based on the quality of its communication services, the scientific discoveries it made available to the public, and from the games it invented. People pay to experience all the things they always wanted to try but are too chicken to do in real life: parachuting, scuba diving, rafting the rapids or even just going on an incredible ride on a roller coaster on another planet. The president, Wilbur Megalot, is the richest man on earth."

"Right," Mitch agreed. "So, with all those millions, Wilbur did studies and found that sex was still too dangerous to have on the Net, even on a complete sensory experience like Virtual Tours."

"So, what you're saying is that if we try to have sex in this program, we'll get arrested?" Flora asked.

"No, nothing so dramatic. It's just useless to try. You can try to excite yourself all you want—it won't work. Go ahead, think of something sexy."

Flora closed her eyes. At first, she smiled, but then her eyebrows drew together as her look of concentration deepened. She opened her eyes. "Nothing. Absolutely nothing." She looked at the other woman. "You try it, Dana."

"I already have. My husband and I went on the Virtual Tour last winter. I thought it would be a romantic second honeymoon. What we got was parachuting and scuba diving." She grinned. "It was a disappointment, but we got over it. I discovered the joys of jumping out of airplanes."

Mitch patted Flora's arm. "You'll still have fun, I promise."

"It was worth a shot." She shrugged. "Tell me something else, then. What about those mutants I've heard about? Come on, Dana, fess up. You must know about them, working in Washington. What's the story behind the mutants?"

Dana made a face. "Believe me, I've checked. I'm a journalist, and my dream would be to get that scoop. Just imagine: proof that mutants exist. But if they do, no one is talking. I've tried snooping in CIA files, I've contacted friends in the FBI, I've even hired hackers to check the Net. Nothing. Nada."

Flora rubbed her arms. "Look at me, I've got goose bumps. Just thinking about mutants makes me nervous. Especially here in a virtual world. I keep thinking one is going to...oh!"

"What?" Dana dropped her strawberry daiquiri on the sand.

"Sorry, it's nothing." Flora gave a nervous giggle. "All that talk about mutants, and I got scared when Penny and Michelle stood up in the water with their snorkeling gear on."

Mitch raised his arm and flagged down a passing waiter figment. "What would you ladies like for lunch? We can have a table set up here or go to the dining room."

"Let's eat here." Dana waved at the two other women. "We'll let our two mutant friends dry off first."

"Oh, very funny." Flora looked a bit pale. "I tell you, I have nightmares about those things. I even hesitated about coming on this trip."

"Don't worry," Dana said to her. "They don't exist. I promise."

Mitch was silent, his feet digging into the cool sand. Mutants. Myth or reality? He wished he knew for sure.

Chapter Three

I believe a leaf of grass is no less than the journeywork of the stars,
And the pismire is equally perfect, and a grain of sand, and the egg of the wren...
Walt Whitman, *Song of Myself*

M-6—Mahler.

I am dreaming. I am flying. Clouds open and close around me, giving me glimpses of indigo water a thousand meters beneath. If I want, I can make the clouds soft as cotton balls so that I can feel them. There, it is done. Clouds upon which I can walk. They hold my weight because I weigh no more than a feather does.

I have lustrous skin the color of mother-of-pearl. It shimmers and shines with blue, green and gold highlights. I am wearing nothing. Sexless, there is no part of my body that says man or woman. No hair, no breasts, no genitalia: I see no use for all that. In my perfect world, I am androgynous. Weightless, I have the power of flight, but having no wings, I am at the mercy of each breeze, each whisper of wind.

That matters not. I am the wind. In my world, I go where I please, I see what I please, and I feel whatever it pleases me to feel.

My world is uninhabited. I am alone with a mirror ocean in a silence filled only by the sound of waves crashing on rocks and the wind whistling through tall eucalyptus trees. My world is a palette of blue and gray hues, and the dry-grass whispers. Even the eucalyptus trees have silvery leaves. I made dark gray beaches upon which the sea throws itself in a white, lacy froth. The clouds scud across the sky, borne by the same wind that carries me. Perhaps I spread my arms, I don't know. I feel clean, free, unfettered. The air is redolent of seawater and the fresh, spicy scent of eucalyptus.

That is my world, and I return whenever I can. Bit by bit I built it, hiding it from everyone else. You must be made of my world to attain it. I can slip into it, and no one can find me. Only I can go there. Only I can find it.

It makes Dr. Djusky quite mad. When too much time goes by without a sign from my body back in the Center, he invariably throws an electrical current through the gas clouds in my chamber. I perceive them as lightning flashes in my perfect world, and when the storm rises, I know it's time to head back.

There's no use angering Dr. Djusky. He can dream up the most aggravating punishments. Once, when I was very small, he nearly blew my circuits. You didn't get it, did you? That is a joke. We all say, "He nearly blew our circuits." Mutant humor takes getting used to, I suppose.

All of us are 'M's: M-1 through M-19. We are all M.O.C.P.'s, short for Mutant Organic Computer Programmer. I *am M-6, the eldest male child. My sisters, brothers and I are called mutants by most people, although some refer to us as freaks.*

I have thought sad thoughts. Now, like Peter Pan, I can no longer fly, and I must return home. Goodbye, Never-Never Land. Lightning bolts sizzle and flash around me. He must be quite angry this time.

* * *

Professor Toutbon strode through the dimly lit hallway on his way to see the mutants. His face was pale, and a faint sheen of sweat showed on his bald pate. He wore a white lab coat over a gray suit. The coat flapped around his long, thin legs as he walked. He was losing papers, one by one, from a huge sheaf he held under one arm, and that didn't help his mood at all.

The papers fluttered to the floor as if he were leaving himself a trail to find his way out of the labyrinth of corridors. He'd been walking down these same hallways for twenty years now. Twenty years of silence and secrecy. Twenty years of responsibility for nineteen entities, whose existence was denied by everyone. Twenty years, and now this! The Net had sent one of their Net Reps to see him. Him! Professor Toutbon had to answer questions posed by a Neanderthal in a business suit!

That was insulting enough, but no, the anthropoid had listened to the entire story and said, "What you're saying is, these mutants have escaped your control?"

"I didn't say that!" protested Toutbon.

"You told me that sometimes you didn't know what program the mutants entered. That they could penetrate any program on the Net, and that you couldn't be sure exactly where they were. They could be anywhere, even in top secret files for all we know." There was no inflection to his speech. He might have been saying, "Cotton is one of the staple exports of Egypt," and not accusing Professor Toutbon of letting his mutants run amok in the Net.

"We have never been able to develop a method to trace them," Toutbon admitted, "but they tell us exactly where they went. We file everything. What is wrong with that?"

"Because they could lie," the Net Rep said tranquilly.

"Lie?" Toutbon sputtered. "They can't lie! They are simply organic programs for computers. You give an order and they execute. You ask for a report, they print it out. Every move they make is easily verified the same way you check a computer's records. What more could you ask for?"

"Something fishy is going on."

Toutbon gaped. "Something fishy?"

"A man was killed in a Virtual Tour under very strange circumstances. He was literally screwed to death. He died with a smile on his face from unrequited sexual release. The main cause of death was a massive heart attack, but we're most interested in the sexual part. As you know, the potential for sexual stimulation is strictly repressed. Someone has found a way to break through barriers we thought were invincible."

Repressed—that was a word that made Professor Toutbon very nervous. He darted a glance at the Net Rep sitting unmoving upon the chair. Strange. He had no nervous ticks at all. No fidget, no shuffle, no glancing at a watch or even blinking an eyelid. Toutbon amused himself for the next five minutes trying to out-still him. It didn't work. He searched for something to say; he was obviously supposed to respond to that last cryptic statement. "I don't know what we have to do with this, um, story."

"We are very interested in Virtual Tours. We have great plans for them. However, if there is the slightest chance that a virus has been introduced, one making death through sexual nirvana possible, we must act immediately to snuff it out."

Sexual nirvana? Snuff it out? Toutbon peered closely at the man to see if he were joking in the slightest. He wasn't. "What can I do to help you?" The second the words left his mouth, he regretted them. Nothing but trouble ever came from those words. He was right.

"I need all the records of the last thirty hours of all the programs your mutants have infiltrated in triplicate, in hardcopy, before five pm."

Toutbon clenched his teeth together so hard he heard a distinct crack. "No problem," he heard himself saying. "Let me contact Laurel, my assistant, and we'll get right to work. Would you care to wait here? There is a bathroom around the corner, a water fountain over there, and if you're hungry, our cafeteria is on the third floor."

"Do you mean the minus third floor? You're underground here."

"Oh yes, quite." Toutbon stood and nearly shook hands with the Net Rep, but Net Reps don't shake hands. Toutbon's hand hovered in the air a moment before finding a handy pocket to hide in. Then, with a curt nod, he left.

He waited until he was in the elevator before giving vent to his temper; he kicked the stainless steel wall so hard the fire alarm went off, deafening him. By the time he reached the twelfth floor beneath the ground his head felt as if it were about to explode.

"Will someone fix the damn alarm in the fucking elevator!" he screamed.

Laurel raised her head. On her face was polite interest. The alarm was deafening, but Professor Toutbon knew it was useless to berate her. She was already deaf and couldn't hear the shrieking siren. Taking a rather shaky breath, he mouthed, "Shut the fire alarm off, please."

His assistant raised her eyebrows, a spark of amusement dancing in her brown eyes. She pushed a button on the console in front of her. Instantly the noise ceased.

"Thank you." Toutbon tried desperately to recover some semblance of calm. "I need your help." He looked straight at Laurel as he spoke. After five years of working together, it had developed into a reflex. He was also proud of the fact that his sign language was almost as competent as Laurel's was. However, most of the time he spoke looking straight at her, and she answered with her small, deft hands.

Laurel nodded and signed, "I was watching on the monitor. How strange they need everything in triplicate. Isn't that a paradox that the Net needs hardcopy? I'd have thought I could just e-mail everything."

Toutbon made a face. "Just do as he says. Get Carlos; he'll help you out. Don't take too long. I'm going to see the mutants. I can't believe he thinks the problem is coming from here. And who the hell told him about us, anyway?"

Laurel rolled her eyes. "You think the Net doesn't know everything that happens in the world?" she signed, her expressive face showing amazement. "You've got to be kidding. No one had to tell them anything. They have spies in all the programs. It wouldn't surprise me if they had their own mutant program." Her hands flew as she signed this, and she gave a curt nod. "You'll see. They'll try to blame this on us so their own program will become exclusive. Be careful, Professor, the Net is watching you!" She jabbed her finger at him and laughed silently at his horrified expression.

"Laurel, stop joking around and call Carlos. This is not a laughing matter. Lord, listen to me! I'm starting to sound like that ape-man upstairs." He shuddered, straightened his rumpled coat and found a sheaf of paper for the copy machine. Paper! The stack was way up on the top shelf, and if it hadn't been a clean environment, it would have been a foot thick in dust. They rarely used paper anymore.

He was unused to carrying the slithery sheets, and he left a fluttery trail of paper behind him as he walked.

* * *

Laurel picked up the telephone and poked at a number. When Carlos answered, her hands flew over the keyboard, tapping a message that arrived verbally in Carlos's headset. He answered and his words trotted across Laurel's screen. "Be right there, Bright-eyes."

Laurel blinked, then shook her head. Carlos was always teasing about something. Usually it was about her hair. Because she worked in a sterile atmosphere, she shaved her head. Nearly everyone who worked below the tenth floor had shaved heads. It made life so much easier. No paper hats to wear and no worry about a stray hair or dandruff clogging precious circuits. It also made the 'denizens of the deep,' as Carlos called them, look like a tribe of mushroom people. Carlos chose not to shave his head. He wore his long, black hair in two tight braids and sometimes poked eagle feathers in them. He loved to tease Laurel about her baldness, the shiny heads of her fellow workers, the white lab coats and the silence that reigned in the perpetual dimness. Well, silent until Professor Toutbon kicked something and set off the alarms.

There were few lights, and the ones that shone were tiny, halogen pinpricks, spotlighting certain computer screens. Lights made heat, attracted dust, and showed the horrible color the walls were painted. Who had chosen that particular puce? Had he or she been color-blind or just a sadist, gleefully picking out a yellow-brownish-green so horrible it brought to mind no natural phenomenon except maybe vomiting? Whatever reason, it made the darkness a blessing, hiding the walls and making it very easy to take a nap whenever the need arose.

Laurel put on some lipstick and checked her make-up. If her hair grew in, it would be golden-brown, sleek, and very straight. She would look like a normal person and could go on dates in a nearby town. However, she was bald, her skin was as white as perpetual darkness could make it, and she had no social life beyond going to minus three and hanging out in the cafeteria. The nearest large city was a three-hour drive away through a burning desert, and her bedroom was a cubbyhole on minus nine. People worked odd hours, were discouraged from going to the 'surface,' and were paid a fortune to keep their mouths closed. Laurel put her money in bonds, played the stock market religiously and waited for the day she could retire at thirty-five.

She would buy herself a homey, beachfront house and spend the rest of her days sitting on a dune surrounded by miles of waving saw grass. She would watch seagulls float stiff-winged in the sky and dolphins rise rhythmically out of the waves. In her mind, she imagined the whole scene. The house would be built of wood gone silvery gray with age, and a rickety dock would spike its way straight out into the water from the smooth, sandy beach. Perhaps she would have a small sailboat, but as she'd never sailed she would have to go slowly at first, staying well within sight of land. Her house would be isolated, with a marsh behind it. At night while fireflies blinked in the whispering grass, moths would flutter around candles outside the filmy netting surrounding her king-sized bed. Beside her, stretched out on white linen sheets, would be the smooth, brown body of Carlos, with his black hair and his harsh, Indian face. Laurel closed her eyes, a faint blush rising out of her lab coat to infuse her pale cheeks.

* * *

Carlos stepped out of the elevator. In the single beam of light over her desk, Laurel sat with her head tipped back, an expression of soft delight on her face. Usually, a million expressions chased themselves across her small features. Her eyes were generally crinkled in concentration while her mouth worked silently, mouthing the words that her hands danced in the air. He'd never seen her face in repose, its features as pure as if she were sleeping. He was used to her monkey mimics, her wide mouth stretching, her eyes fierce as she worked overtime making herself understood in an effort to breach the wall of silence that surrounded her.

It was a revelation seeing her like this. His heart lurched, and he frowned. His first instinct was to step back into the elevator and come back in ten minutes, but the door slid shut behind him. He was alone in the darkness watching a slender young woman dreaming in a pool of light. At that moment, Carlos Blue Jay Lakota fell deeply and instantly in love with the slim, mute girl. He ran a nervous hand through his long, black hair. He was going to have a hard time explaining this to his tribal elders.

* * *

Professor Toutbon stood in the darkness in front of nineteen large, glass cases. Floating within them, nearly hidden from view by a thick cloud of opaque gas, were the mutants. Some were nearly humanoid. One or two could pass for human with no trouble at all. The others were bizarre, with deformed heads and bodies that had atrophied. It was inexplicable why some had developed normally and others had become freaks.

Fifty embryos had been taken from their mothers' wombs after just three months' gestation, and computer chips had been grafted into their brains. They had developed in liquid, a thick, viscous, amber juice that nourished them as they grew. Out of fifty, thirty-five embryos had made it through gestation to be 'born.' Five had died in the first year of life so that there were thirty of them left six years later. Six years of programming their brains while their bodies grew in gas-filled chambers that enabled them to float weightlessly. Electrical impulses flexed their muscles, keeping them fit. Lungs and hearts developed normally, but their consciousness was transmuted into human machines.

When they were seven years old, ten of the mutants were culled for testing.

The remaining mutants were part of an on-going experiment undertaken by the federal government. It was a CIA program, with the tacit participation of the FBI. They had been hoping for secret weapons or defense; what they'd gotten so far was money. The mutants proved themselves extremely lucrative when they started to develop virtual worlds. However, the government, paradoxically, had little control over the program. In making the program so secret, it had lessened any credible power they had over it. Now Professor Toutbon ran the program, and the government was content to stand back and watch closely. Another close watcher was the Net. It made Professor Toutbon very nervous to think of the Net Government having anything to do with the mutants.

A sound made him jump. The elevator doors slid open, and Dr. Djusky, the biologist in charge of the mutants' physical welfare, stepped into the room. He blinked as his eyes adjusted to the light. He noticed Professor Toutbon, and a frown flitted across his face.

Professor Toutbon's hands twitched. He forced his mouth into what he hoped was a friendly smile. "Ah, Dr. Djusky. Do you have a moment? I have a couple questions for you, if you don't mind."

"What is it, Toutbon?"

Professor Toutbon scratched his chin. "I wanted to ask you some questions about the mutants."

"You came to the right person. But you know enough about them. What can you possibly want from me?"

"I'm not familiar with certain of their physical characteristics, and I'm not privy to the information the FBI and CIA have amassed over the years about them. I'm simply in charge of the game programs, in liaison with the owner of Virtual Tours."

"Get to the point." Dr. Djusky peered into a glass case and tapped it with his finger. "Hello there, M-5."

The mutant didn't respond.

"I assisted the program founder, Dr. Tergiversate, you know."

Dr. Djusky straightened and looked at him from over the top of the mutant's case. "I know. But Dr. Tergiversate is dead."

"That's part of what I'd like to talk about. I've been going over those transcripts, and I wondered if you could help me. From what I pieced together, M-20, a female mutant, went insane. Neither Dr. Tergiversate nor I were informed of this when it first occurred. I would like to determine if there were any precursors to the incident, like failure to respond to stimuli, that sort of thing."

"You know there was no precedent or warning. Nobody noticed anything unusual. M-20 just started banging her head against the side of her cage one day."

"At the time, nobody but your team was allowed in the room, correct?"

Dr. Djusky narrowed his eyes. "If I had my way, you would still not be allowed here, nor anyone else, for that matter, except my own staff. What's bothering you, Toutbon? Can't sleep at night? Nightmares haunting you? See any flying men?"

Professor Toutbon winced. "When Dr. Tergiversate found out the mutant was apparently attempting to damage herself, he asked you to treat her, but nothing worked."

"I didn't have time to try everything before your precious doctor intervened. I was against his idea of taking her out of her case. Mutants are fragile, expensive pieces of biological machinery. They are not meant to be taken out and played with."

"He contacted the CIA. There were FBI agents. Everyone was there. It shouldn't have gone wrong."

"If I'd been allowed to continue my treatment, nothing would have happened. If Doctor Tergiversate had listened to me, he'd still be alive."

"How can you be so sure?"

"I was there, remember?" Dr. Djusky grinned at Professor Toutbon. "I saw him fly."

Professor Toutbon shuddered as he recalled the scene. Dr. Tergiversate had uncovered her case, letting clouds of gas float into the air, and reached in to touch her.

No one present at the time could say exactly what happened next. Billowing clouds obscured cameras on the walls, and the dim light made it hard for the assistants to view the scene.

Doctor Tergiversates had levitated into the air. Before anyone could react, he flew across the room and hit the wall with a horrible crunching sound. And then, M-20 stepped out of her glass case. She had been nearly seven feet tall. Her body was sculptural, perfect, with long, golden hair and high, round breasts. She had stood in front of everyone, staring at them with her strange eyes. They were gray and covered with a silver frost, making them gleam in the dim light. She'd stretched, raising her arms above her head, and laughed softly. Her red lips had twisted in a half smile, and she'd opened them to speak, to say something after fifteen years of silence. After fifteen years of floating in a glass case full of clouds.

At that moment, a machine gun volley had ripped through her rib cage, spraying blood, bone chips and lung tissue over those standing nearby. The glass case behind her had shattered in a sparkling fountain of glass splinters. Blood sprayed everywhere. A stray bullet struck one of the lab assistants, and he died, kicking his heels on the ground. Another technician vomited, staggering around, moaning and clutching his stomach. A woman crouched and screamed.

Professor Toutbon had been paralyzed, absolutely petrified, as soon as the mutant had stepped over the edge of her glass case, her long, perfect legs swinging almost insolently over the side. He hadn't been able to take his eyes from her even to look at Doctor Tergiversate's crumpled body. The Junoesque woman had mesmerized him. His breath caught in his throat, and he found himself waiting almost painfully for words she was never to speak. What had she wanted to say? He would never know. It was one of several mysteries surrounding that day.

"Toutbon! Either ask me what you want to know or let me get to work." Dr. Djusky stood impatiently beside the terminal attached to one of the mutant's cases.

Toutbon blinked. "I was wondering if you knew who killed M-20."

"It's been seven years. Are you implying that I'm free to speak now?" Dr. Djusky gave a barking laugh. "Don't be stupid. I haven't the faintest clue who killed her. I was there, remember? I was right next to you. Anyway, if you used your brain, you'd be able to figure it out. The FBI or the CIA. They were the only ones who could destroy a million-dollar piece of machinery. They were hoping for a secret weapon, but what they got was a sex goddess." He snickered.

Professor Toutbon took a deep breath. Dr. Djusky was often hard to take, but he kept the mutants healthy. "Well, actually, we have a problem with the Virtual Tour."

"That's not my department."

"I know, but you recall our reactions when M-20 stepped out of her case. Our physical reactions, I mean." Professor

Toutbon flushed. "The simple sight of a naked woman can't explain our instant, um, arousal. There was something overpowering about her that made us react on an instinctive level. None of us could have fired a single shot at her. At least not in the state we were in."

Dr. Djusky looked sharply at Toutbon. "Just what are you getting at?"

"I don't know. I was hoping you could tell me something about the mutants' physical capabilities. Are they all like M-20? Can they all inspire uncontrollable sexual attraction?"

"No." Dr. Djusky walked to another case and peered inside. "And I won't elaborate, if that's what you're waiting for."

"The Net Rep wants me to give him a hardcopy transcript of all the mutants' movements in the last thirty hours."

"That's your domain. Imaginary worlds and make-believe games." Dr. Djusky snorted.

"The Net Rep is a strange man," Professor Toutbon ventured. "A certain Mr. Frank Dinde. He speaks in clichés."

At that, Dr. Djusky let out another harsh laugh. "Frank Dinde? Don't tell me the head of Net security frightens you?"

Professor Toutbon dug his nails into the palm of his hand. "I don't think it's a joking matter. A man died on a virtual tour, and the Net sends the head of security here to collect data. I don't like it."

Djusky pointed to Toutbon. "Don't worry, Net Reps don't eat humans. Just give him what he wants and he'll leave without making any trouble."

"I feel like the trouble is only beginning."

Dr. Djusky snorted. "Being confined in this Center for twenty years has certainly done nothing for your intellectual capabilities. Why don't you take a trip to the surface once in a while? No, don't answer that. I can see why you don't want to leave."

Toutbon felt Dr. Djusky's gaze rake over him and he shivered. There was something sinister about Dr. Djusky. Then again, anyone who could take ten seven-year-old humanoid mutants and dissect them had to be twisted. Maybe that was why other employees rarely sat next to Dr. Djusky in the cafeteria.

"Well, if you're going to be down here printing for long, I'll come back later. I prefer to work alone." Dr. Djusky flicked his fingernail against one of the mutant's cases and left the room.

Toutbon stood in front of the mutants' cases chewing his nails. Then he sighed, printed the papers he needed, and left the room to its deep, underwater silence.

Chapter Four

Dancing and laughing along the beach came the twenty-ninth
bather,
The rest did not see her, but she saw them and loved them.
—Walt Whitman, *Song of Myself*

Jonathon wriggled his toes in the soft sand. When he arrived at work he'd been hustled into the sending room, attached to the monitors, and hooked up to the IV immediately. Digby hadn't answered a single question, shaking his head, muttering about Arthur's heart attack and nearly didn't find a vein on the first poke. It made Jonathon nervous to see Digby's hands shaking so much.

Before Jonathon dropped off to slip—what the programmers called slipping into the tour—Digby had frowned, looked straight at Jonathon, and said, "I want you to lock the door to your bedroom. No questions—just do it. I'll explain later."

Now, sitting on the beach in the shade cast by a large boulder, the sky a bright, blue bowl of porcelain cupped over his head, Jonathon thought about Arthur. He hadn't known him all that well, but he had seemed like a decent guy. He rubbed his arms, his nerves prickling. At any rate, when he got back to the hotel he'd lock the door. He picked up a handful of warm sand and let it slide through his fingers. The four women on the tour had asked about Arthur of course, and he'd answered evasively. He'd received no orders about what to say, but he preferred not to admit Arthur was dead. Poor Arthur—he was so young. Still, heart attacks could strike at any time.

One woman in particular seemed upset about Arthur's absence. She'd sulked all morning. Jonathon had arrived early, before anyone was awake, thanks to Digby's manipulation of time in the program, and he'd been able to cajole her into coming on the boat trip. He'd taken his tourist charges to a beautiful beach. They'd sailed in a large catamaran to another island, Virgin Gorda, and anchored in the famous bay known as The Baths.

It was a beautiful place. Huge granite boulders, some the size of houses, lay in a titanic jumble at the southern end of the island. A small beach nestled in between the boulders, and the gigantic rocks leaned against each other, forming a labyrinth of caves and grottos where the sun sent shafts of light into hidden, sandy caverns. Water reached into some of them, creating rivers of ethereal beauty. You could crawl through a narrow tunnel in massive stone and find yourself in an enchanted vault of granite, with a white sandy floor and a private pool of clear aquamarine water.

The Baths were practically inaccessible by land. A long, rutted, dirt road led to them, but it was so rugged that the best way to get there was by boat. The bay was small, so usually only one or two boats anchored there at a time. Today, the catamaran bobbed all by itself. On virtual tours, you weren't surrounded by hundreds of other tourists, one of the reasons they were so popular.

Jonathon loved The Baths and took his group whenever he was a guide. The tours were adaptable. You could decide what you wanted to do; you weren't restrained by any set schedule. It was nice to be able to do things on a whim.

Jonathon liked change. He loved travel and hated the idea of a nine-to-five job. A Virtual Tour Guide was the perfect vocation for him. It certainly helped that he was tall, dark, and had eyes that smoldered like live coals. His smile was devastating. To coax the women into a better mood, he'd packed a picnic and brought them here. When they saw the pristine beauty of the place, they had perked up considerably. They hadn't mentioned Arthur's name in an hour.

Jonathon watched as three of his charges spread their towels on the sand and started to unpack the picnic lunch. The other girl was missing, the sulky one who had pestered him about Arthur. He sat up straighter and scanned the beach. There was no sign of her. Where could she be? He hoped she wasn't lost in the maze beneath the rocks. Sometimes you had to climb topside to find your way back. He sighed and got to his feet.

"I'll be right back," he called to the women. "Leave me a few crumbs, will you?"

They laughed at him, waving gaily. One popped the champagne bottle open and squealed as white bubbles frothed over her hands. "Come back quickly, or we'll drink it without you!"

He brushed the sand off his shorts. As usual, he was faintly amused to notice that he could hardly feel his groin. The numbing effect of the program caused your nether regions to feel like cardboard.

Not that the girls had anything to gain from flirting with him. He much preferred his own sex. He had a steady boyfriend, and they lived together in a tiny village in the countryside. The house they'd bought had been an old mill a hundred years before, and they'd renovated it. All Jonathon's wages went towards antiques he gleaned from country fairs. He'd been annoyed when he'd learned he had to go on another virtual tour because he and Alec were just heading to an antique show.

Now Alec was on his own, and he'd probably buy a stuffed moose head to hang over their stone fireplace. There was a blank space and the two men were at odds about how to fill it. Alec wanted something truly outrageous while Jonathon wanted to get a turn-of-the century, Grandma Moses type painting. The thought of a moose, a knit cap on its head and a briar pipe stuck in its mouth, made Jonathon smile in spite of his ire. Whatever Alec got, it would be a surprise.

The smile was still on his face as he ducked through the narrow passage leading to a small cave. It was empty, but he saw footprints leading off through a tunnel on his right. He had to crawl through the small opening on hands and knees in the dark for roughly twenty meters. Then the passage gave way to a huge vault, as three massive blocks of granite leaned against each other over a pool of clear water and a patch of pure sand.

Blue sky showed through a triangular opening formed by the rocks overhead, and a shaft of golden sunlight fell upon a woman floating on her back in the crystal-clear water. At first, he thought it was Rhonda, the missing woman. As he drew closer, her face and body shifted. She seemed to shrink, then stretch. No, it wasn't...exactly...Rhonda. He'd never seen this woman in his life. Jonathon stopped, startled. Several thoughts flitted through his head. Who was she? Where did she come from? Perhaps ten seconds elapsed while he stared. Then she opened her eyes and smiled at him.

A feeling he'd never experienced swept over him. It was as if there was a switch in his body that until then had been turned off. He found himself struggling for breath. At once, the air was too hot, too thick, and his limbs quivered.

The woman stood up and started to walk towards him. Water shed off her skin in shining beads of light. Her feet sank into the white sand, and it powdered her insteps and ankles. Her body was small, compact, and perfect.

She stopped barely six inches from him. The top of her head just reached his sternum. He could feel a sort of force field around her body, as if he were standing in front of an electrified fence. She raised her eyes. They were immense, the color of dark, frosty plums. There was something frightening and compelling in her regard.

"What is your name?" she asked, reaching out to touch his chest. Her finger traced a line from his collarbone to his nipple.

"Jonathon," he whispered. "Who are you?"

"I'm the smallest one in line. The smallest girl is Madeline," she said softly, breathing into his ear.

"Madeline?" He was trembling all over, his skin shuddering like a nervous colt's. "Where did you come from?" The idea that she was a trick fluttered through his mind. Was Digby up to something? Was Virtual Tours trying an experiment? Why hadn't they warned him?

"Madeline, is this your real body?" His voice was breaking. He could hardly draw a full breath. His own body was acting in the most incredible fashion. Waves and waves of desire were rushing through him, engulfing him. He tried to fight it, but it was as if his head and his body were two different entities. Hot lust bloomed in his groin while his mind struggled in panic. He had never had the least bit of desire to make love to a woman; he'd tried it before, and it had been a mediocre experience. Nothing he'd ever wanted to renew. Until now.

"Alec!" he cried. He tried to push her away from him but his arms refused to obey.

"Stop resisting me." A sigh escaped her. She leaned into him, pressing her body against his, and he realized that he was as naked as she was, although he had no recollection of taking his bathing suit off.

He fought the surge of passion, struggling against it as if he were drowning. He was caught up in the embrace of this strange woman and his body was betraying him with an eagerness that confounded him. The fight didn't last long. His mind became clouded with desire and his body took control. With a hoarse cry, he threw himself against the yielding woman, falling with her onto the sand.

They rolled in the soft powder, his feet scrabbling for purchase as he thrust madly into her. The feeling was indescribable; he forgot all else in his haste for release. When it came, it shook him to his very bones. He shuddered, spent, his breath coming in great gasps.

The woman reached down and touched him ever so lightly. An electric spark seemed to jump through his skull. A new wave of pleasure submerged him. Once more, his body strained towards the woman, demanding, giving. She laughed with delight and opened her legs wide.

Ecstasy, he was awash in ecstasy. Nothing he'd ever dreamed of compared to this. He couldn't stop, he couldn't even slow down. Between each orgasm, each shattering, bone-jarring orgasm, he had no respite. The woman never spoke. She only gave soft cries and arched her back, begging for more.

Their bodies slipped and slid together, as arms, legs and bellies grew slick with sweat. Skin glided against skin, slithery and hot. Fingers and tongues roamed and prodded, finding nooks and crannies that begged to be explored. Each touch shivered with electrical delight. The heat was overwhelming, choking Jonathon. He rolled over into the pool of water, and at first, the cool water was a blessing.

It closed over his head as they sank together to the sandy bottom.

The woman kept breathing underwater. So did Jonathon. Her hair floated around them in a swirling cloud, her mouth opened and shut as she moaned. Her legs encircled Jonathon's waist, her hips moved in an incessant rhythm older than time, and her arms held him tightly.

He could not breathe; perhaps she was holding him too tightly. He tried to escape but something was wrong, dreadfully wrong. Desire for the woman was growing stronger every minute but release eluded him. If anything, each time he reached orgasm, pleasure was magnified. He struggled vainly, only vaguely aware of what was happening. His body still strained towards fulfillment, but his heart gave out and he began to die. As oblivion spread over him, he was conscious of only one thing. Bliss, sheer bliss was gilding his body in light.

When he died, his virtual body vanished.

The woman was left alone, floating in the warm water, her eyes open and unseeing, an expression of wonder on her face. Her hands stroked her body, her breasts, and her thighs.

"He loved me," she murmured, and she smiled.

* * *

"Holy shit, holy shit, holy shit…"

Digby paced back and forth, his face a picture of misery, his arms crossed over his narrow chest. Every now and then, he broke off pacing and stared at the scene on the other side of the glass partition where the emergency medical team rushed about. The glass partition muffled their cries, but the body on the chair never moved. Then he started pacing again.

"Holy shit, holy shit, holy shit…"

* * *

The virtual tour was hastily brought to an end. The tourists were all awakened, and so was Mitch.

It was a strange experience, ending a virtual trip before the voyage was complete. The beach dissolved, sand and sky merging into a single gray entity. The women were sitting around, eating their picnic, when the food suddenly vanished in a shower of crumbs. The champagne evaporated and the scene around them wavered and shifted, colors bleeding into one another. The women's faces vacillated, and one suddenly grew old before their eyes, her brown hair turning gray, her face wrinkling, her mouth drooping downwards. All sound ceased, and a scream born in one throat was bitten off as a curious whooshing took its place. A steady thump, thump, thump grew louder and louder. As the light dimmed, the colors all turned gray, then dark. Then blinding light once more stabbed their eyes, and they found themselves staring at the faces of the medical team bending over them, their heartbeats loud in their helmets.

The nurses had strained expressions, and everyone's questions went unanswered. Hot tea was pressed into their hands, warm blankets went around their shoulders, and they sat in bemused silence.

"What happened?" asked one tourist, sipping her tea and plucking at her gray curls meditatively.

"I have no idea, but it is the first time that ever happened to me," another woman said with a strong French accent.

"It's very curious. First one guide disappeared, then one member of our group went astray. Oh, there you are, I nearly didn't recognize you. Where did you go? You missed the picnic."

"I think virtual travel is one big rip-off," she complained. "I have no recollection of going anywhere or doing anything."

The other women gaped at her until the psychologist entered the room. He smiled brightly. "Why don't we talk about it?"

"I don't want to talk, I just want my money back," snapped Rhonda.

* * *

The orders were formally written on thick, cream-colored paper. The Net Rep had handed them to Professor Toutbon as soon as he'd walked in the room, startling him so much he'd dropped his cup of coffee.

The message was short. "Prepare Mutant of your choice for transfer immediately."

Two people had signed the note: the first was Wilbur Megalot, president of the Net Government and king of the Virtual World. The other signature was that of Toutbon's direct superior, the director of the CIA. His hands clenched on the paper, but it was such fine quality that its satiny smoothness and creamy texture didn't change a bit.

* * *

Professor Toutbon watched as M-18 lay in a storm cloud, dreaming peacefully. The mutants dreamed their lives away. Most of the time, they could be reached quickly, but sometimes they seemed to be so far away they wouldn't respond to the stimuli of their console. Then you had to shock them awake. It was for their own good, reasoned the scientists, so that they wouldn't get lost somewhere in Virtual Outer Space.

M-18 had a nickname. It was Monkey. It had nothing to do with his physical appearance, and Professor Toutbon didn't know where the nicknames came from. The sobriquet was written on a sticky tab and stuck to the side of his console. All the mutants had a tag, all starting with the letter 'M'. Now Monkey was about to go on a journey into the real world, one he'd never seen before. Monkey had experienced games and the programs, strolled down virtual streets, driven virtual jets, and shot virtual hydras with virtual laser guns. Professor Toutbon doubted this made him capable of confronting real life, but he had no say in the matter at all. He could simply wait, his foot tapping nervously against the console, until Monkey came online.

"Hello, Professor." The voice was rusty, as if he'd woken up from a deep sleep.

"How are you, Monkey?"

"Fine. What can I do for you today?"

"I have orders to take you out of your case."

There was a long silence. Behind him in the dark room, in the other cases, Professor Toutbon thought he caught a whisper of agitated tension. He had often wondered how closely the mutants were interconnected. They were remarkably evasive when questioned about this.

Finally, Monkey said, "The real world?"

"Yes. I wanted to prepare you. The Net Government wants to take you to their headquarters in Dallas. It will be temporary, never fear. But you will have to walk, and dress, and use the facilities."

A puzzled pause met this statement. "What are facilities?"

Professor Toutbon winced. This was going to be harder than he'd imagined.

* * *

"Are you trying to tell me that they were both raped to death?" Andrea's voice rose despite her effort to stay calm.

"I believe we could put it that way, yes." The doctor wiped his hands on his coat, leaving damp spots.

She stared at him. "What other way could you put it?"

The reception room door opened and a white-haired policeman entered, his hat in his hands.

"Here's Captain Walker." Relief was evident in the doctor's voice.

Andrea nodded. "What's going on?"

"I have no idea what happened," the policeman said, a frown creasing his face. "What I do know is that two men have died in the space of twelve hours here. Mr. Brims tells me that in their world more than three days elapsed between the two deaths."

Andrea glared at the doctor. "Don't you have something to do?"

"I'll go see if the other guide is awake now."

"His name is Mitch Palo," Andrea snapped. The doctor gave a feeble nod and bolted out the door.

Andrea's gaze swept the reception room. A straight line of navy blue chairs sat primly in front of a long, low glass table. Neat piles of brochures dotted the table, and a bouquet of fresh white lilac sprouted from a polished silver vase. Sally always made sure the reception room was impeccable. At this hour, it should have been bustling. Instead, an eerie silence filled it. Except for a dry cough. The police officer shifted his weight and coughed again in a blatant attempt to catch her attention.

"Excuse me, Captain Walker. Now that I've filled out my deposition, what can we do?"

"I don't think we can do anything. Mr. Brims has already copied all the information concerning the tourists. He's gone over all the transcripts, and so far, has found nothing out of the ordinary. The problem, as I see it, is how to investigate within the virtual world. There is no police force there. As far as I know, there is no official law and order force at all in the virtual world." The policeman tucked his hat under his arm and scratched his head. "Just the Net."

"Just the Net," Andrea repeated slowly.

"Are you thinking what I'm thinking?" Captain Walker asked .

"I hope not. Excuse me, please." Andrea walked back to her office, then picked up her private phone and dialed David Willow's number. He was her current boyfriend, but more importantly, he was a senator for the Net. He answered on the first ring.

"Andrea! What's going on?"

"Another tour guide is dead. I think someone planted a virus in my program. I want you to get your ass over here right now. I'll give you ten minutes. Otherwise, I'm calling Bernard Draper at CVN. He'll want to hear all about this."

"You don't realize how powerful the Net is," David snapped. "I don't think you're in a position to give orders here."

"What the Net had better realize is that its very size and power is its own Achilles heel. Virtual voyages are the newest, most lucrative program, and the Net has invested heavily in Virtual Tours. New tours of all sorts are in the programming stages. I happen to know that the incredible success of Virtual Tours caused the Net to speculate far more than it should have. If Virtual Tours becomes a fiasco, the Net will sustain a huge loss. Huge losses mean cutting back essential programs, putting thousands of people out of work. Like you, David. Think about it."

"All right, Andrea. Tell me what happened."

"What's happened is that someone has found a way to break through all the barriers the Net set up to protect the tours. Worse, that person has found a way to use the Net for murder."

"How is that possible? A virtual world is just that—virtual. How can someone, or something, within the program kill someone's physical body just by interacting with his neurons?"

Andrea bit her bottom lip hard enough to taste blood. "I don't know. But you'd better get on the line to someone who can find out. But most important of all, you have to stop the tours."

David sputtered over the phone. "I can't do that."

"Then send someone who can. Send Ms. Andrews. I'll talk to her." Andrea hung up and rubbed her temples. What was going on with her tour?

Chapter Five

(Only what proves itself to every man and woman is so,
Only what nobody denies is so.)
—Walt Whitman, *Song of Myself*

"This is a men's room. You go into the one with the little symbol for a man. The other door is for women."

"How interesting. Tell me, Professor Toutbon, why are there no toilet facilities in the virtual world?"

"I really don't know." Toutbon shook his head. He'd never thought about that.

"Am I doing well, Professor Toutbon?"

"You are doing just fine, Monkey, just fine."

It was true. The mutant had proved to be docile and curious. He didn't seem to be nervous, and except for a rather tense moment when he'd passed in front of a mirror, everything had gone smoothly. Toutbon congratulated himself for choosing Monkey. The mutant was one of his favorites. A bit of a daydreamer, sometimes hard to reach on the console, but easy enough to communicate with once he'd been removed from his glass case. They hadn't wanted to make any mistakes. They had told Monkey everything they were about to do and given him time to settle down before they advanced to the next step.

Monkey's case had been put into a private room. All women were kept away. Toutbon remembered his reaction to the female and didn't want to take any chances with a male. The lights were slowly brightened to give his eyes a chance to adjust from the dimness of his cloud-filled case to harsh artificial lighting.

His muscle tone was amazing, thanks to constant electrical twitching. He had a bit of a problem balancing, though, and would suddenly pitch forward. The first time he did that, he didn't even try to catch himself and had bloodied his nose. Afterwards he put his arms out each time he fell. He learned quickly. He'd worn clothes in the virtual world but hadn't fiddled with zippers or buttons. Right now his fly gaped open and he'd put his shirt on inside-out. Toutbon pointed to his own pants and then to Monkey's pants. The young mutant gave him a blinding smile, then yanked his zipper up so hard he nearly broke it.

Toutbon was confident he could drive a car, fly a jet, use a phone, climb stairs, or shoot a laser pistol. Not that he would get the chance to do any of that, except climb stairs, perhaps. He was still temporarily plugged into his console with a Net shunt attached to his temple. Shunts were simply fine wires that connected into a computer terminal at one end, and to an electrode at the other. An electrode pressed against a person's temple and allowed the user's brainwaves to interact directly with the computer. In Monkey's case, it went deeper than that.

As a mutant, he had a metal plate in his temple that connected to the shunt. At any moment, Toutbon could put him back to sleep and communicate with him purely on a data processing level. He wasn't sure if Monkey realized this. For now, he sat, eyes wide, his mouth working comically as he spoke.

It was unnerving for Toutbon. It was as if his word processor suddenly sprang to life, asking questions and touching things around the room. He had the most candid stare, and that unsettled Toutbon. He felt, obscurely, as if he needed to safeguard Monkey.

He smiled and patted his hand. "You're doing very well. I'm proud of you." Tears pricked his eyes, and he blinked rapidly as emotion submerged him. What was going on? The thought of sending Monkey away to Dallas made him want to weep. He had the strongest impulse to protect him. He was just a child; he knew nothing about the real world, nothing.

"It's all right." Monkey leaned forward and touched him lightly on the arm. "I'll be fine. From what I gathered, I'll be in one of our Virtual Programs, trying to catch a certain virus. Have I understood my mission correctly?"

"Yes, you have." Toutbon took his glasses off and wiped his eyes. He cleaned his glasses on a corner of his lab coat and sighed. Soon he had to take Monkey to the fifth floor where the Net Rep was waiting with an armed guard to take him away.

"I will be back soon."

"I hope so," Toutbon said, "I certainly hope so. Now, let's go over it once more. You drink, you feel certain urgency in your bladder, you go to the room with the little man icon, and then what? You tell me."

"I use the facilities!" Monkey said, proudly.

"Don't forget. Unzip your pants, take your penis out, and point it in the right direction. Don't get your clothes wet, don't urinate outside the urinals, and don't forget…"

"Always wash my hands before I eat!" crowed Monkey. "I remembered!"

Professor Toutbon shook his head. He was terribly anxious. Monkey had spent his entire life in a protected environment. He'd never caught a single cold. He was about to go out into a world full of germs. He'd ordered Monkey to wear special masks, and Monkey had a supply of them in his vest pocket.

"Don't forget your mask when you go outside," Professor Toutbon said sadly.

"Don't worry, Professor. I'll take care. You'll see; I'll be back before you know."

Professor Toutbon couldn't answer. He was too busy pretending to wipe a speck of dust out of his eye and blowing his nose.

* * *

Sally threw herself into Mitch's arms. In her haste, she tripped, so it was a good thing he caught her firmly around the waist.

"Hey, little lady, going somewhere?"

"Mitch! I was so worried about you!" She kissed him hard on the lips.

"Hold on, I need to take a shower and brush my teeth before you ravish me here in the middle of the hallway."

"I'm sorry, it's just nerves." Her voice dropped. "I need to talk to you."

"Can you wait until I get out of the shower? You know how groggy I feel after a voyage, and I just woke up. I'll only be a minute. Wait right here. Don't move." He grinned. "I promise, I'll be quick."

Sally paced nervously back and forth. As she paced, she chewed her nails. She checked her watch; it was nearly ten p.m. She should have been home in bed, curled up beneath her patchwork quilt, her head on Mitch's shoulder, while they watched the stars twinkle through the huge skylight above their bed. They both disliked television and loved classical music. There was an overflowing bookcase next to the bed. Mitch could reach out, grab a book, and read aloud. He loved stories. His favorite books were by Ray Bradbury, and he had a nice reading voice. Sally would rub his back while he read. It was part of the deal. Whoever read aloud got a massage while they were reading.

Then they would make love. Mitch would usually start, sliding his hand down her thigh, giving a soft sigh when his fingers touched her skin. Then he would lift the covers over his head, giving her a wicked grin before he disappeared beneath the sheets. Always that wide smile before he vanished beneath the covers. She loved that grin; it preceded the feel of hot breath on skin that was so sensitive the slightest touch was too heavy. A finger, no matter how smooth, felt rough. Only a tongue, a soft, velvety tongue, could...

"Miss Child, what *are* you doing?"

Sally dropped her purse with a shriek. Her eyes had been closed, her head tipped back, as her back pressed against the wall. She glared at Digby. "Don't you ever scare me like that! You'll give me a heart attack!"

"Sorry. You looked as if you were about to go to sleep standing up, and I didn't want you to fall and hurt yourself."

Sally ran a shaky hand through her curly hair. "No harm done."

"Where's Mitch?"

"In the shower. Why?"

"He has to come with me. The head Rep wants to see him."

Sally blinked. "Head Rep? Wants to see to Mitch? What about?"

"He's a witness in the case."

"Case? What are you talking about, Daniel?"

"The Net seems to think the program has been infiltrated by some sort of virus, a ghost glitch, and they want to catch it and whoever slipped it into the program."

"A ghost glitch?"

"That's the name I invented for it." Digby shrugged.

"How can a virus in a virtual program kill a body back here in the real world?" Sally's hand crept to her mouth and she nibbled on her nails.

"I have no idea. Isn't that weird? I have no idea at all."

Mitch stepped out of the locker room, his hair still damp. His smile slid off his face like water when he saw Digby. "Hey Danny-boy," he said cautiously. "What's up?"

"I hate it when you call me that. It's Digby, or Daniel. And what's up is you're our chief witness for the defense."

"The defense? Who's prosecuting?"

"The Net."

Mitch stood perfectly still. He didn't even seem to breathe. "They didn't tell me why they woke me up nearly ten hours too early; they just shuffled me out of the room. What's happening? They don't think it was an accident, is that it?"

"That, my friend, is what we'd all like to know." Digby took a deep breath. "It's not official yet, so no one is saying anything about this. For now it's not being called an investigation, it's being called a case. You're the one chosen to find the ghost glitch in the program."

Mitch gave a faint grin. "That sounds like one of your handles. Ghost glitch. Is that what you're calling the virus?"

"The Net thought it was fitting."

"Why me and not you?" Mitch asked.

Digby frowned. Evidently, he would have preferred to have been chosen. "You're familiar with the tour. I'm just the technician. You'll be able to sense if something is not right. After all, you practically live in the virtual world."

"What does the Net know that we don't?" Sally asked, her fingers tightening on Mitch's arm.

Digby looked at her. "All I've ever heard are rumors. But now I'm beginning to think that they were true."

"Meaning?" Sally urged.

Digby tightened his lips and shook his head. "Let's just say I hope Mitch doesn't find anything wrong with the program. Well, shall we go? The Net Rep awaits, and she doesn't look like the type to be kept waiting."

"Where am I going?" asked Mitch.

"Dallas. Didn't I tell you? You're going straight to the top, Mitch. To the headquarters to take part in a hunt for a ghost glitch. Isn't your skin just prickling with dread?"

"Dallas? You're kidding."

"Nope, got your plane ticket right here. Do you have a toothbrush in your bag? Yes? Well, you're all set." Digby took Mitch by the arm. "Come on, let's go. The sooner we get this cleared up, the sooner we can all get back to life as usual."

"Why can't I do it from here?" Mitch asked, a puzzled frown on his handsome face.

"They have some new virus-catching program set up in a secured room. It should be interesting. Let me know what you think of it. They loaded the main terminal and packed it in a spray-foam box just ten minutes ago. The tour guides' sending room has been stripped. They took two chairs and all the electrodes I had. They even had their own technician come and ask me how to hook everything up correctly, although I could tell he already knew what he was doing. Don't worry, Mitch, you'll be in competent hands."

Mitch gave a short laugh. "Don't worry? Are you kidding? Let me get this straight. I'm on my way to Dallas to find a virus in the program because the Net Government is in charge all of a sudden?"

"They have always been in charge. We just didn't realize it, that's all. I don't think you want to keep them waiting."

"Wait," Sally protested. "Can't I have just a minute with him?"

"Hurry up," Digby said.

"You can't leave me without a kiss." Sally embraced Mitch tightly and buried her face in his chest.

Mitch gave her a quick kiss, touching her lightly on the cheek. "Don't worry, Twinkle Star Sal, I'll be back in a flash," he whispered.

"I love you," she replied.

Then he left, practically dragged down the hall by Digby. Damn that Digby, anyway. Dallas was a long ways away, and two men in the program had died. Sally gnawed on her thumbnail. If anything happened to Mitch, it would destroy her. She glanced up at Andrea Girt's office. If only she was more like Andrea. Nothing seemed to perturb her. She stayed calm, cool, and never bit her nails. Sally looked at her fingers and sighed.

* * *

The building echoed with the sounds of heels tapping on the floors, of sirens, of tense voices and the steady whistle from a teapot somewhere. Until midnight, the offices had been crowded. Afterwards, when the last police officer had left and the tourists were herded into vans and taken away, the Net technicians had finished loading up the material they needed and the door slid shut with a final *ping,* the silence rushed in.

Andrea stood in front of the plate-glass window and stared unseeingly at the lights below. Her head was ringing, her eyes stung, and she wanted to curl up in a big, soft bed, and cuddle with someone strong and dependable. Only *dependable* wasn't how she would describe the men she dated. A small whine startled her, and she spun around.

Cocotte stepped daintily out of her wicker basket and trotted to her mistress. Her claws made a light clicking sound on the green stone floor. She looked up at Andrea, shiny nose twitching, eyes pleading. She whined again, her plumed tail wagging silently.

Andrea reached down and ruffled her silky ears. "Everything is a mess, Cocotte. You won't believe what a mess it is." She straightened and sighed. "Dave Willow is such an unfortunate wimp." She paused and looked at her dog to make sure she was listening.

Cocotte tilted her head to one side.

"He said something about someone named Frank Dinde. Do you know who he is? I checked. He's in charge of the security division of the Net. That means whatever happened here has shaken them badly. They feel their control slipping, and that scares them. It scares me, too."

A flashing blue light in the street distracted her for a moment. "I can't believe I'm dating such an idiot, can you?"

The dog whined again.

"You're right, they've all been pretty bad. I promise after this I won't have any more boyfriends. I'll either get married or become a nun. How does that sound?"

Cocotte barked.

Andrea frowned at her dog. "You don't seem to agree. I guess I'd make a lousy wife and a worse nun." She made a face. "David Willow sweats too much for me to get serious about him."

She picked up the dog's leash and snapped it on its collar. "You know, David told me the Net is disturbed about a virus. I think the Net is more interested in catching whoever planted that virus and I wouldn't want to be in that person's place when they do. They'll probably send him to a virtual torture chamber. Did you see Ms. Andrews? She looked colder than an ice cube. Poor Mitch. I hope he has better luck getting her to smile than I did. Well, I suppose she's under pressure with this new virus cropping up. I would like to know where it came from, though. Did it come from Virtual Tours?"

Cocotte panted and gave a small *woof.*

"I didn't think so. I have confidence in everyone who works for me. I only hope that the Net will keep their part of the bargain and not sell any more tours until we work this thing out." She shrugged on her coat and grabbed her purse. "It's odd, Cocotte, but I feel as if I could tell you anything, and you actually understand what I'm saying." She laughed shortly. "Our ride should be here. Let's go."

The distance to her apartment was about thirty blocks. Before she'd inherited Cocotte, she used to walk. However, the dog was old and couldn't keep up with her long strides. Even after two blocks, the aged spaniel had to sit and pant a while. Therefore, Andrea had hired a chauffeuring service to pick her up in the morning and drop her off every night. The chauffeurs were very professional, dressed in black uniforms with patent leather shoes. They had caps with shiny brims, and each time they held the door for her, they clasped the cap across their chests. Tonight Andrea was glad to see Tony, her favorite. He was young and handsome, but more than that, he always had a genuine smile for her and for Cocotte.

"At least something went right," she told Cocotte as she settled in the wide leather seat. Cocotte curled up on her lap, and she stroked the little dog's silky ears.

"Good evening, ma'am," Tony said.

"Will you drop the ma'am, please? You know my name." Andrea caught his gaze in the rearview mirror.

"Sorry, Andrea. It's late, isn't it? I was surprised when I got your address."

"It's very late. It's been a terrible day and I haven't even had time to eat dinner." She realized she sounded peevish and frowned.

After a minute Tony said, "I know a nice place by the river."

There was another silence. "Is that an invitation?"

"It sounds like one to me."

Tony looked at her. His eyes were very green. Andrea didn't drop her gaze. "All right," she said slowly. "Let's go to the river."

* * *

After dinner, Tony and Andrea strolled down the riverside. The breeze lifted Andrea's hair and when she reached to smooth it down, her hand encountered Tony's. They stopped and leaned towards each other like swimmers in the deep, moving slowly and in silence. Tony drew Andrea to him and kissed her, while Cocotte nosed through the tall grass and the night birds called to one another.

* * *

Once in the airplane, Mitch thought he'd be able to talk to the woman who had accompanied him all the way from the Virtual Tours office building. She'd been polite, if distant, and they'd spoken a bit in the shuttle cab on the way to the airport. He'd learned her name was Ms. Andrews and that she was the head of the Net Representatives. He was looking forward to finding out more from her.

He was mistaken. When he asked for a briefing, Ms. Andrews had stared at him with her pale eyes and said, "Get this straight. You're a tour guide, not a tour operator. Your job is to go into the tour and see if anything seems out of place while the

Net's virus scanner does its job. There won't be any tourists this trip, so your work won't be taxing. Just go to the places you usually go to and keep your eyes open." Then Ms. Andrews sat down, took a small white pill, and slept for the entire three hours of the voyage.

Annoyed by the Net Rep's dismissal, Mitch waited until she was asleep, opened the overhead luggage compartment and took down her briefcase. The double electronic lock consisted of both a combination lock and a fingerprint ID. The combination lock was no problem. With a tiny, portable computer he had in his back pocket, Mitch ran all the possible combination of numbers through the machine. Next was the fingerprint ID. The woman remained sound asleep while Mitch carefully pressed her index against the small, iridescent square just under the handle. He held his breath as he heard a small *click, zzzz, click.*

"Well, well, well." Mitch lifted a thick sheaf of papers out and shuffled through them. He scanned a couple pages, then came to a paragraph that caught his attention. He read it, then read it again. It took a while for the information to sink in. When it did, he shuddered and took a deep breath.

"Mutants," he whispered, then pursed his lips and looked askance at the woman next to him, now snoring sonorously. "So they exist after all. I always suspected as much. What I'd like to know is why the FBI and the CIA felt the need to keep this program secret all these years. It doesn't make sense. The mutants are harmless, from what it says here."

The papers were in triplicate, faxed, and of a poor quality that made reading them a chore. Mitch browsed through them, a thoughtful look on his face. When the flight attendants came to offer drinks, he shook his head.

Mitch became absorbed in the contents of the papers. He read for the better part of two hours. Then he packed the documents back into the briefcase. He searched the case carefully, to see if he missed anything, but there was nothing except a black plastic beeper with a tiny red light blinking regularly on one side of it. He turned it over in his hands a few times, looking for an outlet or a button, but there was no seam in the plastic. Finally, he snapped the briefcase shut and put it back in the overhead luggage compartment.

He thought about mutants for the rest of the flight.

* * *

Laurel and Carlos ate dinner together in minus three. Their hands kept colliding, the salt shaker kept tipping, their cups wouldn't stand straight, and their feet, beneath the table, found each other and started a caress. Laurel's skin was mother-of-pearl under the bright cafeteria lights, and her cheeks glowed pink coral as their feet entwined. The table before them was an immense stretch of beige sandstone; they were alone in the room. The walls were sea-foam green, and the floor was made of shiny, indigo tiles. Against the ocean colored background, Carlos thought Laurel looked like a mermaid's exotic child, fetched from beneath the waves and deposited on a white beach.

They didn't use sign language, and Carlos didn't speak to her, although he knew she read lips perfectly. He ate, or pretended to eat, for his stomach was tight as a balled fist. Then their feet touched, their eyes met, and Carlos couldn't look away from her.

After dinner, Carlos led Laurel to an elevator that took them up, up, up to the surface where a full moon cast silver light over the empty desert.

Laurel had been to the surface many times, but never at night, and never with Carlos. They held hands as they walked, which put a serious crimp in their conversation. Carlos felt no need to communicate. He knew their thoughts ran along the same path.

Carlos was familiar with the desert. He took Laurel to the edge of a secret canyon, and they sat beneath the vast sky on a smooth, flat rock that still held the heat of the sun. The moon was so bright that the cactus and the aloe cast shadows on the sand. Lizards, thinking it was still daytime, basked in the moonlight, scales shining like tiny beads. A hungry coyote trotted across the wash, yellow eyes intent. A deer stepped out of the night to drink briefly from the narrow silver thread that was the stream. Drops of water fell like diamonds from its muzzle. Without a sound, it faded back into the darkness.

An owl's shadow floated soundlessly across the ground, and Carlos knew what Laurel felt, encased in the stillness of the night. Here, they were equals. Here, under the huge, sparkling vault of the sky, Carlos reached through the wall of silence and pulled Laurel to him.

* * *

Sally went home alone, her heart heavy. Her fingers drummed nervously against her thighs. She opened her mailbox and found a letter from her mother written with silver ink on purple paper. By holding it up to the light, she managed to read most of the writing. It was like deciphering shiny snail trails.

Dear Twinkle Sally Star, I hope you are well and in nirvana. Today the sun is so bright it reminds me of your smile. Sweet Twinkle, my first baby, I miss you so much. I have met the strange ghost who lives in the farthest corners of my mind. He says his name is Deer and tells me that I could have been an opera singer. Don't you think that's wonderful? I sing all the time. Time, what a marvelous invention. If someone would invent a time machine, where would you go? I would go back to when you were five years old and kiss your precious chubby cheeks all over again. I miss the feel of a child's hug. I feel quite happy today. It stopped raining and I will take a walk to see the flowers blooming. I speak to Deer about you. So far, he has only told me that you were fine, and he said you chewed your fingernails. Please don't do that, Twinkle; he says it looks dreadful. I hope you are fine. Nirvana to you, sweet baby, your mother who loves you.

Sally tilted her head to one side and considered the letter. It was the most sensible letter she'd ever received from her mother, an ex-hippy who still lived in a commune. And except for the strange, shiny-transparent ink, it looked almost normal. Whoever or whatever the strange ghost named Deer was, he seemed to be a good influence. She made herself a microwave dinner and ate alone. The night was deep, but she wasn't tired. She was waiting for Mitch to call her and tell her everything was all right. Then she would be fine. She put her fingers in her mouth for comfort, but for once, she didn't chew her nails.

Chapter Six

This hour I tell things in confidence,
I might not tell everybody, but I will tell you.
—Walt Whitman, *Song of Myself*

M-6—Mahler

Somewhere in the farthest corner of my world, there is a crystal tree. I created it with thoughts of moonbeams and ice and with the feel of glass and blue silk. It grew like a crystal, branching intricately the way frost does on a winter morning windowpane. Because it is so beautiful and fragile, I surrounded it with mist, sparkling with millions of diamond-bright raindrops. The result is so ethereal and resplendent that I must stay away from it. Otherwise, I can become lost in contemplation, forgetting everything else. I forget to eat, to drink, to breathe, even, staring hour after hour, day after day, at the marvel. The sun rises and sets, light flowing up and down the branches. At night, each star picks out a branch and confers its lambency to the tree. The moon is in love with its silvery splendor and covers it with kisses made of light.

The tree is not alive and responds not in the least to all this adoration. I call it the Mother Tree.

Today a strange rumor echoed in our worlds that one of us is gone, and shivers of horror iced our limbs. The last time we started to disappear, none of the missing ever returned. Where did they go? All we knew was that there was no answer when we tried to make contact. Their secret worlds were gone as well, vanished in an emptiness that was terrifying after the gorgeous splendor of their existence.

M-18 is gone, the one they call Monkey. His absence leaves an ache behind him, an empty space. Although we have never actually spoken, we have communicated many times. We feel each other's presence keenly for we are all related, taken from the same human woman's eggs and multiplied.

How do I know all this? You seem to forget. We have access to all records kept on the Net. We are the Net's bastard children, unacknowledged and anonymous. The Net is our father, and our mother abandoned her eggs to science and never attended our birth. Hard parents, indeed. I know. I have studied psychology on the Net, been to chat forums, and participated in grief sessions where all my angst of not having a normal family was partially abated. The rest is poured into the roots of my Mother Tree and it flourishes, nourished by my pain and love, a blindingly beautiful monument to my inhumanity.

I consider myself the eldest male of the remaining mutants. My code is M-6; the name on my glass case is Mahler, perhaps given by a scientist with a bitter sense of humor. I looked up Mahler on the Net, and his sixth symphony is called 'Tragic.' Perhaps I'm simply being too sensitive. The first five M's, one through five, are all females. They are a closely-knit group, rarely participating in our discussions, except to be bossy and to give orders. Are all older sisters like that? I believe so. The rest of us are fairly independent. The scientists like to work with the five sisters-they do most of the mathematical work-and right now, they are busy scanning the universe for signs of radioactivity.

I am more attuned to the others than any of my siblings are. The scientists often use me to find out what is wrong with one or another of our group. A moment ago, they asked me to contact everyone and reassure them, to tell them that M-18 has just gone for a small trip.

To tell you the truth, I don't know if this reassures me or calls attention to the fact that so many others disappeared and were never spoken of again. I will meditate on the command.

The Mother Tree is below me. I open my arms and swoop from the sky, gliding through the cool mist, to land on the smooth rocks. The tree is on a cliff. Beneath it, the sea crashes against huge boulders, sending glittering spray into the air. I tip my face to the sky and feel the water droplets on my skin. How akin to tears they are. Monkey, Monkey, can you hear me? Take care of yourself. Don't get lost out there; the real world is a terrifying place for mutants.

* * *

Monkey was lost. He'd taken the hallway leading to the restroom, found the correct icon, and used the facilities with only a slight mishap. He had yet to become accustomed to zippers; his boxer shorts were caught and the metal teeth wouldn't let go. Monkey urinated the best he could, pulling his penis out of the small hole the zipper left. He shook the remaining drops off the end, as Professor Toutbon had showed him. Then he washed his hands. Washing his hands was fun; he could stare into the mirror and see his face and body, something none of the mutants could ever do. He had no idea if he was handsome or not, and it didn't matter. He enjoyed the way his mouth moved, the way his eyebrows went up and down, and how he could wink one eye, then the other. He had an expressive face, and it amused him to feign fear, surprise, joy, and sadness in quick succession. His own face fascinated him. After he washed his hands, he dried them by pushing a button on a machine that created gusts of hot air.

He left the bathroom and stood uncertainly in the hall. He had no idea if he'd come from the left or the right. The man accompanying him, Frank Dinde, had gone to some place known as the *cigarettemachine.* He tilted his head, considering his options. Left or right? He opted for left and walked down the hallway. Once he fell down, too occupied with looking up at the lights, but he put his hands out and caught himself.

* * *

Mitch was strolling down the hallway, looking for the men's room. He was impressed by the headquarters, still amazed by the luxurious entranceway, which looked more like a five-star Venetian hotel than the headquarters for the Net Government. Italian tiles in muted terra cotta and pale blue covered the floor. The walls were stained brick red and the windows were all copies from an Italian palace in Venice. Very nice, indeed. Copies of Renaissance paintings hung on the walls, and overhead hung small, crystal chandeliers.

Coming down the hallway in front of him was a man walking with his nose in the air. He seemed to be examining the lights, stopping now and then to gape. He was very young, or seemed so, with a smooth, pale face and candid eyes. His hair was a riot of red curls, as bright as polished copper, and his fly was open. His underwear poked out like a handkerchief, and so did his penis. The young man wasn't walking as much as he was swiveling. His legs seemed to be unsure exactly where they wanted to go. Once he pitched forward, his torso advancing before his feet, but he gave a funny leap and caught himself, then stood grinning, pleased with his effort.

He caught sight of Mitch and his grin widened. "Hello," he said, in a warm, joyful voice. "Can I help you?"

Mitch was caught off guard. "I was just going to ask the same of you," he admitted. He cocked his head. "Did you know your fly was open?"

The man looked puzzled. "Which one is my fly?" He opened and closed his eyes, his mouth, and his fists. "Is it closed now?"

Mitch pointed. "No, your fly's still open. It's there. And unless you want to get arrested, I'd put your pal back inside."

"Oh. My pal? What a funny name for a penis. Hold on now, everything seems to be stuck." He tugged and tugged, oblivious to the danger a suddenly unstuck zipper posed to a tender penis.

Mitch jumped forward. "Wait! First tuck him back inside. If you get him stuck in the zipper it's straight to the emergency ward."

"Is that supposed to happen?"

"Supposed to?" Mitch frowned. "No. Take this end and hold that side down, steady now, I'll pull here and you yank up." There was a ripping sound and the underwear was free.

"There, good as new. You're presentable again." Mitch stuck out his hand. "I'm Mitch. What's your name?"

"Monkey. Pleased to meet you."

"Um, you usually let go of a person's hand after the first minute or so." Mitch removed his hand from Monkey's grasp.

"I like holding your hand." He said it simply, like a child.

"Do you?" Mitch blinked, then his face cleared. "You're one of the mutants, aren't you?"

"I am, yes." Monkey blushed and put his hands behind his back, then in front of him, then held them stiffly at his sides. "Professor Toutbon didn't have time to teach me everything. I've been relying on the experiences I encountered in virtual worlds on the web. So far, I haven't seen any dragons. I would like to see a real one; do you know where they sleep? First, I'd better find a light saber. Have you any idea where the magic swords could be hidden? I've been looking very carefully for secret spaces, but so far, everything has been as it appears."

Mitch smiled. He shook his head. "I'm afraid dragons only exist in virtual worlds. We're all out of magic swords at the moment, and secret spaces are usually hidden behind mirrors. We're frightfully ordinary in all aspects, otherwise. Will you come with me? I have to go to the men's room, but then we can go get something to eat. I have a feeling the cafeteria here has excellent Italian food."

"I would like that very much." An enormous smile lit his face. "I'm so happy to meet you." They walked together down the hall, Monkey hanging tightly to Mitch's hand.

As they passed, the eyes in one of the paintings followed them.

* * *

M-6—Mahler

There are secret worlds everywhere. Some are hidden behind mirrors, some are in spaces created by computer programmers, and some are invented by the mind. Some simply exist and no one knows how they came into being.

In my travels, I have seen the worlds created by men in the virtual programs. There are worlds of magic, sorcery, dragons and demons, worlds of splendor and fear. There are worlds made to entertain, with parachuting, deep sea diving, and roller coasters galore. The most interesting worlds are the museums, developed for educative and cultural purposes, with hands-on demonstrations and scientific explanations. Of course, that is just a personal opinion. Chat forums are very popular with mutants. We like to communicate with humans; the interaction is vital for our well-being. Speaking to the scientists through our consoles isn't enough.

Most of the people working with us ignore the extent of our need for communication. The reason, I believe, is our penchant for disappearing into the Net and being hard to recall on our consoles. The scientists have gotten used to waiting for hours, sometimes, for us to come online and answer them. From this, they have gathered that we are often dreaming in our own private worlds. Hard to boot up, is an expression they use.

Do they even know about our worlds? Do they believe, on the other hand, that we are so machine-like that the space of time before we answer their call is simply the same thing as a computer booting itself up? Perhaps they think that because of our complexity, we need time to open all our circuits for trading information. I have never asked Professor Toutbon, the head of our department, about any of this. And I never ask Dr. Djusky anything at all. I think it's necessary to cultivate a bit of mystery concerning us. We are so dependent upon the scientists. It is purely a survival instinct that causes me to say nothing. My five elder sisters, too involved in each other to participate in my life, have agreed with me in this. As the others tend to follow our lead, there has never been the slightest whisper of the fact that we roam upon the Net in all liberty, taking part in discussions meant for humans, exploring museums, game worlds, and riding roller coasters to our hearts' delight.

Our own worlds are different from the places we create for the tourists. Our worlds reflect our reality, and the restrictions humans live with have no meaning for us. We try to spend as much time there as possible, but some of those locations are hard to reach, even for us. The scientists believe we sleep most of the time, like computers in rest mode. The inverse is true. We hardly sleep at all, and when we do, our dreams are full of strange longing.

Chapter Seven

Logic and sermons never convince,
The damp of the night drives deeper into my soul.
—Walt Whitman, *Song of Myself*

Carlos was a technician, not a scientist. He was also the official liaison between the secret complex beneath the surface of the desert and the natives living not far away in their traditional tribal village.

The murders committed upon the Net were none of his affair until the orders came.

Professor Toutbon called him on his interline.

"Carlos, can you check the mutants' whereabouts during the last three days? I want a full report, in triplicate."

"Isn't that what you gave the Net Rep?"

"It is, but this report is for the police. They're starting to gather information for the inquest."

"The police know about the mutants?"

"No, it's for the federal police. The Net called them in. They're not stupid, you know. They're also covering all the bases. If someone planted a killer virus, the Net wants to prosecute them fully."

"Is there a suspicion the virus came from the mutants?"

"No, I don't think so. The Net believes it came from outside."

"What about the feds? What do they think?"

"They're starting a murder investigation. They're not guessing about anything right now; they're just gathering information."

The Professor didn't usually speak in such subdued tones. "Is everything all right?" Carlos asked. He turned on a floating video screen, and the professor's face came into view.

"I'm worried about Monkey. I should never have agreed to send him without a proper escort. I should have insisted in going myself."

"He arrived in Dallas and everything is going smoothly."

"How did you know that?" Professor Toutbon asked.

Carlos hesitated. "Laurel told me."

"Oh. That was last night. Anything could happen in a day. He could fall down the stairs, get hit by a bus...anything."

"He's worth a fortune, and the Net will probably have a guard with him every second. Professor Toutbon, I'd like to ask you a question, if I may, but you don't have to answer if it's none of my business."

"What is it, Carlos?"

"Why is the Net so concerned about this? I mean, why didn't they bring their equipment here and plug it into a mutant?"

"I'm not sure I would have liked them to come here and start poking around. At any rate, the Net has a new virus-catching program in their headquarters. It's highly protected and can't be accessed from anywhere but there."

"But what exactly has the Net got to do with this?"

"The companies linked to the Net started asking the Net Government to help develop imaginary worlds for their game programs. The Net Government then contacted the federal mutant program, asking for technical help."

"They knew about us?" Carlos gave a little cough. "No, forget I asked that."

Professor Toutbon chuckled over the phone. "The mutants were being used for various tasks, both trivial and important. Developing imaginary worlds for recreation or games was a novel idea. It was also a lucrative idea, and the Virtual Tours program was born. From within the computers themselves, the mutants invent, create and expand worlds that no human could imagine. That was not their primary use, of course, but it is highly profitable one, and the Net encouraged game companies to take out contracts with them, never telling anyone who was really creating the virtual worlds. The mutant program remained a secret while the Net or private companies got all the credit."

"That doesn't sound fair."

"We wanted it that way." On the floating video screen in front of Carlos, Professor Toutbon's face became grave. "Most people would be frightened at the thought of mutants."

Carlos nodded. "You're right. We haven't told the villagers about the mutants. The only ones who know this isn't a biological weapon research center are the tribe's elders."

"You see? They're more comfortable with the idea of deadly viruses than mutants."

Carlos touched the bottom of the screen, sending ripples through Professor Toutbon's image. "I'll see what I can do to get the transcripts."

"Ask Mahler. He's the eldest mutant, and he'll be able to get them for you the fastest."

"All right. See you later, Professor."

* * *

Laurel concentrated on the glowing screen in front of her. At least she appeared to concentrate. Actually, her mind was far away, in the middle of a nighttime desert, with her lover lying beside her on soft, warm sand.

She imagined his hands, his capable, sure hands, as they caressed her trembling body. She knew each place his lips had touched; his kisses were branded on her skin. She could still feel the velvet hardness that nudged her legs apart.

She blushed, and warm color flooded her pale cheeks, making her eyes brilliant. In the faint, green glow of the computer screen, she looked more than ever like a mermaid, underwater with the obscurity of the depths around her. In the darkness, her hand fluttered over the keyboard, typing symbols her eyes saw but her mind didn't process. She was dreaming, deep within her well of silence, but no longer alone. She could sense Carlos now, a second heart in tune with hers. She knew where he was, and if he stepped out of the elevator at her back, she would still feel his body's vibration and turn. They resonated to the same note and could feel each other even when they were too far apart to touch.

The elevator doors slid open and Laurel swiveled her chair around. Carlos stepped out, as she knew he would. He paused. When she smiled he gave an answering grin, and she realized she'd been holding her breath. She stood and held her arms open. He came to her, and she kissed him on the mouth. To tease him, she stroked his thigh and signed, "Hello, handsome lover."

A faint flush reddened his cheeks. "Hello," he signed. "Did you sleep well?"

"Of course. I wish you could have stayed with me," she answered wistfully.

"I would ask you to come home with me, but I live with my parents." He grinned and shrugged.

She laughed silently. "My room is a cubbyhole and only has a twin bed."

"That's all right. As long as it doesn't rain, we can stay outside."

"When will it rain?"

"In the desert it rains once, maybe twice a year. I bet you've never gone camping, have you? I have a tent, sleeping bags, and I toast a mean marshmallow. Will you be afraid to stay with me all night long in the desert?"

Laurel cocked her head. She looked at him, considering. Then she smiled. "As long as I'm with you, I'm not afraid of anything." They kissed. Then Laurel pulled away. "Do you know anything about boats?"

He shook his head. "I've never been on a boat."

Her face lit up as she signed, "Me neither. We'll have fun learning. You'll see."

"See what?" he asked, but she shook her head.

"It's too early for dreams," she replied.

"I need to speak to Mahler. Will you take me to meet him?" Carlos asked.

* * *

Laurel and Carlos walked down the hall pausing intermittently to allow Laurel to speak with her graceful gestures. She tapped her head. "Mahler seems to be the most attuned to our way of thinking. The others can sometimes be hard to understand."

Carlos nodded. "Are you sure you won't get in trouble for letting me talk to him?"

"No, of course not. Your blue badge gives you access to the mutants' consoles, and that means you can talk to them if you wish."

"I never realized that." Carlos frowned.

"They don't encourage outsiders to come and chat," signed Laurel, regret on her face. "I think it's a mistake because everyone needs stimulation from the outside or they develop psychological disorders."

"I'm sorry—some of your words are not familiar to me in signs."

"I'll carry my light pen next time," she motioned with a smile.

In front of Mahler's glass case, they stood shoulder to shoulder, peering through the thick vapor at the mutant floating within. Sometimes he was nearly obscured by clouds. Although his eyes were open, he claimed he rarely registered what he saw. All his thought images were supplied through the console. It was his doorway to the outside world, a doorway his mind could use but not his body.

Mahler had auburn hair. It floated in coppery curls about his wide shoulders. His torso was beautifully developed, but something had hampered his legs—they were small, twisted things that seemed to have no bones. It was a pity, because if his legs and hips had developed as his upper body had, he would have looked like a young god. Instead, he looked like an alien. The swirling clouds of gas and the fine, shiny wires attached to various parts of his body didn't help. When Carlos started typing on the console Mahler opened his blue eyes and stared at them through the thick glass. His lips curved in a smile, and as usual, when she saw him, Laurel felt a pang of sorrow so acute it brought tears to her eyes. She turned away, looking instead at the screen where bright letters chased themselves across a black background.

"Hello, Mahler, I'm Carlos. I'm one of the technicians. Are you with us?" Carlos used the keyboard instead of the microphone out of deference to Laurel.

Green words flowed across the screen. "Hello, Carlos, I am here."

"I want to talk to you about what's going on here. A few days ago in a place called Virtual Tours, two men were killed while hooked into the Net. We have no idea how they were killed. They were guides in the newest program created for Virtual Tours with the help of your team. The Net has taken M-18 to their headquarters in Dallas to hook him up to a new virus-catching program they've developed in hopes of finding something in the Tour."

"So that's why he is missing. We wondered."

"No one told you why he was gone?" Carlos looked intently at the console.

"No, should they have?"

"They could have," he temporized. "The police have asked for a full report on all the mutants' movements during the time the Virtual Tour was in operation. Do you mind if we give them all the transcripts?"

There was a pause while little stars flowed across the screen, a sign Mahler was thinking. Finally the words appeared. "Why do you ask?"

"I wanted your permission."

"You don't need it. You can print out anything you wish from our records. All our movements are described. There is nothing to ask for."

"I think it's time we started to communicate more fully," Carlos replied.

"We communicate with the scientists constantly."

"But you haven't communicated with me. For me, communication means something that goes two ways. So far, we haven't truly spoken. We give you orders and you execute. When have you ever asked for anything?" Carlos finished the sentence despite Laurel tugging frantically on his arm.

"I never knew we could ask for anything," the mutant admitted, and within the glass case his body rotated. "Tell me more. Do the police think we have something to do with the deaths?"

"I don't know," Carlos typed.

Laurel stood quite still, staring at the mutant. Her body was oddly stiff.

"I want to know more. How did the men die?" Mahler's face never changed expression; it remained serene and angelically smiling.

"I don't know. I wasn't allowed to read the reports."

"If the police have them, I will be able to access them." Mahler turned slowly, floating in his foggy bed.

"Who worked on the program in the beginning? Which of you...mutants?" Carlos typed that last word hesitantly.

"I know what you call us." Mahler's smile didn't waver. His face, close now to the side of the case, came into clear focus. Its beauty was astounding. It looked as if an angel were staring out of the clouds. His eyes were so blue they appeared electric. "It was the youngsters. That is what we call them. M-16, 17, 18, one boy and two girls. M-12 through M-19 are all used to create the games and virtual worlds. They are artists: masters of illusion, emotion and imagination."

"Are they younger than you are?" Carlos asked.

"No, not physically. But they were awakened a few years later than the rest of us, putting their intellectual ability above ours and their emotional development on the level of a fifteen or sixteen-year-old."

"Why would waking them later enhance their intellect?"

"They spent more time shunted and received more capacity than we did. We are all different, you know. Or did you know? Each of us is unique. The scientists in charge of the program experimented in many different ways."

"Clarify." Carlos typed a curt order, then as an afterthought added, "Please."

"M-1 through 5, mathematical programming, analysis, data storage and scanning. They can stay awake for one hundred and fifty hours without losing the slightest bit of concentration. Perfect for scanning the furthest reaches of the universe, hooked into the Saturn III telescope, searching for signs of life. Main function: exploring the vast nether regions of outer space.

"M-6, M-7, and M-8 were developed primarily for communication analysis and development, also used for research, clarification and explanation of different subtle movements in the dynamics of world weather changes, crops, and earthquakes. We are intimately linked to several thousand sensors around the world, sensors measuring heat, light, vibration, and air and water currents.

"M-9 through M-11 were born blind, deaf and dumb. They are the middle children, as we call them. We care for them and answer for them, because they will not answer you directly if you use their consoles. In fact, when you see the writing on their screens, it is actually myself or M-7 who is answering for them."

"I didn't know that." Carlos, threw a startled look at Laurel, who raised her eyebrows, shrugging to show him she didn't know either. "Does anyone else know this?"

"Professor Toutbon, Dr. Djusky, and the main technicians working on this floor."

"Why do they not answer?"

"They never learned how. They have not mastered communication through words. In your world, children such as these are called autistic. They live in a different world, have other ways of communication. They are dreamers, and we use their dreams for various things. They are geniuses in the realms of math probability and statistics. We believe they can alter, in a certain way, time."

"They can change time?"

"Only for themselves," Mahler said.

Carlos signed at Laurel, "What do you make of all this?"

"I had no idea." Her hands flew, agitated. "It makes no sense to me. I had no idea the program was so complex. The mutants never admitted that they had so many differences, and Professor Toutbon has never encouraged anyone to come and socialize with them. They are only used for their programs."

"It's a crime," Carlos told her angrily.

"What would you do with the mutants? Would you just turn them out in the world? What would become of them if they weren't taken care of here?" Laurel replied, her expression worried.

"I never thought of it that way. Do you believe him?"

"The professor says they cannot lie."

Carlos turned back to the console. "More questions," he wrote. "Which mutants work on the Virtual Tour programs now?"

"Almost the same group as in the beginning. M-9, M-10, M-11, M-16, M-17, M-18 and myself. I was asked to help supervise, although most of the work was done by M-18. He's quite proficient at developing worlds."

"You developed tour programs about places that actually exist, with everything exactly as it is in real life. Is that unusual, or do you use imaginary worlds as the basis for your programs?"

"It is more common to use existing worlds or places. It is much easier, for one thing. Furthermore, it is not certain your minds could comprehend a world that we mutants made up from our imagination. Our perceptions of reality are so different from your own..."

The words broke off. An eerie stillness descended upon the room. And then, in their cases, nearly all the mutants started moving, their limbs waving slowly, as if they were swimming.

"What is it? What is wrong?" Carlos typed.

"You may send the transcripts to the police. It doesn't matter to us. To answer your other two questions, you had better leave. Dr. Djusky is coming in the elevator, and he doesn't seem happy."

"How do you know this?" Carlos asked, stunned.

"The middle children can see outside their cages. They seem to be able to project their minds to a distance of up to three miles from this point. Go now, but come back soon. I would like to speak more with you, Carlos."

Carlos and Laurel left, after waving goodbye to Mahler. He waved back, his face serene.

"Did you notice something?" asked Carlos, as they rode the service elevator towards Laurel's bureau.

"What in particular?"

"In the last phrase he wrote so quickly. He wrote cage, instead of case."

"I don't think it was conscious," Laurel signed.

"That makes it even worse."

Chapter Eight

I heard what was said of the universe,
Heard it and heard it of several thousand years;
It is middling well as far as it goes—but is that all?
—Walt Whitman, *Song of Myself*

Andrea woke up from a dream of floating in blue water. Keeping her eyes closed to hang onto the last, faint images in her mind, she reached her hand out to turn off her alarm clock before it rang.

It wasn't in its place. Instead, her hand encountered a warm expanse of smooth skin. Her eyes flew open. On the pillow next to her head, there was another head, turned away, and a broad shoulder rose out of the sheets like a mountain, cutting off her view of the table. She froze, her hand hovering over Tony's back, while her other hand groped for a clue to tell her where her clothes were.

She was naked under the sheets, no silky nightgown crumpled on or under the covers. She shifted slightly and peered out the window. A cold, gray light showed feebly under the shades. Her hand continued its search, feeling for a shirt, a skirt, anything to wear. Nothing. There was nothing she could reach. Her eyes, becoming adjusted to the dim light, made out her blouse on the other side of the room hanging over her lampshade. A pair of men's shorts lay on top of it, and a tie curled like a snake over everything. There was a chauffeur's cap sitting on the chair closest her bed, but that was it.

Tony didn't stir, and he didn't snore, which was a blessing. His skin was warm and soft, and her hand lowered itself of its own accord and draped over his side.

Andrea watched as her traitorous fingers stroked the white skin just under Tony's arm. The bed was so warm and inviting; why think of leaving it? It smelled of roses and musk, her expensive perfume, and something that might be Old Spice. Her body curled itself up next to his, pressing against his back. He murmured something in his sleep and rolled over. His arm crept over her shoulders, pulling her closer.

There was a moment of silence, of sweetness, when Andrea felt a keen joy. Serenity filled her spirit and she slid her hand down beneath the covers.

The alarm went off with a noise like a mad siren.

* * *

Monkey had spent a most fascinating night. First the helicopter ride, then the taxi, and then there was the Net headquarters. He had been so happy to meet Mitch, with whom he felt an instant and deep affinity. His hand had been comfortably warm, not cool and damp, or quivery, like the Net Rep called Frank Dinde. Furthermore, Mitch had truly spoken to him, not treating him like a mutant. He had looked at him straight and even joked around and helped him choose what to eat from the buffet table at the cafeteria.

Mitch was his friend, he felt sure of that. He hadn't wanted to go to his room by himself so Mitch had suggested they share a double room.

Monkey was grateful. He had been terribly apprehensive about sleeping alone in a strange room in a bed. Beds were something he'd never had to get used to; his body had always floated in a buoyant cloud. After only one day out of his case, his muscles were sore and he ached all over from the stress and strain of remaining upright. He had good muscle tone and wasn't exhausted, but he felt worn out, fragile, and he was thankful Mitch volunteered to room with him. No one else had wanted to.

Now he opened his eyes and sat up. There was no light, so he got out of bed and raised the window shades. The cold, pale light of dawn flooded the room. It cast a faint, pink glow on Mitch's face, and he moaned in his sleep and put his arm over his eyes.

Monkey perched on the end of Mitch's bed and waited patiently for him to awake. After a few minutes, he felt the urge to go to the facilities and he did so. Then he put his wet boxer shorts into the sink. He looked at his face in the mirror for a while. He brushed his teeth, which he liked doing very much. He brushed his hair as well and then took a bath, filling it first with cold water, then adding hot.

The bath overflowed onto the floor, but that was all right. There were plenty of towels to soak up the water. When he finished, he discovered that all the towels were wet, so he padded around the room naked, waiting to dry off. He started to shiver. He woke Mitch by shaking him none too gently.

"What? What is it?" Mitch asked groggily.

"I have bumpy skin and my teeth chatter."

Mitch groaned, turned on the light and peered at Monkey. "You're naked. Put some clothes on. You're just cold, that's all," he added, reaching out and touching his arm.

"I'm cold," Monkey agreed. "You're warm. Move over." He crawled into the bed with Mitch and huddled next to him, trembling. Mitch uttered a loud sigh, and then he moved over. Monkey's body relaxed. He snuggled into the warmth of the bed and sighed happily. "Thank you, Mitch. You saved my life."

Mitch uttered a surprised laugh. "Don't be silly. Next time you take a bath, dry off and get dressed quickly. That way you won't get chilled. Are you feeling better now?"

"So much better." Monkey sighed deeply, then he paused. "You know, it's funny, but my little pal, as you call him, isn't so little anymore."

Mitch rolled over and raised his eyebrows at Monkey. "What do you mean?"

"He's quite stiff and pointing. I feel, I don't know, strange somehow." His voice rose and quavered in fear. "Am I dying again? Am I sick?"

Mitch's mouth twitched, but his expression remained serious. "It's normal. Your body is telling you that it's feeling horny. In your virtual worlds, didn't you ever..." He sat up and frowned. "Get up, Monkey, I'm going to take you to breakfast. We'll talk about this in more detail."

"I'm not sick?" Monkey asked. His fright was ebbing. He wondered why Mitch looked so solemn all of a sudden, though.

"No, not at all."

"I can't get dressed. My shorts are all wet and the zipper is broken on my pants."

Mitch dug through his suitcase and found some extra clothes. "Here are some clean shorts and pants. Didn't Professor Toutbon give you anything to wear?"

"Only one outfit." Monkey put on Mitch's clothes and admired himself in the mirror. "I look very nice in blue. We have the same color eyes. Except mine are darker blue and yours are very, very pale. I like your eyes better. I wish mine would look like yours."

Mitch smiled and patted his shoulder. "Yours are great, don't worry. Come on; let's go out to eat. I saw a diner from the window that should be open." He glanced at his watch. "It's nearly six a.m., the best time of day for hash browns."

"Hash browns?"

"You're going to love them."

"What about my mask?"

Mitch shook his head. "I don't think they'll let us out if you wear it. Look, I imagine you've had your vaccinations and all your shots, or you wouldn't be here. A few germs won't hurt you. Just don't touch any doorknobs, all right? Hey, that's a joke. Lighten up. Smile!"

Monkey felt shaky and unsure of himself. But going out to eat something sounded good, so he pasted a stiff smile on his face and followed Mitch, being careful not to touch the doorknob. Joke or no joke; he wasn't taking any chances. Professor Toutbon had managed to frighten him with his stories about germs.

They walked down the stairs to the lobby. Mitch nodded politely to the guard and gave him false names. Monkey wondered about that, but the guard opened the door and Mitch dragged him outside before he could ask. They went across the street to the diner and sat on shiny red seats. Monkey loved the napkin holder and would have pulled all the napkins out if Mitch hadn't stopped him.

Mitch ordered for both of them while Monkey amused himself with the saltshaker. The hash browns arrived and Monkey loved them. They were so crunchy and tender, so salty and sweet. He put a bit of egg on them and tried that, then ate some toast. He adored the tartness of orange juice, thought coffee was bitter, and bacon made him sneeze for some reason. The waitress, a pretty girl with a red dress and a little pin that said 'I'm Sarah,' poured coffee into their cups whenever the level dropped the slightest bit.

Mitch took his time explaining the facts of life to Monkey, who gave him all his attention.

"You're saying that sex is something men and women do together for recreation?" Monkey asked.

"Men and women, yes, but also men and men, and women and women. The important thing is not the act but the emotion that accompanies it. It's called love. When you fall in love with someone, you want to spend the rest of your life with him or her. You want to have children and grow old with that person at your side. Sex is just a tiny part of the whole picture. Unfortunately, it's a very strong impulse."

"You're saying I should learn how to control this impulse?" Monkey asked, his face serious.

"Yeah, that's about right."

"You also said that if I do something called masturbation, it would be easier to control?"

"Right again." Mitch grinned. "You learn very quickly."

"If I understand correctly, I should use my hand to satisfy the strange urgency in my pal, wait until I fall in love with someone, and then have sex."

"It sounds rather cold-blooded if you put it like that, but yes, I think that's what I would tell my own son."

"What exactly do I do with my hand?" Monkey's face was perfectly candid as he asked this question.

Mitch choked on his hash browns. "Haven't you ever gone to a chat room on sex?" he asked.

"No." Monkey raised his eyebrows. "Will I learn all there is to know about sex on the Net?"

"You might learn the mechanics, but sexual feelings in virtual worlds have been repressed by the Net Government. Still, I suppose you could go to a sex education site and read about it."

Sarah poured some more coffee. "You know, I'll be glad to help you if you need a hand." She blushed as she said this, but her eyes didn't leave Monkey's face.

He stared, fascinated. "Are you a real woman?"

"I'm about to go on break. Why don't you follow me and find out?" She put the coffeepot down on the table and walked to a door in the back of the room.

"I can't go in there," Monkey said, agitatedly. "It has the wrong icon!"

"If you're invited, you can go wherever you want," Mitch said. "It's up to you now."

"What would you do in my place?" he asked.

Mitch tilted his head. "In your place? I don't know." He drew a little circle in the spilled salt on the table. "When this is over, you'll be taken back to the Center, won't you?"

Monkey nodded. "Why do you look sad, Mitch?"

Mitch shrugged. "After all my talk about true love and how to handle sexual frustration, I just realized you're going back to your case, and it won't ever apply to you, that's all."

"What are you trying to tell me?" Monkey asked. "Are you saying I should follow I'm Sarah?"

"Yeah, I guess so." Mitch brushed the salt off the table with the flat of his hand. "Go on. This might be your one chance to find out what the fuss is all about."

Monkey wasn't sure what Mitch meant, but the door with the woman's icon still beckoned. He rose, his heart starting to thump in his chest. Whatever was behind that door was more frightening than all the monsters of Zorg and more exciting than any game he'd ever played. Carefully, without touching the doorknob, he entered the room.

* * *

Mitch sipped his coffee slowly. Monkey had been gone for twenty minutes by his watch. Then the waitress came out, her face flushed, patting her hair down and straightening her skirt. Monkey followed a few moments later. He drifted across the room and sat down, a huge smile on his face.

"Well?" asked Mitch. Monkey's dazed expression reminded him of the first time he made love to Sally. He couldn't suppress a grin.

"I'm never going back to my glass case." Monkey's face was very pale and his navy blue eyes glittered. "That is the most amazing feeling, as if my insides were turning upside-down. I don't know if it's love, but it must be close. I feel as if I could jump to the top of the building and float down."

"You can't. It's the real world here. But it sounds like Sarah knew what she was doing."

"She did." Monkey took a sip of his orange juice and sighed deeply. "Wow."

*   *   *

All day long, Carlos thought about what Mahler had said. He couldn't concentrate on his job; his mind was on the alien floating dreamlike in his cloudy world.

"Cage, cage," he muttered. "Why did he let that slip? Was it intentional? Why did he warn us about Dr. Djusky?" The questions went unanswered, just as his work went unfinished while he stared pensively at the poster in his cubbyhole of an office.

Finally he went into the system and called up the conversation they'd had that morning on his monitor. He studied it carefully, tapping a pencil against his teeth as he tried to recall the mutant's expressions. Not that he'd had very many. His face had been like marble, with the same white perfection as stone.

Several phrases caught his attention, though.

He put his face in his hands and thought. What he wanted to do was to speak to the tribal elders about all this, but he didn't have the time.

When the five o'clock buzzer sounded in the complex, Carlos donned a white lab coat, put a call through to Laurel, and took the elevator back down to the mutants' level. In his hand was a small paper. Upon the paper were several questions he needed Mahler to answer. Then he would talk to his elders and they would tell him what to do.

* * *

Laurel accompanied him. One of her particular talents, directly linked to her deafness, was her ability to read facial and body expressions.

Mahler was waiting for them. His face, pressed close to the glass, was unearthly in its pure beauty. Mist obscured most of his naked body, but his smooth, powerful shoulders were visible. Laurel had never used sign language with the mutants. There were not many times when she'd had the opportunity to communicate with them, even though she was Toutbon's assistant. In fact, she avoided them whenever possible. The beautiful, otherworldly faces in their foggy cases disturbed her.

Now, as she drew near, she tried to concentrate on each of Mahler's movements, to perceive a hidden meaning behind his words. She stood at Carlos's shoulder, able to see the screen and the case at the same time. The first questions were easy, and Mahler answered them readily.

"Will you please explain what you meant when you said that M-9, M-10 and M-11 could change time?"

"They can only change time for themselves. Sometimes they can stretch out spaces of time so that they are doubled or tripled. The scientists have been trying to understand the mechanics of their talent, but they have yet to comprehend. We use them with the virtual tours to make the three days seem like a week. Hadn't you wondered about that?"

"I didn't realize that," Carlos murmured. He typed, "The scientists haven't made any of their studies about that particular aspect of the mutants known yet."

Laurel caught the barest flicker in Mahler's eyes. She was troubled by the way the interview was going. There was too much revealed on Carlos's side, and Mahler was doing his best to withhold important information, she was sure.

Carlos moved on to the next two questions. "You told us that you considered the last group of mutants the youngsters. Mentally, you said, they were more advanced than you were, but emotionally you placed them on a fifteen-year-old level. Can you be more explicit? How do mutants mature? Do they experience an adolescence as we know it and what role do hormones play in your body's development?"

Mahler's mouth quirked. "Ah, Carlos. I can see what you're leading up to, but I will answer you anyway. We have the same emotions that you have. Fear, hate, love, joy, even lust are born in our minds, but our bodies are not like yours. They are half machine, half alive, and do not respond to your stimuli. Our hormones are the same as yours, but we discipline them. We live in worlds of our own making, and any emotions we need to exorcise or want to empower are ours to control. From what I gather of the real world, most of the time you cannot control your emotions or your reactions. We not only control them, we create them or destroy them. We live in our own worlds, so you can imagine that we form them to suit our various needs."

Carlos looked thoughtful. "Another question, please. Have you read the transcripts from the police?"

"Yes." Mahler shifted ever so slightly in his cloud.

"Print them out for me, please," Carlos wrote. The console hummed and a sheaf of paper slid out of a bottom drawer. Carlos perused them, hesitating at one or two places. "What do you think of their idea of using M-18 as a detective?" Carlos asked.

"I didn't think much of the idea." The mutant shook his head slowly. In his glass case, his hair floated around his head, weightlessly, as if he was underwater. It was almost like watching a marine creature.

"You must have some idea of what happened," Carlos said. "Don't you?"

"Why should I? Actually, I don't. It's very curious, and I will have to meditate upon it. The thing I don't comprehend is the sexual part of the murders."

"Do you know what the police will do with Mitch Palo?"

"I have no idea." Mahler's grave expression never changed.

"In the report, it says that Mr. Palo is a witness for the defense. He was a tour guide with Virtual Tours. Why do you suppose the police want him as well as M-18 in Dallas?"

Mahler turned his face, so that all they saw was his clear-cut profile. "Is that a rhetorical question, or do I have to answer?"

"I'd like you to answer," Carlos said.

"He's the bait," Mahler replied, and for the first time, he smiled.

* * *

Carlos poked the campfire fire a bit, sending red sparks into the air. He looked at Laurel and smiled. Light flickered on her skin and bald head. They sat side by side on a sleeping bag, their faces towards the fire.

Laurel took a light pen from her pocket and wrote in the air in front of her, leaving green glowing filaments. The words floated, sparkled a bit, then dissipated in the faint breeze. "Mahler was lying," she wrote.

"About what?" Carlos asked. The statement caught him off guard. He'd been thinking how pretty she looked in the firelight.

"I'm not too sure. He was very clever. He knew I was watching him and he was very careful not to show me his feelings. I don't know how, but he knew I could read him."

"Does he know you're deaf?"

Laurel winced. "The mutants say they don't mind if you call them mutants, but I don't like to be called deaf."

"Sorry. What do you prefer to be called?"

"Laurel, if it's all right with you." She wrinkled her nose and laughed silently. "All right, I'm being silly. Hearing impaired is such a vulgar expression, and deaf is so absolute. I like to think of myself as silenceful. That's a word I made up. It's graceful and more feminine than deaf."

She stopped writing and sat very still for a moment, looking out over the desert. "It's very silenceful out here at night, isn't it?" Laurel's light pen flashed as she wrote, and the letters wavered as the breeze moved them. They sparkled green and gold before vanishing.

Carlos nodded. The breeze moved the tent flap, and a coyote howled from far away. The moon was still fat and round, but tonight there were small wisps of cloud clinging to it like a filmy veil. He stirred and asked, "What did he lie about, exactly?"

"He lied about nearly everything he told you, or if he wasn't lying, he didn't tell you the whole truth. He was using you, Carlos. I wish I knew how, but he was using you for something. He knew you were going to come back to talk to him, and he was ready."

"How do you know that?"

"Did you see how close to the glass his face was? He wanted to be sure to see you."

"He could have moved there when he saw me coming."

"No, Mahler is nearly paraplegic. He can't move his whole body except with great effort."

"I didn't know that."

"You don't know very much about the mutants, but to tell you the truth, I don't know much more than you do."

"I need to know what he lied about," Carlos said patiently, taking her wrists and holding her still while he spoke.

Laurel licked her lips, then she pulled her hands free. Her pen moved quickly, dancing through the night air. "He lied about two things in particular. When you asked him about emotions and hormones, he nearly didn't answer you. Instead, he turned the question to his advantage, but what he told you was mostly untrue. The mutants went through a particularly painful adolescence. They suffered depression, mood swings, and one or two tried to commit suicide. It lasted for about six weeks until the scientists found a way to speed their growth and stem their hormonal surges. It was very brutal for some of the mutants. I know that one of them became partially paralyzed from a stroke. I think it was M-3."

"One of the older sisters?"

"Yes. Mahler lied when he said that the mutants could control their hormones. They cannot. The scientists do it for them."

"Perhaps he doesn't realize this." Carlos was silent for a minute, watching the fire, his eyes following the sparks as they rose into the sky.

Laurel made a face. "I don't know, but he was lying about something."

"But Laurel, he couldn't lie to me with you there, watching him."

"It wasn't a direct lie; he was simply evasive. Perhaps he doesn't realize I know about their hormones. It was several years ago and I only learned about it from transcripts." Her mouth twisted as she shook her head.

"All right. What else?"

"He lied about the police report. Either he knows more than he's telling us or he has a definite suspicion about what happened."

"Do you think it's possible the mutants are involved?" Carlos leaned forward and put a stick in the fire. Far off, an owl hooted.

"How?" Laurel shook her head. "I don't see how any of them could profit from murder. Besides, it all seems to be hinged on sex, from what I gathered."

"You gathered correctly."

"The mutants have no idea what sex is. They have no way of experiencing it. They can read about a car and drive a virtual car, but they can't have virtual sex. Reading about it isn't going to help. Especially since all the pornographic sites were removed back in 2010."

"Good old 2010. Sex is simply hormones."

"Aren't you romantic?" Laurel wrote the glowing words in the air, rolling her eyes and touching his chest. "Is that all I am for you? A way to empty your overflowing hormones?"

"Ha, ha, ha." Carlos kissed her on the tip of her nose. "For your information, I haven't overflowed since I was in diapers. But this is serious, Laurel. One thing is certain—someone called Mitch Palo is in danger, and I don't know what to do about it."

Laurel yawned and cuddled in her sleeping bag, staring sleepily at the flames. Carlos lay down next to her, propping his head on his arms. There came the occasional cry of a coyote and the crackling sound the mesquite wood made in the fire. For Laurel, everything was silenceful, but for him, the night was full of whispers.

* * *

"Mr. Palo, please don't get upset."

"Upset? Not get upset? What should I do, say thank you for putting me under house arrest? I came back, didn't I? We only went to have breakfast, not rob a bank or take the first flight to Brazil. Look, Monkey is just like you or me. He's a person, not a robot, and he's not dangerous. I can…"

"Mr. Palo, there is nothing more to say. You will be kind enough to stay away from him until the virtual voyage. Until then, I'm afraid you'll have to remain in this room."

"Where's Monkey?" Mitch stood up, towering over the Net Rep standing before him.

"He's in his own room. He'll be quite all right, rest assured. We've put him in a very luxurious room and he's got a shunt. He'll be fine until tomorrow morning."

"What happens then?" Mitch asked.

The Net Rep gave a tiny shake of the head. "We'll brief you just before the trip. If you need anything, the console over here will connect you to the service center where you can order food and drinks. If you wish to see a film, there are numerous choices in our video library..."

"What about the Net? Can I surf?"

"I'm sorry. Your shunt has been confiscated." The man smiled thinly, turned on his heel, and left.

Mitch watched him leave, a meditative look on his face. "My shunt has been confiscated," he mouthed at the closed door, "but I have another one."

Then he stood up and, hands on hips, surveyed the room.

It didn't take long to find the cameras. One was thinly disguised as a fire alarm and another glinted from the middle of the curtain rod. He nearly missed the third camera, installed in the painting, but that was because he couldn't imagine the Net being so obvious. He shook his head as he carefully realigned the lens. The bugs were easier; scanning with his portable radio and listening for the static, he soon found them all. He pulled them carefully from their hiding places and set them on a different frequency while staying out of sight of the cameras.

Now that a large space in the room was cleared, he opened his suitcase and removed the lining. Whistling tunelessly, he pulled a long, thin tube from within it. He took the cover off the console with a small screwdriver and plugged himself in, using the material he always had with him. He used just a small mask, not one of the bowling ball sized helmets the Virtual Tours used, thin gloves and fine wires attached to electrodes pressed into his ears and onto his temples. With the mask, electrodes and wires, Mitch could go beyond the normal user's online experience. The cutting edge technology Digby had helped him get allowed him to experience the virtual arena almost as if he were on a virtual tour. Sound and touch were slightly muted, but sight was sharp and keen. He couldn't eat or drink anything—he had no sense of taste at all—but he could go nearly everywhere, within the parameters of where he was visiting.

His teachers had jokingly called him a mutant. Now that he'd actually met one, he wasn't sure how he felt about them. Monkey was so captivating it was impossible to resist him. Mitch couldn't understand how the Net Reps could be hard-hearted enough to lock him in his room despite his entreaties.

Now, he floated in the Net space, intent on finding his friend. If he was, as the Net Rep said, shunted, Mitch should be able to locate him.

In the end, it was easy. Monkey was terrified and he'd retreated to his own world, but he wasn't in the institute and he wasn't in his own glass case. The trail he left was simple for Mitch, although it was doubtful anyone else could have found him. He floated in the traffic area of Net, the place called the highway. It was a vast, vague corridor where paths of different colors wove like stringy rainbows in every direction. Some were easy to identify, and those attached to publicity were the brightest and easiest to follow. Others led to online sites of interest; still others led to private lines. Mail lines were yellow and led only in one direction. Educational programs were colored a certain way, as were certain lines that were encrypted or coded. Those you had to possess a key to enter. Government lines were mostly coded, and they were the easiest for Mitch to unlock. Monkey didn't encode his line, he just hid it. It was so faint, and so ethereal, you could hardly see it unless you were looking for it. Mitch had gotten to know Monkey, so he knew instinctively what to look for.

Monkey's line was flimsy but not very complicated. Mitch found the trace by scanning all the lines leaving the Net building then choosing the one that seemed the most incongruous. Once connected to a line, it was rather like taking a moving sidewalk. Other times it could be like climbing a rope in the gym. Some lines were old and broke apart after a certain time, from disuse or misuse. New lines tended to glow faintly as if they were a bit wet. Monkey's line was not new, but it did glow enticingly. Mitch felt himself drawn towards the filament. He took hold of it.

Mitch was pulled along Monkey's line like a fish being reeled in through a rough sea. Around him, worlds flashed as he caught glimpses of games he'd played and realized Monkey had disguised his trail by stitching it like a thread through several different worlds in order to confuse any followers. After what seemed a long while, Mitch slowed and found himself in a thick fog. A silhouette appeared, drifting out of the mist like a ghost. It was Monkey.

"Hi." He smiled shyly.

"Hey, Monkey, how are you?"

"Not so good, I'm afraid." The image wavered a bit before coming into sharper focus.

With a thrill of shock, Mitch recognized himself. "Why aren't you using your own body?" he asked.

"I only saw myself for the first time two days ago. I don't know myself yet." His voice was plaintive. "Why don't they let us out of our cases, Mitch?"

"I don't know." It troubled Mitch that Monkey was trembling and on the verge of tears. "Hey, don't sweat it. I'm sure everything will work out fine."

"I was doing fine, wasn't I? I was adapting to the real world, wasn't I?" Monkey, in the form of Mitch, stretched his arms out in the position of a crucified Christ. They were both floating in a silver mist that was growing lighter by the second.

"You were perfect," Mitch said. "This is a cool place. Where is it?"

"I made this world myself," Monkey replied. "If you want, I'll show you around. I hope you don't mind that I pulled you in so fast, but I don't want anyone else to find it."

"They won't. I was just lucky I found your line."

"No, I wanted you to see it." Monkey smiled and his face suddenly relaxed. "Here, take my hand and we'll fly."

They soared through thick clouds and suddenly came upon a clear expanse of blue sky. Mitch gazed in delight at the forest below him. A waterfall cascaded thousands of meters down a sheer, red cliff into a jade-green lake. There was another lake in the mouth of a volcanic mountain, and on one of its sides, a river ran uphill towards the magnificent falls. It was like a surrealistic drawing come to life. A shallow creek flowed out of a cave in the opposite side of the lake, twisted around the mountainside, and splashed into the river, which ran back up the volcano towards the waterfall.

"Do you want to swim?" asked Monkey.

"Sure!"

They fell through the air as slowly as feathers floating to the surface of the lake. The water was tepid and calm.

"Follow me." Monkey swam towards the cave.

They drifted, pulled by the current into a tunnel. After a few moments of floating in darkness lit only by the glimmer of thousands of fireflies, Mitch saw the end of the tunnel, a bright arch of dazzling sunlight. When they reached the opening, a small creek swept them down the mountainside as if they were on a huge water chute ride. Mitch whooped aloud as they rushed downwards. When they splashed into the river, it was just a few lazy strokes to a small beach. They hauled themselves onto the warm sand, shook bright water droplets off their bodies and stood in wonder.

Monkey pointed to the trees above their heads, and Mitch saw a yellow cloud of jewel-like butterflies. A blue jay swooped among the branches and a red squirrel chattered high in a white birch tree.

"It's beautiful here." Mitch's voice was hardly a whisper.

"Watch." Monkey put his hand on Mitch's shoulder, and they stood perfectly still, mirror-image twins, in a pristine forest.

The sun rose and fell in an instant, shadows twisting like snakes around their feet. Then the scene shifted, and summer gave way to winter.

It was so sudden, as if a cover was suddenly whipped off the world. Snow sparkled on the ground. A fine powder swirled in the air. The trees leaned as a storm approached, dark clouds slouching across the sky. Snowflakes began to fall. The snow blurred Mitch's vision, but he was not cold. He could see things as if he were omnipotent: a bear in his den, jays huddled in the fir tree, a squirrel curled in his nest and deer lying pressed together for warmth. A pine marten poked his head out of his burrow, and snow frosted his fur. Night came, and darkness settled upon the world.

Then the snowstorm tapered off and the sun rose once more. Everything was bathed in a pink and gold glow. Deer struggled out of their hiding places. Birds shook their feathers and fluttered into the air while the squirrel bounded from branch to branch. A lynx padded across the snowdrifts, his soft fur whipped by a freezing wind. Ice crystals sparkled in the air. Winter passed in the space of a minute. Snow melted, vanished, and plants pushed out of the thawing earth. Crocuses opened purple blossoms while pale spring grass feathered the ground. Leaves budded and unfurled. The sunlight became green, filtering through a dense canopy of trees. A wolf howled as night fell, the moon sailing across the sky like a fat, yellow boat. Mice watched the night sky with beady eyes, and an opossum balanced like a tightrope walker on a high branch, the moon tipping his fur with light.

Mitch saw constellations wheel through space, and then dawn colored the sky pale gray and rose. Spiders knit webs and decorated them with dewdrops. Mist emerged as the sun grew hotter, and the forest was first gray with fog, then green and dappled with gold.

All the while Mitch watched and saw everything. He saw each tree and leaf, each animal and insect. Even the fish swimming under the water and the birds in the sky had no secrets from him.

Then Monkey took his hand off his shoulder, and time snapped like a rubber band back to normal. Mitch sank down on the sand, his legs suddenly too weak to hold him upright.

"Did you like that?" asked Monkey.

Mitch shook his head, incapable of answering. Tears ran down his face as he took a shaky breath. "How did you do that?"

"It's like swimming. You have to learn, but once you do, you realize that you always knew how to swim and that it's easy."

"The Virtual Tour program. You made it, didn't you?"

"We worked on it as a team," Monkey answered, a note of caution in his voice.

"I mean, you didn't need all the movie footage you were provided with, did you?"

"We studied it carefully. The orders were to create a world analogous to the one in the Caribbean, and we did our best."

"You did your best," Mitch said slowly. "Was this," he swept his arm in an arc, "all from film footage as well?"

"This part of my world is from your world. You wouldn't understand the part I created from my imagination."

"I would like to see it," Mitch said.

"Not today. We must return to the real world. Time is almost up for you, and soon they will come get us."

"Get us? For what?"

"I'm not sure, but I think we'll be working together. I hope you don't mind."

"Of course not." Mitch grinned. "I loved your world, Monkey. I hope I'll be invited back."

"Whenever you wish to come, you'll be welcome. Thanks to you, I know what it's like to be a human being. Before meeting you, I was nothing but a freak, a living machine. Now I know what friendship is, what sharing means, and what it feels like to have a woman take hold of my pal and..."

"Um, that's quite all right." Mitch coughed to hide his grin.

"I only hope that I'm Sarah will do that to me again," he said wistfully.

"I'm Sarah?"

"Her pin said that was her name. It's beautiful, don't you think?"

Mitch clapped him fondly on the shoulder. "It's a lovely name. Come on, we'd better go. I don't want the Net Reps to catch me shunted."

Chapter Nine

I have embraced you, and henceforth possess you to myself,
And when you rise in the morning you will find what I tell you
is so.
—Walt Whitman, *Song of Myself*

Andrea floated through the day. Her mind kept drifting back to dinner, then breakfast then... Her cheeks turned pink and she busied herself with her files. Not that there was much to do that day. Until the murder investigation was finished, Virtual Tours was closed for business.

The Net had sent David Willow to check out some sort of new anti-virus program. He'd called her that morning and left several messages with Sally. Andrea had called him back and been very cold. He'd gotten the message. Several red roses had arrived shortly afterwards, with a store-bought thank-you note. It was, Andrea reflected, the most civilized separation she'd ever experienced. She tossed the note into her garbage, put the roses in the silver polo trophy that one of her exes had given her, and patted Cocotte on her silky head.

She sighed. She didn't know if she was depressed or exhilarated. Since yesterday, her life had been on a roller coaster ride. Her office seemed empty without Sally bustling about, but Andrea had told her not to come in that day. In the tour guide sending room, only Digby was present, along with a maintenance technician. There were no tourists sitting in the waiting room, no waking nurses sitting in their cozy station. There was none of the usual liveliness and activity to animate the floor. Instead, a deep silence penetrated the building. The hush of mourning pervaded everything; even the messages on the phone were spoken in quiet, concerned voices.

Andrea tapped her fingernails softly on her desk, her mind oscillating between the sadness of losing two employees whom she had known several years and the joy of discovering Tony. Cocotte whined, and Andrea glanced at her watch. Time for a walk. When she came back, she consulted her answering machine, but the only messages were from Digby.

The clock on her desk clicked as the numbers changed— three p.m., four p.m.—the hours simply dragged by. Digby worked in the sending room, the halls echoed when the cleaning crew walked by, and still her private phone didn't ring.

Andrea tried to concentrate on the letters she'd received via email or on her professional phone line, and she listened with an almost religious fervor to the news. There was no mention at all of the murders, except a terse announcement during the newscast. Her Virtual Tours were being interrupted thanks to technical difficulties. Technical difficulties? That's what the murders were being called? For Andrea, there was no doubt murder had been committed. Then a photo appeared on the screen behind the newscaster. It showed two men shaking hands.

"Here we have Frank Dinde and David Willow celebrating the Net's takeover of Virtual Tours," the newscaster said in a loud voice.

Andrea gaped. Her heart beat painfully in her chest. How could they? They had specified that the deal be kept a secret, that she would remain the president with complete control of the employees, as before. The fact that the Net was now the majority shareholder, since paying off the billion-dollar debt towards the program developers, hadn't changed anything. Why publicize now? Especially now that there was a serious glitch in the program?

The newscaster went on to say that Andrea Girt had relinquished control of Virtual Tours, while remaining as president on the board of directors. "Ms. Girt has not been reached for comment."

Andrea drummed her nails on the desk. The program had been created at her demand, but she hadn't been able to pay for it; the price had been as spectacular as the results. Two days before she was about to put Virtual Tours on the market, the Net had made an offer she couldn't refuse. What she hadn't truly appreciated was the power the Net possessed. Not only had they bought Virtual Tours, they had bought her silence as well. Not reached for comment was a polite way of saying the Net hadn't wanted her to be interviewed. She could do nothing about it. A clause in her contract stipulated she couldn't speak to the press about anything unusual or negative that happened within the Virtual Tours. However, the Net's takeover was a larger breach of contract than she had ever imagined they would make. Perhaps she had a way out of this after all.

Her hand hovered indecisively over the phone. Biting her red lips, she snatched it up and punched out a number before she changed her mind.

"Hello, I'd like to speak to Professor Toutbon," she said, her nails tapping loudly.

"Professor Toutbon here." His voice was soft and timid, not at all what Andrea had been expecting. She punched a button, and a floating screen appeared. In it, she saw a tall, thin man with a shiny, bald head and a sharp nose. He was peering at a point somewhere to his left. When he noticed the floating screen, he gave a start.

"Oh. Hello," he said. "I'm not really used to these yet." He reached up and she saw his finger poking at her. "How amazing. We just installed them in the Center. Quite an improvement to the fixed..."

"Professor, this is Andrea Girt. I'd like to speak to the head of the team that did the work on my Virtual Tour."

The professor blinked and a pained expression crossed his face. "I'm sorry. I don't think..."

"Two men have died in my program. I think I have the right to know what is going on. Has the Net been in contact with you?"

"Of course." He frowned. "Ms. Girt, I hope you understand, but our Center is part of the CIA. For security reasons, I can't..."

"I simply want to speak to the scientist in charge of the development of my program. Is he or she available?"

"I'm afraid that's impossible."

Andrea looked at her fingernails then put her hand flat on the desk. "There's something you should know. I don't own

Virtual Tours. I developed the company and I am the president, but I am not the major shareholder."

Professor Toutbon straightened, and a wary expression flitted across his features. "Who does own Virtual Tours?"

Andrea looked at him. "I think you know."

He nodded slowly. "It seemed strange that the Net would be so interested in your tour. I was surprised when they sent the head of security here."

"Frank Dinde? Why was he sent to you?"

"He came to pick up the person who created your program. He's taking him to Dallas to work with the Net's new virus-catching program. I must admit, I'm extremely worried about Monkey." The professor ran his hand over his bald head.

"Monkey?"

His hand froze on his head. "Did I say Monkey?"

"Yes. Professor, why would Frank Dinde want to take Mr. Monkey to Dallas? One of my tour guides is on his way there too. I thought that the Net was simply trying out a new virus program to flush out whatever killed my two employees."

Professor Toutbon looked undecided. He stared at the screen then down at the floor. Then he sighed heavily and rubbed his face.

"Professor? Are you all right?"

He drew a deep breath. "Ms. Girt, what I am about to tell you must remain a secret for now. It won't be a secret long, but please don't say anything until it is official."

"I'm listening."

"Your program wasn't developed by scientists or computer programmers. This place is officially named the Organic

Computer Research Center by the CIA and the FBI, but we call it the Mutant Center. For twenty years, we've been in charge of a government program so secret only a few people inside or outside the CIA and FBI know about it. One of them is Frank Dinde. The Net has known about us from the beginning—they helped turn this program into a profitable business. But I'm afraid. I'm afraid because the mutants are fragile beings, and the Net…"

"Wait a minute." Andrea held up her hand. It went right through the floating screen, making a gaping hole in Professor Toutbon's head. She licked her lips. "Did you say mutants?"

He nodded. "I represent the mutants, Ms. Girt. Just as you represented the Net and I didn't realize it, so I represent an army of nineteen mutants. And one of them has already escaped the Center."

* * *

Carlos held the phone to his ear and with his other hand he jotted down bits of his conversation with Mahler. He looked up at the clock. It was nearly five p.m. As soon as the buzzer sounded, unlocking the doors for the evening, he would go to his desert village and speak to Chief Black Deer about his actions. His mind was already made up, however. No matter what his elder told him to do, he was going to Dallas before it was too late. No more murders could be committed; otherwise, the entire mutant program might be wiped out by the Net. He'd seen the news. To Carlos it was clear the investigation was a setup the Net was using to gain total control of the mutant program and virtual tourism.

* * *

Laurel sat at her desk, in the darkness, in her complete silence. She had arrived at a different conclusion than Carlos, but the repercussions of what she believed had happened could be just as devastating to the program. She twisted her hands together as she reflected.

Finally, she shook her head and sighed deeply. No matter how she looked at it, the only way to save the program was to let Carlos believe he was right. Otherwise, everything was going to end right here. Before she and Carlos had talked to Mahler personally, she had been able to avoid thinking about her suspicion that the mutants had feelings like any other person, that what was being done to them was immoral. They had been willing employees in her mind, machine-like beings with whom the scientists worked and with whom Dr. Toutbon created virtual programs. The talks with Mahler had forced her to consider the ethics of the situation. The mutants were individuals; she could no longer deny that. And that was, she thought glumly, the worst part. If her theory was correct, then every one of the mutants would be exterminated. There was no way the Center could ever convince the public that the mutants were harmless. She was positive the program had been infiltrated by a mutant who had killed those men. Why? Could it be jealousy? Mahler had said himself that mutants felt everything humans did. If they felt murderous rage, what could possibly stop them from slipping into any virtual program and killing its user?

She looked up when Carlos stepped out of the elevator. The pinprick of light over her desk made her eyes deeply shadowed and mysterious.

"Hello, Carlos," she motioned.

"I'm going now," he said, looking very serious. "First to my village, then to Dallas. I made reservations for the nine o'clock flight."

"The Net will never let you see Mr. Palo when they find out you work for the Center."

"They won't find out I work for the Center. I looked up Mitch's direct superior, a man named Daniel Glover Brims. I'm going to pose as that person for an hour or two. At worst, it will let me warn Mitch Palo before I get thrown into jail."

"I'll come bail you out."

"Do you think this is the right thing to do?"

She nodded, breathing deeply. "Yes, I do."

His face cleared. "I hope so. There's something very strange going on, and I have a feeling the Net is behind it all. I think they want to sink Virtual Tours. They're going to buy up all the stock, and then they'll create their own tours."

"They're already majority shareholders," Laurel motioned. "I saw that on the news today."

"I know, but Andrea Girt is still founder and president, and even if they control the shares, they don't own her. She has more power than they do right now. She still has forty-eight percent of the whole company. There is one percent in public hands, and fifty-one percent belongs to the Net."

"They can out-vote Andrea in any decision she wants to make."

"It depends on the type of contract they made for the takeover. Imagine if she retains right of veto and director's rights. The Net might be limited to collecting the profits, and that's it. I think they want more, and this is how they plan to get the whole business."

Laurel shook her head. "But why point a finger at the mutants? Why risk antagonizing the government? They must know this program is run by the CIA." Her hands flew as she signed, a frown on her expressive face.

"Public opinion will swing in the Net's favor. The public hates secret programs, and the government will do anything to put the blame on the mutants themselves, not the program. In the end, the mutants will be eliminated, but not before the Net can use them. This is the way the Net can gain power over everything. They will own both the Mutant Center and Virtual Tours. That way, they won't have to pay our prices for the programs. It's all about money, Laurel. Remember that the Virtual Tours program is subject to copyright law, and Andrea owns the copyright. If the Net wants it, it will have to pay."

"And us? What will happen to our jobs?"

"We'll be unemployed government workers without any credible references."

"Great." Laurel frowned. "Did you tell this to Mahler?"

Carlos looked shocked. "No, of course not."

"Well, maybe you should."

"Not yet. Wait until I return from Dallas. I'll tell you everything I've learned and we'll discuss it then." He was quiet then, just looking at her. There was not a sound in the room. Laurel had no radio playing soft music. All that could be heard was a slight intake of breath as she reached up and touched his cheek.

They leaned towards each other, coming together in the dimness. Laurel's arms rose, wrapped themselves around Carlos's neck as his lips sought hers.

Carlos bent her backward over her desk, his hands sliding down her waist and slipping beneath her dress. He stopped, startled, and then drew a deep breath. "Where are they?" he asked.

Laurel pointed to a bit of lace on the floor. Her face was mischievous.

"Oh, Laurel!" He moaned as her hands deftly unbuttoned his pants. He was shuddering, standing perfectly still while she pushed his pants down with her feet, holding onto him with her hand. He couldn't move. She raised her knees and lay back on her desk.

He lowered himself onto her, thrusting slowly so as not to slide her off the smooth desk. The rhythm accelerated when she grabbed his hips with her hands, pulling him into her. Her head tipped back off the desk. Her breasts bobbed in time to his movements, her nipples brushing his broad chest.

She felt her belly tighten. Her hips rose and her legs locked tightly around his waist. Her heels drummed his thighs and urged him on. He needed no encouragement. Her fingers dug into his sides. He shuddered and stopped moving, and she concentrated on the faint throb she felt within her. It grew stronger, shaking her belly, arching her back. With a groan she abandoned herself, shattered by the frantic pulsing she felt. Waves of pleasure rushed through her, and she leaned into him as his hips dove into the space between her open thighs.

Afterwards he rested his forehead on her collarbone. A bead of sweat trickled down his temple and landed on her breast. He licked it off. His tongue stirred her nipple and slid down the swell of her breast. His mouth seemed to move of its own accord. He pressed his lips to her nipple again and he sucked sleepily, nuzzling her skin.

Laurel sighed deeply then pushed him away. She rose to her elbows, looking at the tall man splayed on the desk next to her.

"If Professor Toutbon comes now, we'll be out of work no matter what happens," she managed to sign, her hands making short, abbreviated motions as she tried to sit up.

Carlos nodded. "All right. I'll go." He shook his head and kissed her on the lips. "How could I have spent all those years seeing you before and never realizing how utterly beautiful and sexy you are?"

She grinned. "Because you never really looked. I noticed you, and I waited for the day you would finally take heed of me."

Carlos shook his head. "I must have been blind."

"Well, now you see," she quipped with her graceful hands. Her face grew still, suddenly.

"Hey, look at me." He took her chin in his hand and tipped her face to his. "I don't care if you're deaf; I like you just the way you are." He winced and closed both eyes. "I didn't say that right, did I?" He opened one eye, then the other. "Let me say that again, please? Pretend you never saw my lips move. Now, watch carefully. It makes no difference to me that you're silenceful. I love you, Laurel, exactly as you are."

She nodded, wide-eyed. Then her lips moved. "Thank you," she whispered, in her toneless voice. He shook his head.

"You don't even have to try. I can see into your heart, and I know what you're telling me."

She blinked, sending two perfect tears sliding down her cheeks.

Carlos smiled and kissed them away. Then he picked up a pair of lacy panties from the floor. "I believe these are yours, my lady."

* * *

Mitch woke up in his room, still shunted. He unhooked himself and hid the material in its secret pouch. Then, whistling, he took a shower and called room service.

"I'd like to order two dinners from the menu. Yes, that's right, two. I'll have the fresh asparagus to start, and then grilled tenderloin, well done, with the caviar-stuffed potatoes followed by a green salad and raspberry soufflé for dessert. To drink I'd like a bottle of Bordeaux wine. What is your most expensive bottle? Fine, that sounds wonderful! Now, send the same dinner to room 509. Put everything on this credit card number." He recited a long string of numbers by heart. "That's right, Ms. Sonia Andrews. Thank you, ma'am."

Mitch hung up and cocked his eyebrow at the television. "Now let's see what videos you have in your library."

* * *

Carlos stepped off the plane and shouldered his backpack. The interview with his elders had gone as he'd expected. They had been against his meddling in the program in the first place, and now that he wanted to save it, they were leery of affronting the Net. None of the elders had a computer. Chief Black Deer sometimes went to the terminal at the public library and surfed, although his voyages were rapid, usually to foreign countries, and when he came back he always complained about the advertisements that littered the Net. None of the elders wanted to go on a virtual voyage to anywhere, claiming if man were meant to change worlds he would have been born with a shunt.

Chief Black Deer had given his blessing for Carlos to go to Dallas. They both knew that if the Center closed, the village would lose income. The employees, when they ventured into the village, spent a good deal of money in the local supermarket, the pool hall, and at the rodeo. Many of the employees were foreign, and the village was the only place they were allowed to visit. Furthermore, Marilouise, the only Japanese and Russian translator in the village, was Chief Black Deer's niece, and she needed the money to raise her three kids. Chief Black Deer patted Carlos on the arm.

"I know you'll do what's right," he said, "but try not to make any enemies."

"Who do you take me for?" Carlos tried to look indignant.

"My grandson. I know you better than you know yourself. You've decided to save the mutant program, but I want you to remember this: we've always considered this program an abomination. The elders have spent many moons discussing this."

"Many moons?" Carlos raised his eyebrow.

Chief Black Deer grinned then grew serious again. "To most people, mutants are simply a legend. But for us, the tribal elders, they are monsters with no souls."

* * *

The night was sultry. A taxi took him to the Net Building, and Carlos gave a low whistle when he spied it. He walked into the front door, nodding in a friendly fashion to the beefy guard posing as a liveried doorman.

"I'd like to see Mitch Palo," he said when he arrived at the front desk.

The secretary smiled coldly, peering at him from behind green, pointy glasses that looked like a prop for a cartoon character. "I'm afraid that isn't possible."

Carlos didn't return the smile. "I must insist. My name is Daniel Glover Brims, and I have orders from Ms. Girt concerning her employee, Mr. Palo."

"Orders? Let me see your ID and the orders." She pushed her chair away from the ornate desk and took the papers Carlos removed from his vest pocket. She stared at them, then without another word she left the room, muttering angrily. Her high heels tapped a staccato on the mahogany floor, and Carlos winced as he imagined the damage she was doing to the burnished wood.

When she was out of sight, he leaned over her desk and peered at the console. Mitch's room was not hard to locate; there was a red tag with his name on it plugged into a socket. The wire went towards a small screen, and, with a quick glance at the heavy door the secretary had disappeared behind, Carlos flicked the button. The screen lit, and he saw a young man sitting cross-legged on a huge bed. A tray with empty dishes was at his side. As Carlos watched, the man took a bottle of wine from a bedside table and poured himself a glass. Before he drank, he raised the glass and looked straight at Carlos. "Cheers," he mouthed.

Carlos took an involuntary step backwards. He looked for a camera then quickly turned off the screen. The secretary returned a few minutes later, a small, dapper man at her heels.

"I'm Frank Dinde, head of Net Security," he said, but he didn't offer his hand to shake.

"Daniel Glover Brims," Carlos said.

"So, you're Virtual Tours' operator. I've heard much about you." His expression said very clearly that what he'd heard hadn't included the fact that Daniel was a nearly seven foot tall, full-blooded Kiowa, with obsidian eyes and black hair nearly to his waist.

Carlos grinned widely. "You have? How wonderful. It's hard living up to my reputation, but I try my best. Now, when may I speak to Mr. Palo?"

"We can't go to his room right now. You've arrived quite late. I'm sure he's sleeping. You'll have to wait until tomorrow morning. I hope you made reservations in the city."

"Oh, if I know Mitch, he'll be lounging in bed, watching a dirty movie and drinking a glass of red wine." Carlos shrugged. "What can you expect from these playboy types? I'll just give him a call on the phone, and he can come down to the lobby to meet me. We'll go to the diner across the street to talk."

Frank Dinde opened his mouth then shut it. The skin around his nose turned white. "I'll take you to his room."

Carlos hid his amusement behind a blank, Indian stare.

They took an elevator to the third floor and walked down a luxurious hallway. On the walls were several beautiful Italian Renaissance paintings. Carlos stopped in front of one and stared. "Amazing."

Frank Dinde stopped and retraced his steps. "What's amazing?"

"The colors. They are so vibrant. Titian really knew his stuff, didn't he?" Carlos raised one eyebrow and shrugged. "Although it has to be a copy, it's a very, very good one."

"Indeed. Now if you'll please follow me. Mr. Palo's room is right around the corner."

He knocked once, and Mitch opened the door. Behind him, the television was blaring and he was holding a glass of wine. He looked at Frank Dinde then at Carlos standing behind him.

"Can I..." He began.

"Mr. Glover Brims is here. He has orders from Ms. Girt. I must say, I don't approve of your company's way of doing things," he added, turning to Carlos.

"We do our best," Carlos said coldly. "Now, if you'll excuse us."

"When you're through, call the receptionist. We'll send you an escort."

After Carlos shut the door in Frank Dinde's face, Mitch said, "I'd love to see Digby. Have I got some things to discuss with him! Is he in the lobby?"

"No, he's not here. I hope you'll forgive the ruse, but it was the only way to get to see you."

"I'll forgive you if you can get me out of this place. They put me under house arrest, so to speak."

"Your door's locked?"

"Try it and see." Mitch shrugged.

The knob would not turn. "Escort. That's a euphemism for goon, I suppose."

"Goon? Whoever you are, I like you already. Would you care for dinner? If I order now, it will arrive in about twenty minutes. The service is fast and the food sublime."

"I'll have a glass of wine, if you don't mind," Carlos said. "And let's stay in sight and out of sound. Is that possible?"

Mitch cocked his head. "Unless the Net has someone better than me in their service, which I doubt, we can stay right here and talk. I've tuned the bugs to the Puerto Rican Radio de Noche. Right now whoever is listening is getting an interview with this year's new limbo champion."

"In Spanish." Carlos grinned.

"Exactly. So, if you're not Digby, and I can assure you that you're not, who are you?"

"My name's Carlos, and I work with the mutant program."

"Oh." Mitch ran his hand through his hair, ruffling it then smoothing it back down. "Why are you here, Mr. Carlos?"

"Just Carlos will be fine."

"Monkey, I'm Sarah and Just Carlos. I'm collecting a whole load of friends with odd names."

"You've met Monkey?"

"Of course. He's a great guy," Mitch said, a trace of frost appearing in his voice.

Carlos nodded. "I don't actually get to approach the mutants that often, and until lately I had never tried to have a conversation with one."

"That's too bad. You might have learned something." Now Mitch's voice was icy, and the frost had spread to his pale blue eyes.

"I realize that."

"Why don't you let them out?"

"I beg your pardon?" Carlos hadn't expected that question. It caught him completely off guard.

"I said, why don't you let them out? They are perfectly normal human beings except for the fact that they've been kept in cages all their lives."

"I wish you were right, but you've only met Monkey. The others aren't like him."

"They're not?" Now it was Mitch's turn to be surprised. "He didn't tell me that."

"They don't see each other. They can't even see themselves. They have no mirrors, and they float in thick, opaque clouds."

"Why aren't the others like Monkey?"

"Only one or two mutants ever developed a normal physique. A couple of them are literally monsters only fit for a freak show. Some are partially paralyzed; others are autistic and won't communicate in any way that you or I could understand. Monkey was the only mutant we could even consider 'letting out,' as you put it."

"Freaks?"

"Yes, I'm afraid so."

Mitch took a sip of his wine. "I'm sorry. Perhaps you'd better sit down. Here, have a glass of Bordeaux. It's a nice little wine."

Carlos held the glass up to the light, gently swirled the ruby liquid around it, and inhaled. "Nice legs. Black currant, strawberry, banana, blackberry, pepper, cinnamon and lots of tannin. Excellent." He held the glass to the light again. "Almost terra cotta. I'd say about twenty years old."

Mitch raised his eyebrow. "Twenty-one, actually."

"Good choice."

"I just asked for their most expensive bottle," Mitch said.

"Are you paying?"

"Do I look like I could afford a two thousand dollar bottle of wine? I charged it to someone else's account."

Carlos nodded. "A wise decision."

"How did you like meeting Mr. Dinde?" Mitch asked, tipping the bottle over his glass and shaking out the last drops.

"You do know what *dinde* means in French, don't you?"

"I do, and I agree that the name suits him perfectly."

Carlos raised his glass. "Here's to the turkey." He drank deeply.

"Now, perhaps you can tell me why you're here." Mitch lay back on his bed, his arms over his head, a knee drawn up.

Carlos sat down on a chair nearby. "I'm here to tell you to be careful."

"As if I didn't know that already." Mitch grinned.

"I spoke to M-6. He's considered by all the other mutants and the scientists to be the spokesman of the group. He calls himself the elder son."

"Go on."

"I have a copy of the conversation here. I'd like you to read it." Carlos took a paper from his hip pocket, unfolded it, and handed it to Mitch.

There was a long silence while Mitch read. An even longer silence followed, while he considered it, slowly tearing the paper to tiny shreds and dropping them on his sheets. "Bait? Mahler thinks I'm bait?"

"My theory is the Net wants to frame the mutants for the murders so they can get total control of virtual travel. Perhaps they've even developed their own virtual tour, which is why they'd be willing to sacrifice the mutant program."

"That's impossible." Mitch brushed the paper off his bed in a snow flurry. His eyes followed the white bits as they drifted to the ground. "They haven't found a way to create a virtual travel program because it's impossible to do that without the mutants' help."

"What do you mean? The program exists, you work in it, and you should know better than anyone how it was made."

"I know nothing at all about it. I thought I did." Mitch wrenched his eyes away from the torn paper and looked at Carlos. His mouth was quirked in a wry smile. "I'm afraid you've come all the way here for nothing. The Net doesn't dare harm the mutants. They're the only ones who can create the programs. No human being in the world is capable of such a feat."

Carlos sat very still. "I had no idea. I simply assumed that the mutants were the best at developing a tour. I didn't know they were the only ones who could make one." He rubbed his hands over his face. "Do you think the Net knows this?"

"I'm certain that no one knows this. Right now, only you, me and the mutants know who really creates these programs."

"Programs worth billions."

Mitch nodded. "The most precious commodity on earth, manufactured by mutants."

"If the Net doesn't realize that, then you're still in danger," Carlos said gravely.

"Perhaps I am. Maybe Monkey will save me."

Carlos gave a start. "He's going into the program with you?"

"Who else can catch a virtual murderer?" Mitch smiled.

"I thought it was a setup."

Mitch rubbed his face. "I hope the new virus-catching program can flush out whatever is wrong."

"Maybe there is a virus, after all." Carlos felt like an idiot. He hadn't even considered the most obvious situation.

"But who made it? It couldn't just appear."

"Usually you look for the one who will profit the most."

Mitch's smile slid from his face, leaving him looking tired. "No one could profit from killing Arthur or Jonathon. It must be more complicated than that. No, I think you're right somehow. The Net seeks to profit from this, but how and why I don't know."

"The why is easy: money and power."

"And the how?"

Carlos shrugged. "I have no idea." He yawned. "I better get going. I have to be at the airport at dawn to be back to work. I'm catching the five a.m. flight to the base."

"Where are you staying, Just Carlos?"

"I'll sleep in the airport on a bench."

"There's room here. I get lonely if there's no one in bed with me." Mitch grinned at him.

Carlos was startled. "I appreciate your offer, but I'm not interested, thank you."

"Oh, it was made in all innocence. My bed is big enough for two. I'll sleep on this side, and you can have that side, and when you get up at five, don't wake me."

"When this is finished, stop in at our Center. I'll show you around, and you can meet the rest of the mutants. Monkey will be glad to see you."

Mitch shook his head. "Monkey won't be coming back, I'm afraid."

Carlos froze. "Why not?"

"He's discovered the joy of sex." Mitch stifled a yawn. "Seriously, don't count on him trotting back to his cage. He's a free man now. What's more, I'll do everything in my power to keep him that way." His eyes were chips of frozen ice, all friendliness gone.

Carlos nodded. "I see."

"No, I don't believe you do." Mitch picked up the phone. "Shall I call the goons to get you now?"

"No, I think I'll accept your invitation. Move over." He lay down. "If what you say is true, then you're in far more danger than I thought, Mitch Palo."

"Excuse me?" Mitch sounded startled.

"Be quiet, I've had a long day and I have to get up early." Carlos closed his eyes, and was asleep in an instant.

* * *

"What did they speak about?"

"It's very strange. They spoke all night about some sort of dancing contest."

"Let me see that. They spoke in Spanish?"

"Yes, ma'am."

"What are they doing now?"

"Sleeping, ma'am."

"In the same bed?"

"It seems that way. Oh, Ms. Andrews?"

"Yes?"

"The restaurant faxed your bill to us. Shall I give it to you now?"

"No, don't bother, I had a club sandwich and some fries. Send it straight to accounting, and they'll debit it in the morning."

"Very well, Ms. Andrews. Goodnight."

"Goodnight."

* * *

Monkey shifted in his bed. He'd polished off the dinner Mitch had sent him and most of the bottle of wine. He'd never had alcohol before so he'd become very drunk. He hadn't realized it, though. All he'd felt was a sort of slowing of his system, a dopiness combined with a sort of anesthesia of his nerves. He lay in a boneless heap on his bed, his mind full of the things I'm Sarah had done to him, his pal sticking straight up into the air. Mitch's advice came to him, through the wine-induced fog. He grasped his penis with one hand and imitated I'm Sarah's actions. It worked beautifully. After a few moments, he dissolved into the shivering delight of release. He waited a while and started again.

* * *

Down in the back office, where little screens glowed, a man wrote his notes as dutifully as possible.

Masturbation, rest, masturbation, some wine, television, masturbation, sleep.

The notes would ultimately be read by the Net security agent, then by Frank Dinde, and finally, by Sonia Andrews, who would be too upset by a message from her banker to take any notice.

Chapter Ten

Earth of the limpid gray of clouds brighter and clearer for my sake!
Far-swooping elbow'd earth-rich apple-blossom'd earth!
Smile, for your lover comes.
—Walt Whitman, *Song of Myself*

"The coast is clear," Monkey said for the thousandth time as they lay in the sand sipping margaritas. The palm trees rustled overhead, and the frigate birds sailed lazily in the blue sky. Bright notes from a steel-drum band playing Calypso tunes rose gaily over the sound of the waves crashing on the beach.

"Shall we try the next frame now?" Mitch asked.

"I'm almost finished with my drink." Monkey sat up a little straighter and his voice dropped. "I don't sense any signs of a virus in this section of the program, and I've checked out everything around us. There's absolutely nothing out of place."

"Why are you whispering? You said, 'The coast is clear'. That should trigger the virus hunter within the program."

Monkey shrugged and took another sip from his frosty drink. "I don't know why I whispered. There's nothing here, but there's an odd feeling. I just can't place it. Perhaps it's the virus hunter."

"Do you think something could be wrong?" Mitch took off his sunglasses and squinted at Monkey.

"Not exactly. And I trust the Net's virus hunter. When they explained it to us, they were very thorough. Supposedly, if any killer virus were attracted to you, the program would be able to isolate it immediately. But the feeling I get isn't one of danger. It's very strange. Usually I can trace those sorts of things…" His voice trailed off and he frowned. "I don't know, and it bothers me. It's as if I should know."

"Do you want to try another screen?" Mitch glanced at his watch. They were staying close by the two places the deaths had occurred, but so far, nothing out of the ordinary had happened.

"Let's go back into Arthur's room. I want to check out the doorway, and then we can take a sail to Virgin Gorda again tomorrow. I didn't feel anything on the beach there, but in the cave there was a definite eddy or aftershock the program absorbed. I'll try to sort that out."

"You're working very hard, Monkey. Don't you want to rest?"

"I don't want to leave you alone here."

"That was part of the plan, remember? I'm the bait."

"I didn't agree to that plan. You stay with me, okay?" Monkey hesitated. "Besides, I'm not sure which one of us is the bait. I don't think we should get separated."

Mitch didn't argue. He got to his feet, picked up his towel, shook out the sand, and then followed Monkey back to the hotel.

* * *

They woke up after three days and gave a full report. The Net verified everything with the virus trackers installed in the program. Everything seemed as it should be, but Monkey shook his head when Frank Dinde asked if this particular tour could be opened to the public once more.

"No, I don't think so. There's definitely something in there although I couldn't find it. I think you'd better give the program back to the Center and have the team that created it work it over." Monkey grinned shyly as he said this, ducking his head and looking at Mr. Dinde sideways.

"You didn't find anything?" The Net Rep gazed over Monkey's head towards Sonia Andrews. "Then the two deaths must have been accidental. Nothing to do with the program at all. There's no killer virus."

"I didn't say that," Monkey began, but Frank Dinde motioned at him to be quiet.

"I'll take care of everything. Tell Mr. Glover Brims," Frank said to Mitch, "that we appreciate his control visit, but next time he should announce his arrival."

"Monkey said it wasn't safe," Mitch said, speaking for the first time since the beginning of the interview. Monkey gave him a thankful look.

Frank made a negligent gesture. "M-18 said he didn't find anything, that there wasn't any virus within the program. That means that the program is perfectly safe, right, M-18?"

"The program itself is safe," Monkey said. "There is nothing wrong with the program. What I'm worried about is something coming from outside the program."

There was a little silence while the Net employees thought about that. "If the tour operates from a secured location, there shouldn't be any outside agent invading the tour. It's impossible."

"Nothing is impossible." Monkey clenched his fists, looking towards Mitch for help. The problem was, there was no proof that anything was wrong.

"Is the system secure or not?" Frank Dinde insisted.

Monkey nodded absently. On one hand, he approved the secure system, and on the other, he thought it was possible to introduce a virus, but he didn't know of anyone capable of doing so.

"You'll be remaining in Dallas, M-18," Frank Dinde said. "Your assistance with an upgrade to the virus-catching program is necessary."

"How long will he be here?" asked Mitch.

"That is not for you to know." Frank Dinde's eyes flashed with annoyance.

Before they parted, Mitch gave Monkey his address and orders to call him as soon as possible. "Let me know what's going on," he said, giving the mutant a quick hug.

"Goodbye, Mitch." Monkey watched as his friend was led out of the room, then turned to face Frank Dinde. "I'm tired. I'd like to lie down for a while."

Frank expressed no surprise at this, despite the fact the mutant had been 'sleeping' for three days straight. "I'll have you escorted to your room," he said with a nod towards one of the security guards.

Monkey had a sick feeling in the pit of his stomach. There was something bothering him and no one to talk to about it. Mitch was gone; now he was alone within the Net headquarters. He had no friends here. Frank Dinde, head of security, called him M-18 and refused to shake his hand. The others avoided eye contact and flinched if he accidentally brushed against them. Even Ms. Andrews, the head representative, looked at him as if he were a monster.

When he arrived in his room, he wandered about a bit, looking out the window and flicking the television on and off. There was no shunt in his room, although there was a computer outlet in the wall. He called up a floating screen, but the only channels he could access were closed-circuit. He found the security channel and easily deactivated the block. Now he could see the whole building and watch Net Reps as they passed certain cameras. He amused himself by poking his finger through the screen and making ripples appear in their bodies. He swirled Ms. Andrews' face into a grotesque blob.

The paper with Mitch's address was folded and carefully tucked into his pocket. Every now and then his hand strayed to it and he touched it lightly. He'd heard that the program was to be re-opened the next day. His protest had gone unheeded because he couldn't pinpoint any actual errors. All he knew was that something had penetrated the program and had left without a trace. And there was no one capable of doing that unless it was one of the other mutants.

He closed his eyes and pressed his forehead against the wall. His hand reached into his pocket and he drew out the folded paper Mitch gave him. He wouldn't call Mitch—the calls would all be monitored. But it made him feel better just to know he could. He unfolded the paper Mitch gave him, and a thin silver wire fell out. It winked in the light. Monkey held his breath and picked up the wire. Then his shoulders sagged in relief. It was a shunt.

* * *

"Are you kidding?" Andrea slammed her fist on the desk. It didn't make the noise she wanted, so she picked up her serpentine pencil holder and hurled it onto the floor.

The Net Rep, Ms. Andrews, didn't even blink as the green stone shattered. "I never kid. Tomorrow morning, six a.m., the president of the worldwide Net will be here in person to take a Virtual Tour. He will be accompanied by his staff and three bodyguards. They will all go on the tour with him. He has personally asked for Mitch to accompany him, and there will most likely be news coverage. You will have everything ready."

"Mr. Megalot?" There was a catch in her voice.

"President Megalot. Yes, he will be coming here tomorrow morning to partake in a Virtual Tour. It was his own idea." The Net Rep rubbed her hands together.

Andrea sat down in her chair. "Didn't you read the report, Ms. Andrews?"

"Call me Sonia, please. I did, and it was quite clear to me. There was no sign of a virus of any kind. The ghost glitch never existed."

"And you knew about the mutants?" Andrea still had a hard time believing in mutants. If Mitch hadn't told her about Monkey, she would have been tempted to disbelieve Professor Toutbon.

"Of course I knew about the mutants." Sonia Andrews sighed. "The Net found out about their capabilities and used them. What's wrong with that?"

"How do you explain the two deaths?"

"Coincidence. Unfortunate accidents. A cardiovascular attack killed the first man, and apparently, the second tour guide died of a nervous disorder linked to an embolism in the brain." Ms. Andrews smiled. "Just worry about getting ready for tomorrow. We need good publicity right now."

Andrea licked her lips. "All right. But before we do anything I want to have it in writing."

"Have what in writing?"

"That I am in no way responsible for the Virtual Tours anymore. That I am in no way to be held responsible for any kind of accident that may befall the president. I want the paper signed and on my desk by five o'clock, and I want the check the Net promised me. A cashier's check made out in my name, for the total amount the Net promised me if I decided to abdicate my position as president. My forty-eight percent is worth thirteen billion dollars. Subtract what I owe the Net and pay me the rest. It's all yours. I want nothing to do with it anymore." Her face was deathly pale, but her eyes glittered with determination.

"You're quitting?" Sonia Andrews looked stunned.

"Yes," Andrea replied. She stood up and walked to the door, her shoes crunching on the bits of smashed stone. "Now, if you'll excuse me, I have a lot of work to do before tonight."

After the Net Rep left, Andrea went to the broom closet in the hallway and got a sweeper. She didn't want Cocotte to cut her paws on the sharp pieces of serpentine. Then she pressed a button on her console.

"Sally, would you please tell Digby to come to my office? And get Mitch. You'd better bring maté for everyone, too. On second thought, make that whiskey. Yes, whiskey! I want everyone to hear this."

She put her face in her hands. She wanted Tony to be here so she could confide in him. She realized that she'd always confided in him. Ever since he'd become her chauffeur, she'd talked to him about her worries, her triumphs and even her problems with the Net. He'd always listened and always managed to say the right thing to her. She rubbed her face and looked out the window. A whiskey was just what she needed. And then a long talk with Tony.

* * *

After Mitch, Sally and Digby left and the express courier brought her papers and check from the Net, Andrea stared at the telephone and willed it to ring. *Tony. Please call me, Tony.* Her lips moved as she whispered his name. It was six p.m. and he was two seconds late.

The phone rang and she jumped, then her hand shot out. "Andrea Girt."

"It's me," he said simply.

Her heart did a sort of jig in her chest and she knew she was grinning idiotically. "Will you come and pick me up tonight?"

"Of course." He paused. "I want to ask you something important."

"I'm listening."

"Not over the phone. I'll see you in a few minutes."

Andrea replaced the receiver as if it were made of glass. She looked under her desk at Cocotte, curled up and sleeping in her little bed. "I have the check, and I have the signatures on the letter. Now we're going to go out and celebrate. I will be free in exactly three days, as soon as President Megalot wakes up after his trip. Then you and I will walk out of this office and we will never come back."

The dog twitched her ears and raised her head, yawning widely.

"Come on, let's go hear what Tony wants to tell me." Andrea snapped the leash on her dog's collar.

* * *

Digby saw Sally bite her nails as she stared at Mitch. She wouldn't go home, begging him to let her stay until the trip was over. Still subdued after Andrea's meeting, Digby had relented. Now he was sitting by his console, his fingers trailing lightly over the buttons, his eyes unfocused as he thought about the implications of Mitch's news.

Mitch had told them all about his trip to Dallas. The part about the mutant had fascinated Digby. He desperately wanted to meet him and learn his secrets, even if he didn't like the part about the mutants' role in creating the virtual worlds. He'd thought that he had done most of the work himself, except for the necessary time-lapse factor, which had stumped him and all the programmers under him. Then the Net had hired a group of scientists—the mutants.

Self-doubt was trickling into his brain, numbing his fingers and causing his teeth to seek his lower lip and gnaw restlessly.

How was it possible? How could it be true? Mutants were just a rumor. Mitch must be mistaken. A mutant. A real mutant, a cyborg! A man so intimately linked to the machine he could cast his mind into it and delve into its deepest secrets. A mutant!

Digby shook his head a bit and sighed. His eyes focused on the console and automatically checked the status of his voyagers. Thanks to the new virus-catching program the Net had devised, he could trace the voyagers' movements much more closely. Mitch was in his own room, and the president was in the bar, drinking a piña colada. Fine. Now Digby could follow their movements with some precision. Not perfectly, of course, but closely enough to feel secure. Two Net Representatives were with him now in the console room. They were trained technicians, and already they had spent more time than he had watching their president.

They were part of the new group that would move in after this trip was done. Everything was finished here, for him. He had handed in his resignation, along with Mitch and Sally. Andrea had made things very clear. The Net was taking over, and there would be no room for the upper level employees in the new incarnation of company.

With his knowledge of the system, Digby could probably have stayed, but he thought better of it. Mitch's description of their attitude towards the mutant and the way the Net employees had kept them both prisoners made him suspect the Net offices would not be a good place for him to work.

Sally had made the same decision, but hers was because of Mitch. She went where he went. The little diamond on her finger sparkled as she wrung her hands together. Her face was drawn and her eyes had huge circles beneath them. She'd pleaded with Mitch not to go on the tour, but he had simply kissed her and lay down on the sending couch. Now she paced up and down in front of the plate-glass window or came into the room to stand next to her lover. Digby couldn't order her to leave, not with her distress so palpable. Instead, he motioned to the Net men sitting at their table in the far corner.

"Will you fellows take over for a while? I need to get something to eat."

He took Sally by the shoulder and led her outside. "Where are we going?" she asked.

"It's time for dinner."

They saw Andrea getting into her limousine. That didn't surprise them. They were amazed, though, when she leaned through the window and gave the chauffeur a long, lingering kiss on the mouth.

* * *

Mitch stared at the moray eel, his eyes widening in shock. The amazement he felt was not because he was scuba diving with the president of the Net. It was because the eel had just whispered into his ear.

Wilbur Megalot floated in the crystal-clear water, his eyes magnified behind the scuba mask. His expression was beatific. He motioned to Mitch, pointing to a leopard ray moving lazily through the water. He had been pointing at everything; he was one of those people who couldn't admire something without having everyone else admire it too. Mitch nodded vaguely and gave him a thumb's up. A school of angelfish hovered over the staghorn coral. A parrotfish swam by, its green and blue scales looking like fine turquoise mosaic. One of the president's bodyguards floated near the surface of the water. Mitch wasn't watching any of this. His eyes were fixed on the moray eel.

"It's me, Monkey. Don't tell anyone I'm here. Don't worry. I'm going to protect you."

Wilbur Megalot, president of the worldwide Net and the richest man in the world, motioned to Mitch and swam towards the surface. In the virtual world, you didn't have to worry about decompressing. Actually, you didn't need to wear the scuba gear at all, and you could swim underwater all you wanted. However, Mitch never told his clients this, and no one ever asked. Sometimes, when he was alone, Mitch would dive without gear. It was like dreaming.

He splashed out of the water, climbing up the ladder onto the rocking boat. He took the president's scuba tank from him and handed it to a figment standing nearby. Another fig helped the bodyguard onto the boat. The figs, known as Diver-1 and Diver-2, could handle scuba gear and drive the motorboat to well-known diving locations. There were underwater wrecks and portions of the reef entirely reconstructed from real landscapes. Diver-1 knew every location and could find them with no help from the map taped to the navigation console.

"Ah, this is the life." The president sighed as he sat on a comfortable chair on deck and took the cold beer Diver-1 handed him. He popped the top and slurped the foam noisily. The sun made him squint, so he asked for a pair of sunglasses. Diver-1 pulled a pair out of his pocket. Mitch knew that the pocket was simply a virtual pathway. The president could have asked for a Thanksgiving turkey, and after processing the order, Diver-1 would have pulled it right out of his pocket. Some orders were easier to process than others; sunglasses and sunscreen were available right away. A funny order to process was a fishing pole. The figment would pull it out of his pocket with a perfectly straight face, never realizing the incongruous sight it made.

Mitch dried himself off with a fluffy towel then pulled on his T-shirt. It was the official guide's shirt with Virtual Tours written across his chest.

"Do you need anything else, sir?" he asked the president.

"No thanks, son, this has been a wonderful trip. Since I've been here, I've done nothing but relax."

"That's why you're here, sir." Mitch nodded to the figment to start the boat.

"That and to check out my newest acquisition."

Mitch nodded. Andrea had been very clear that night. As they sipped their whiskey, she'd explained that the Net had just bought Virtual Tours and that she was relinquishing her shares. The president's voice interrupted his thoughts.

"What are we doing tonight?"

"There's a limbo dancer on the patio, and we're having a steel-drum band come especially from Tobago to play for you. Dinner is stuffed grouper, our chef's specialty, and we have lime ice for desert. I promise you'll love it."

"I'm sure I will." The president grinned at Mitch, showing his famous dimples. His silver hair was also the same, but aside from the dimples and hair, it was doubtful his wife would have recognized him. He'd chosen his younger self for the trip, jokingly saying that he'd always wanted to be rejuvenated. "What a great trip. I was crazy not to have tried it sooner. I'll have to come back every month and bring the wife. What do you say, Boris? Are you up for a monthly appointment in paradise?"

The bodyguard nodded, his arms crossed over his chest.

Mitch smiled weakly and rubbed his forehead. The boat chugged across the water, and he could see the docks in the distance. He wanted to be alone in his room because he figured Monkey could talk to him then. He had a couple questions to ask.

* * *

My name is Madeline, the littlest girl in line. I am an orpheline, *which is French for orphan. Am I truly an orphan? I tried for years to find a mother but never discovered who she had been. The father was easier. Chips and sparkles, dazzles of silver metal and a frosting of diamond-bright electrodes, slender wires in every rainbow color, and* voila, *the father.* Le père.

I like France. The Louvre is a wonderful place to visit, and I wander through its echoing corridors long after everyone else has gone. My world is like the museum, with beautiful Greek statues staring at me, their eyes empty, and paintings of heroes hanging on gilded walls. My world is enclosed, with a doorway leading out of it into the real world. Don't ask me how I escaped; I only know that one day I discovered a pathway that led me to paradise.

I was a prisoner in the program. I longed to be free. I created my own world, and I used it to escape the glass case where I grew up. Then one day I found a gateway leading to the real world. The real world! I stood in the sun, I felt sweat trickling down my chest, between my heavy breasts, and I sighed deeply. My hand crept to my throat, slid down, over my collarbones, over skin made slick with sweat, and I felt myself for the first time. I felt my body, I felt it breathe and move, and

I felt desire. I looked upon another human being and he saw me for what I was. His eyes grew heavy-lidded and his mouth became soft.

I pressed myself to him, needing to feel him holding me. But there was more, so much more that I needed. My whole body was awash in a sensual rush of delight.

Now my head spins when I think about it. I wish that I could live forever in the real world, giving in to my body's every desire. But the path is only open for brief amounts of time. I slip in and out, in and out, in and out...my breath is coming faster and faster, my heart speeds up and sweat trickles down my chest. Or is it my light fingertips? I will return to the real world. Love is the most important thing in the universe, and I will worship it until I die.

* * *

Mitch searched his room. There was nothing out of the ordinary; it looked just the same as it always did. Right down to the usual bouquet of hibiscus. He touched one of the blossoms pensively. It giggled.

"Wha—!!" Mitch jumped backwards as if he'd been stung.

"It's me," Monkey said. The blossom nodded sagely.

As Mitch stared, the flower bent its stalk and seemed to peer around. "I think we're alone." The petals of the hibiscus moved like huge, red lips.

"Why don't you take your own form?" Mitch asked. The talking flower gave him the chills.

"It's easier for me to become something that's already in the program." Monkey's voice was sad. "That way, no one can trace me. I'm not supposed to be here. I'm back in my room, using the shunt you gave me. "

Mitch was silent for a moment, digesting this. "You do know what happened," he said finally. It wasn't a question.

The flower shed a petal. "Yes."

"Am I in danger?" Mitch asked.

"I think so. I'll stay with you, watching. Don't worry."

"No, you should stay near the president. My God, Monkey, if anything happens to him…"

"I won't leave you."

"Will you…" Mitch licked his lips. "Can you tell me what happened to Arthur and Jonathon?"

The flower shivered a bit. "There are many discrepancies. I think it was another mutant, one of us. I'm sorry, Mitch."

"No, I'm sorry." Mitch approached the flower and stroked it gently. "You couldn't hurt anyone. Whoever murdered Arthur and Jonathon was evil. He wasn't like you."

The hibiscus blossom tilted backwards to look at Mitch. Another petal fell silently. "I don't know yet what happened. But I have a feeling we'll find out soon."

"How soon?"

"There's an eddy in the program. Someone is approaching. Whatever happens, Mitch, don't worry. I'll be around."

Mitch tried to grin but his mouth felt dry. "I'm not worried." The blossom lost all its petals and vanished. "Now I'm worried." He looked around the room with wide eyes. But nothing moved, and nothing spoke to him.

Suddenly the room shivered and a waft of sweet scent filled his nostrils. He froze, unsure of what was happening. There was no knock on the door. The door didn't even open. Instead, a young woman stepped through it as if it were tissue paper or smoke. She gave him an enigmatic smile, and her eyes took on a strange, silvery cast.

Mitch gasped involuntarily. His body reacted so physically to her smile that it astounded him. Suddenly his whole consciousness was concentrated in his loins. His penis was so stiff it was painful, and his breathing was ragged, his teeth chattering.

When she approached, he didn't move. His legs were locked tight. Not that he wanted to flee. He wanted to touch her. She didn't take her eyes from him, but her hand reached up and caressed her own throat. Delicately she drew a line downwards with her fingers, tracing a path to her full breasts. She parted her robe and Mitch gave a soft moan. Her breasts were round and heavy, swaying like soft…

There was no warning. A hard blow to his head, and then his vision darkened. He saw the floor fly up to meet him, but he was unconscious before he hit the ground.

* * *

Monkey looked up, but the girl was gone. She'd vanished when he'd appeared, frightened by his sudden appearance. He picked Mitch up and put him on his bed. Tenderly he smoothed his hair from his face. He leaned over and kissed his lips. Then he sat up and put his face in his hands. There were too many variables, and he didn't know how to react. Saving Mitch had been instinctive, but now he was lost. He loved Mitch. The president and the others would have to learn to take care of themselves. Yet…and yet, he hadn't sensed any evil, just danger. If only he had his magic sword.

He flexed his fingers. He would go talk to Mahler; perhaps he would know what to do. Time, the problem was time. A smile pulled at his lips. Time could be twisted if you knew the right equations, or if you had the right acquaintances.

* * *

Monkey stepped out of the Virtual Tour world and onto a rocky seashore. He knew Mahler was there. It was a question of finesse, and Monkey had the lightest touch. He could follow anyone, and no one ever knew he was being followed.

A silhouette stood on the edge of the cliff, looking down at a fantastic tree below. A wave crashed at its roots, covering it with a white shroud of foam. Monkey approached slowly. He knew he was intruding, but he had to act quickly. He clenched his hands and waited until Mahler noticed him. He wished he'd taken the time to pass through the world of Zorg. His magic shield and sword would come in handy now. If Mahler decided to take offense at his trespassing, he could probably kill him.

* * *

Mahler stiffened. There was an intruder in his world. His first reaction was anger. Then he saw who it was. Monkey, the dreamer. He relaxed and extended his hand. "Come," he said. "Admire the Mother Tree with me if you wish."

"I want to ask you some questions." Monkey lowered his chin and grinned.

Mahler nodded and sat on a rock. Next to it, his legs were as shiny black as gunmetal. He flexed his foot. "What is it?" he asked.

"Love…and sex," added Monkey.

Mahler gave a little start. His smile faded as his eyes strayed back towards the Mother Tree. "I have risen above all that. There is nothing left of passion in my body. I willed it to be so. It was causing too much confusion in my brain."

"In your brain or in your circuits?" Monkey wrapped his arms around his knees. In the distance, clouds scudded across the sky. The sea was one solid color without nuance. The water was dark blue and the waves wore white foam on their crests. The rocks were black and glistened with water droplets. The sky was pale gray, except for a faint silver line on the horizon.

"Both, perhaps," Mahler said, finally.

"How long ago did you discover love?" Monkey asked. "In what world did you go to experience such a thing?"

"It was before you were woken," Mahler admitted. "There were worlds that catered to sex, although love seemed to have no part in them. Whenever I fell in love, it was misinterpreted. I grew tired of deception. The physical aspects of love intrigued me for a while, but even they grew stale when I discovered I could not share more than my passion. It was frustrating to have my partners disappear after one bout of lovemaking. Conversation or sharing was never a part of it. I concluded that I had to eradicate desire from myself in order to gain serenity. I have done so."

"Do you remember when you were still in the stages of discovering love?" Monkey asked. "Were any of our kind with you?"

"Yes, the first five M's were with me. We grew up together and passed that part of our physical growth at the same time. Then the scientists discovered our hormone imbalance and corrected it. Sex became less of a compulsion. We were able to control it. Why all these questions? Don't the scientists control your hormones?"

"Perhaps they do." Monkey sounded sad. "But one of us has escaped control. It's M-19, I believe. I saw her today. She was trying to seduce a friend of mine."

Mahler glanced at the sky. Dark clouds were gathering on the horizon, blotting out the watery light. In front of him, the crystal tree shimmered as the waves slammed into it. Water glistened on each of its slender branches like diamond beads.

"Do you know M-19?" Monkey asked.

Mahler nodded. "I've been watching her. She was M-20's twin. Her sister's death unbalanced her. They were very close and shared the same world. She is going through a particularly difficult time. She searches for love like the rest of us search for knowledge."

"I want to protect my friend."

"Then you mustn't touch him. Perhaps you don't realize what kind of effect we have on humans. In the real world, we are formidable. We have powers..." His voice trailed off. "At least, some of us do. There is a conflict within our own matrix. It is the human within us trying to overcome the machine. The difference is passion, my son. Only our emotions distinguish us from the machine. In some of us, the difference is overdeveloped. M-19 spends too much time in her own world, locked within her own desires."

The wind whistled as the storm gained power. Huge, darkening clouds roiled in the sky. Lightning stabbed through the heavens, touching the sea with jagged fingers. Monkey raised his head. Tears, or maybe it was rain, streaked his face. "They're calling us. I'm afraid I will be too late."

"Don't worry. I can ask the time-twisters to send you back. That's what you wanted, wasn't it?"

"Yes, that, and to protect the ones I love."

"Did you ever play with M-19 in your secret garden?" Mahler's voice was gentle.

"You know she can't play," Monkey said. "You know what she's really like."

"Somehow she overcame all that." Mahler's voice was admiring, a little frightened. "Come back and tell me what has happened as soon as you can." The gale whipped his voice into shreds.

Monkey opened his mouth to answer, but the wind was too loud. A swirling portal opened in the sky in front of him. He turned to bid farewell to Mahler, but the doorway sucked him in and he was swept into darkness.

"Come back soon!" Mahler raised his hand, but his world was empty now. Monkey had gone. The storm struck then, and lightning sizzled up and down the Mother Tree.

* * *

There was a strange tingling as his brother sent him back to the Virtual Tours world, only half a minute after he'd left it the first time. He reappeared on the bed, perched next to Mitch who was still unconscious. A noise startled him. He raised his head, listening. It came from nearby. A feeling a dread crept over him as realization sank in. He looked once more at Mitch, lying motionless on the bed, and his heart lurched.

"I could kill you with a kiss," he whispered. His eyes were bleak. Mahler would have to wait.

* * *

The president hummed as he undressed. His virtual body glowed with a new tan, and his taut muscles moved under smooth skin. He moved in front of the mirror to admire himself. Another face stared back at him. He gasped, whirled around, then laughed weakly.

"You certainly frightened me, dear," he said. "I didn't ring for room service. Are you the new maid?"

"Hush." It was a whisper. The girl was looking at him from beneath long lashes. Her eyes were a strange, frosty plum color that made his knees weak and started his heart pounding uncomfortably.

Wilbur Megalot thought that he'd never seen such an exquisite beauty. The girl's face was a pure oval, her mouth slightly open, showing white, pearly teeth. Her hand strayed to her throat and trailed down her chest, drawing his eyes along with it. Her breasts were heavy, round, like fruit waiting to be plucked. His own hand drifted towards her, even as his brain told him very sternly to stop that nonsense.

His body told his brain to shut up.

When he touched her, an electric shock stunned him. He lost concept of where he was or what he was doing. All he could feel, or think about, was the tremendous heat building in his loins. The hard passion of youth astounded him. He felt as if all his years had suddenly vanished, and he was a teenager in front of a nude girl for the first time. The hardness of his desire was thrusting against the satiny thighs of the girl. She smiled, her hands sliding up around his neck.

"There's a soft bed over there," she whispered.

Wilbur Megalot couldn't answer. His mouth was open, gaping, but he was too busy gasping for breath. Waves and waves of physical pleasure were washing over him. His muscles were tingling and sexual passion was making any sort of coherent thought impossible. He wanted to push her down on the bed and throw himself onto her. She took his hand. He let himself be led to the wide expanse of white sheets. Without a word, the girl lay down and spread her legs.

"Please," she whispered, with a tiny moan. The tip of her pink tongue parted her lips.

Wilbur Megalot was panting. In a second, he was sure he would explode. He lunged onto the sweet, compliant form beneath him and buried himself in her body, thrusting madly to end the incredible pressure he felt building inside him.

But the release he felt only aggravated his desire, and as the girl moaned and squirmed beneath him, he felt his whole being drawn into the vortex she created. A huge vacuum that could never be filled. His moans and gasps turned into harsh cries as his heart, back at the Virtual Tours sending room, gave out.

* * *

"What have you done?" Monkey rushed into the room.

"What do you mean?" The girl raised her face. It was deeply flushed, and her hair hung in a dark tangle over breasts. She didn't appear surprised.

"You killed him. He's dead." Monkey's heart thudded in his chest. He closed his eyes.

"He isn't, he just disappeared for a while to rest. How silly you are. And anyway, who are you?" She stood up and stretched voluptuously. Sweat beaded her forehead and belly, and she sighed. "It's so hot and humid here, as if I'm breathing blood instead of air." She gave another sigh and peered at Monkey. Her red lips curved in a sultry smile. "Do I know you?"

"Don't you remember me?"

"Have we met before?"

"My name is M-18. You are M-19. Now do you know me?"

"My name is Madeline." She pouted. "Madeline, not M-19."

"We'd better get out of here. Can you hear those bells? That means the program is being shut down. Quick, before we're trapped." He grabbed her hand.

"This isn't a program," she said, her voice petulant. Monkey didn't pay attention. He pushed her into a portal. For a minute they hovered, grayness all around them.

"Where do you want to go?" she asked.

"Take me to your world," Monkey ordered.

A lurch, a swirl, and then Monkey found himself standing in the hallway of the Louvre. It wasn't quite the Louvre, actually. The museum was empty and the sky outside the windows was a hard turquoise color that hurt the eye. He turned away and contemplated the walls instead. They were covered with gold leaf. Paintings hung in no particular order, their frames covered in glowing jewels. Monkey noticed that they were mostly of nudes.

"Is this your world?" He looked around. "It's very interesting." A curtain made of blue and green glass beads moved in the breeze, clicking softly. Overhead, squawking scarlet macaws flew back and forth along the long corridors. Just ahead, in a doorway, a peacock appeared. It pecked at something on the marble floor then moved on.

"Let me show you my favorite statue." Madeline tugged his arm, her voice girlish and high.

"Why did you do it?" he asked her. He felt tired, all of a sudden.

"I didn't do anything. You won't tell, will you? You won't tell Dr. Djusky?" There was more than a shade of fear now in her voice.

"I promise," Monkey said soothingly. He let himself be led down the echoing corridors to a small room. In the middle was the statue. It was M-20, Madeline's twin sister, dazzling in the perfection of white marble.

"Do you like it?" Madeline asked, her eyes bright.

"It's lovely," Monkey said, still in his gentle voice.

"I've been looking for her for so long. She went strange and then disappeared one day. I think she went to the real world. I miss her, Monkey. We loved each other. She was all I had."

Monkey felt tears pricking his eyes. He turned to look out the window, rubbing his hand over his face before turning towards her once more. "I don't know what happened to your sister. You should have asked someone before looking for her. Perhaps Dr. Toutbon can help you."

Madeline spun around. "You don't know anything." She tossed her head. "I can show you something you never thought of doing." Her eyes grew sly. "Come here, M-18. Let me show you something wonderful. Everyone does it in the real world. Come on, let me show you. I promise it won't hurt. And then you'll understand why I ran away to live in the real world."

"Madeline, that wasn't the real world." Monkey's eyes were sorrowful.

"Of course it was. As soon as I find the key, I'm going to stay there forever."

"No." Monkey sighed as she ran her hands up and down over his chest.

"Kiss me," she begged him. "Please, kiss me." Her frosty, plum-colored eyes were pleading.

"Look." Monkey reached down and put his hand right through her body. It was as if she was made of mist.

She jumped backwards with an exclamation of shock. "How did you do that?"

"It's because that isn't your real body. We're in your world. And the world you think of as real is only another virtual world, one that I made. You can only get to the real world if you leave your glass case and take an elevator."

Madeline swung her head slowly from side to side. Her face took on a haunted look. "I don't believe you. Look at me. I can see myself now when before I could not. In the other world, there were mirrors, and I could touch people. They could touch me too, and in ways...in ways that I only dreamed about before. Listen, they do these things, oh M-18, will you let me show you what they do?" Her eyes were all pupil, her mouth slack. Her breathing deepened as her hands roamed over her own body. "They touch you here, and here, and down here. Oh, it feels so good," she moaned.

Monkey spoke firmly. "Stop, Madeline. That's enough."

She stopped. "Do we have to go back? Was Madeline naughty? I didn't mean to be bad, I was just so lonely. I wanted them to love me, the way I love my statues and my paintings. Look, aren't they beautiful? Aren't they perfect?"

Monkey nodded. His face was as pale and expressionless as white marble. "Go home now, Madeline," he said gently. "I'll close up here."

She nodded, her small hands clenched by her side. "Goodbye, M-18," she whispered. Then she was gone.

Chapter Eleven

Press close bare-bosom'd nigh—press close magnetic nourishing
night!
Night of south winds—night of the large few stars!
Still nodding night—mad naked summer night.
—Walt Whitman, *Song of Myself*

Nothing made sense. Bells rang, sirens shrieked, and the president of the Net died. There was a stunned silence in the sending room.

The two technicians and the mobile emergency unit worked frantically on the body until it was obvious nothing would bring him back.

The emergency unit, two female doctors and a male nurse, packed their needles and electrodes away, their postures slumped in exhaustion. The technicians nodded in stunned silence as the doctors explained the cause of death. Then the doctors shook hands with them and left, the doors closing with a loud ping. A minute passed.

The door slid open, and two Net Reps walked into the room. One was a woman with pale hair pulled back in a tight chignon, the other a man with a red tie decorated with tiny Christmas trees. Odd, it was September. The technicians stood up straighter. Wary, they watched as the dark-suited man and woman approached. The man peered at the president's body, his eyes lingering on the smile that twisted the president's mouth and the damp stains like egg white on his skinny thighs.

The two technicians backed away uneasily. One tried to speak, but the words died in his throat. Finally, his partner stuck out a hand. "I'm Jim Lockheart."

The Net Reps both ignored the outstretched hand. The man said, "I want a full report in triplicate."

"My God, sir, he's dead!" blurted the other technician.

"Heads are going to roll," the Net Rep said coldly.

If he hadn't been so shaken, Jim Lockheart would have laughed.

* * *

Frank Dinde and Sonia Andrews looked at each other. "What do we do now?" Frank asked.

Sonia licked her dry lips. "What were you told to do in such a situation?" Her voice wavered. She felt as if she'd just fallen into a deep well.

"Snap out of it!" Frank's voice, on the other hand, was sharp. "I don't need you to fall apart now."

"We have to call the vice president."

"The hell we do. This is a security breach. I'm security. Go get that mutant, M-18 or whatever the Hell he's called, from his room. I have some questions for him."

Mitch and the president's bodyguards were still asleep in the chairs. Dinde turned towards the two technicians still standing rooted next to the president's body. "Wake up the rest of them. I want to speak to them immediately. Hurry up!"

"It will take a moment to unhook the electrodes and take out the IVs."

Frank Dinde glared at the technician, and the man fumbled with the monitors, his hands shaking so badly he dropped the bottle of alcohol used to sterilize the electrodes. The glass broke, and a sharp scent filled the room.

* * *

Mitch was in the president's room with Monkey. They were standing by the bed, the window was open, and the palm trees outside were gently rustling in the wind. There was no sign of the president, his bodyguards, or of Madeline. The bed was rumpled, and an echoing vibration in the air made Mitch's head ache. Or perhaps it was the bump. He fingered it gingerly. Monkey's explanation made no sense to him.

"Are you certain it happened that way?" he asked, rubbing his forehead. The bells were ringing now; soon the scene would fade and he would wake up. His head throbbed.

"I think so. She never meant to hurt anyone. She only tried to love them. You must understand!"

Mitch tried to grin, but his face felt frozen. Horror was seeping into his bones, freezing them. He felt as if he was in a nightmare. Perhaps it was all a dream, and when he woke up, the president would still be alive, Digby would be laughing at him, and Sally would be holding him tightly. "I'm sorry," he said. "I'll have to tell the police. You can see that, can't you?"

"I'll take care of Madeline. Don't let anyone hurt her. Do you promise?"

"I can't promise anything; I have no power at all in the real world. All I can do is warn Andrea. You'll have to go to the Center and speak to Professor Toutbon. Maybe he will be able to protect her. I can't. I'm sorry."

"Sorry, sorry—everyone's sorry." Monkey frowned and turned his head. "I have to go now. The picture is fading. I can't see you anymore. Goodbye, Mitch, until we meet again."

Mitch struggled against the fog, but it swept in, filling his eyes with mist and numbing his body. There was a sickening jolt, like an elevator coming to an abrupt halt, and then a feeling of weightlessness and cold. For a minute, he floated in a deep gray cloud, deprived of his senses. He wondered if the mutants lived like this, encased in a cotton silence, neither in nor out of the world, simply existing. Then lights blinked on and he gasped for breath, as he always did when he woke up. There was an indistinct murmur of voices, and someone draped a warm blanket around his shoulders. A cup of hot tea was pressed into his hands.

"Mitch, are you all right?" It was Sally, the color leached from her skin and her eyes immense in her small face. "I was so worried. When we heard the sirens I thought...I thought it was you." Tears spilled out of her eyes and dashed down her smooth cheeks.

"I'm fine." He smiled at her. It was so easy to smile when she was there. His heart resumed its normal rhythm. Sally was with him and he was all right.

Digby dropped to a crouch near his sofa. "Hey, Mitch." His face, too, was pale and his eyes glittered strangely behind his glasses. Mitch darted a glance behind his shoulder. Frank Dinde and Sonia Andrews were approaching. "The virus catcher put a name tag on two mutants. Do you know what happened? Can you tell me?"

Mitch winced. "Two?"

"M-18 and M-19."

Mitch shook his head. Tears threatened to spill. If only he didn't feel so helpless when he woke up. He was still dizzy. But the Net Reps were nearly in earshot. He tried to speak clearly. "It was just an accident. She never meant to kill anyone. She didn't even know what she was doing."

From the way Frank Dinde stiffened, Mitch knew he'd overheard. His hands tightened on the cup of tea. There was no backing out now. If he wanted to save Monkey, there was only one way he could do it. The Net would need a scapegoat, and he didn't want it to be Monkey.

* * *

Digby stood up as the Net Reps drew near. He wiped his hand on his lab coat and stuck out a hand. "I'm Daniel Glover Brims."

The two Net Reps looked at each other, then down at Mitch.

"I think you have some explaining to do," Frank Dinde said, the skin around his mouth whitening in rage.

Mitch looked at Digby, still standing with his hand hovering in front of him. "If you don't both shake his hand and introduce yourselves properly, I won't say a thing to anyone. I'll take the Fifth Amendment and let Virtual Tours—let's see, how would you say it, Frank? Go down the drain. That's it. I'll let the whole bloody mess go right down the drain." He lifted his tea and took a long, deliberate drink. His face was pale, but his eyes flashed.

Frank Dinde shook Digby's hand.

* * *

Officially, it was called the killer virus.

The Net flew Monkey to the Virtual Tours office in New York that evening to secure the program from viruses, human intervention and, most importantly, other mutants. Any mistakes, they said, would mean the end of the mutant program. He could do that, of course. The program was already secure from viruses and outside agents, but who would have thought to secure it from mutants?

No one knew how easy it was for him, however, so nobody wondered why he spent all night in the room, alternately hooked to a shunt or standing in front of the console, a pensive look on his angelic face.

"The program is ready," Monkey said, finally. His face was haggard, his magnificent eyes bruised with fatigue.

Frank Dinde nodded. "Thank you, M-18." He refused to address him any other way. "I'm sure Dr. Djusky at the Center will be pleased with your work here."

"I'm sure he will, sir. Am I going back to the Center now?"

Frank Dinde smiled. "As soon as we clear up the mess here, M-18."

Monkey nodded, too tired to argue. "She didn't mean to hurt anyone," he said for perhaps the hundredth time.

Frank Dinde didn't blink. "That makes her even more dangerous, then, doesn't it?" he said quietly.

Chapter Twelve

Space and Time! now I see it is true, what I guess'd at,
What I guess'd when I loaf'd on the grass,
What I guess'd while I lay alone in my bed,
And again as I walk'd the beach under the paling stars of the
morning.
—Walt Whitman, *Song of Myself*

Andrea wore her new engagement ring. Whenever she felt her patience slipping, she would glance at it, take a deep breath, and smile at David Willow. He had inherited her post as Virtual Tours president.

"Shall we start over this section again? You have to know exactly how the process works or else you can't possibly direct the company."

"You wrote this whole book?" David lifted the heavy manual and made a face. It fell on the desk with a loud thump.

"Yes." Andrea glanced at her ring again and opened the book to page four hundred and fifty. "This section tells all about the company's structure. I set it up…"

David reached over the desk and shut the book. "I'm finished for tonight. Just tell me the truth. Are only the mutants capable of creating a virtual world?"

Andrea leveled a cool glance at him. "It's true. If anything happens to the mutants, Virtual Tours will collapse. The only way that we've been able to stretch two days into two weeks is thanks to the mutants."

"How can that be possible?"

"Who knows? But if they disappear, the only things left will be the games created by humans fifteen years ago and substandard tours. And, of course, educational sites." Her voice was almost amused. "Fifteen years of progress, down the drain."

"We could get it back," he insisted.

"Perhaps, but it would mean all the money you sank into the program was a total waste. It's better this way, believe me."

"We can't control them."

"They can be restrained." Her ring winked at her, reassuring. "I'm done for the night, too. I have plans for dinner."

David ran a hand through his thinning hair. "I'll see you tomorrow, then."

Andrea gazed at him for a minute. "We're not enemies, you know. I'll be working with the mutants and you'll be working with the public. Instead of three parties, there are only two, and we'll communicate better. Mistakes like the one that killed Wilbur Megalot and the tour guides won't happen again."

"Three parties?" David looked confused.

"The Net, Virtual Tours, and the Center. We were all fighting for control. Now we know who has it, and it's balancing itself out."

"The mutants are the ones in control," he said bitterly.

"God no, don't you understand anything? They don't even exist in our world."

"Except M-18."

"He's an exception," Andrea admitted.

"He should have stayed in his case."

They glared at each other. Then Andrea's face softened. She could never stay angry with an old boyfriend. Once she'd slept with them, they became part of her. "Let's not start out with a disagreement, David. I'm glad they chose you to take over here. I'm looking forward to starting a new program directly with the mutants."

"You didn't have to accept blame for Wilbur's death. The papers you signed absolved you of responsibility."

"Who else could? I had already left Virtual Tours. No one could hurt that program, and besides, the Net is protecting it now."

"And so you formed your own company. How did you know the public would react the way it did?"

She smiled. "The public is terribly predictable. Let them know about a secret program—any secret program—and they'll scream scandal. Poor creatures, they honestly believe they have the right to know everything."

David smiled uncertainly. "So you saw the breach in the wall and offered to fill it up."

Andrea nodded. "I'm leaving in three days to start a new life. It's my choice, and as chance would have it, it means we'll be working closely together. Let's stay on good terms, shall we?"

"I'll put it a different way. The public screamed scandal, the government wanted to dump the mutant program, and you somehow came up with the idea of starting a new company with the mutants as its assets. Now everyone is grateful. The CIA because you took responsibility for the Net president's death, claiming that the Virtual Tours program had been flawed from the very beginning. The Net because you managed to portray them as a savior when Monkey repaired the program and everything was restored to order. Even the Mutant Center is grateful, because you're taking over their business program and you'll make it as successful as Virtual Tours ever was."

"I hope so. It's going to be interesting, working with them. Mutants—who would have thought they really existed? People are going to be begging to go on virtual tours made by mutants now that they aren't secret any more. You're going to have your hands full."

"What page were we on?" David picked up the book and leafed through it.

"Four hundred and fifty. Chapter nineteen. I wrote it for laymen. You'll be running this company like a pro in no time. But finish reading it yourself. Right now, I'm going to dinner." Andrea picked up Cocotte's leash and walked out of her former office.

* * *

In the dark, in the deep, several miles beneath the surface of the earth, there were many happenings. Love and death, betrayal and hope, all were swirling together. In the maelstrom, a loss occurred. It was a small loss but would have important consequences.

Laurel was the first to notice Mahler's disquiet.

She had been speaking to him daily, asking his advice about dealing with the different mutants. Since the Net president died, the Mutant Center had been restructured into something resembling a corporation and not a laboratory. The three top floors were opened to the public, and although the mutants remained hidden, their presence was discussed regularly in corporate meetings.

"I don't like that document." Mahler's lips moved as the words formed on the crystal screen above his case.

"What document?" Laurel checked her records.

"The one about Madeline. I don't like what the Net Representatives are planning to do."

"Ms. Andrews?" Laurel raised her eyebrows. Sonia Andrews, or 'The Ice Queen,' as Laurel had dubbed her, was, along with Frank Dinde, one of the representatives the Net had assigned to the Mutant Center.

"No, just Frank Dinde."

"How did you get this document?" asked Laurel, typing quickly.

"Do you really need to ask?" Mahler shifted in his case. "Dr. Djusky is helping them. Did you know that?"

Laurel shook her head, startled. "No, I didn't. What else do you know?"

"There are talks. Professor Toutbon isn't in on them. No one knows what to do about M-19."

Laurel nodded. M-19 still floated silently in her glass case, but she was totally isolated, kept within the Center and out of the Net. She could not escape to her own world; even that was blocked to her. She spoke to no one. Laurel's fingers flew over the keyboard. "What are they thinking of doing to her?"

Mahler stirred. His face came closer to the glass and Laurel was shocked to see tears on his cheeks. "They will set her free," he said finally.

"Is that so bad?"

"She is too fragile. She is like a deep sea creature pulled up to the surface. The pressure will be too great for her." Mahler paused. "Don't tell Monkey. Please?"

"Why not?"

"I don't want him to worry. He worries too easily."

Laurel smiled. Monkey did tend to worry. Since the Center had become public, Monkey was the mutants' representative to the clients. Andrea had trained him, and he was now working under Laurel as an assistant to Professor Toutbon.

"What about Ms. Andrews?"

"She's not privy to this news."

"Maybe she can help us." Laurel looked at Mahler, but he shook his head and disappeared into the depths of his mist-filled case.

* * *

"Monkey, why don't you go get us some coffee?" Frank Dinde jerked his thumb at the door. "This conversation doesn't concern you."

Andrea nearly called Monkey back but didn't want to lose her temper in front of him. When the door closed behind him, though, she let Frank Dinde know exactly what she thought of him, which was not very flattering.

Dinde just waited until she was finished and shrugged. "We're talking about a mutant, M-19. I don't think he should hear this. It will just upset him."

Andrea tapped her fingernails on the desk. He had a point. Monkey was still too sensitive to emotions. He had not been put back into his case, and Andrea had given him several jobs. One job was to coordinate the communication between the mutants and the engineers. Digby headed that group, with Mitch as his assistant. Sally was still Andrea's private secretary. That hadn't changed, although the office was now on the ground floor of the Center. Huge bay windows revealed stunning views of the desert instead of the city streets. Tony was still her chauffeur, although the limousine had given way to a solar-powered four-by-four.

Cocotte still dozed in the wicker basket beneath Andrea's desk, her silken ears twitching as she dreamed.

Andrea was pleased at how well everything was going but wished Dr. Djusky and Frank Dinde would go for a walk in the desert...and never return. Sonia Andrews was proving to be extremely competent, and if she would only relax a bit, Andrea thought she might even get to like her. She wished Sonia were here right now.

"I won't let you harm her in any way." Andrea leaned over her desk, placing her hands flat on the smooth, red marble surface.

"She is more dangerous than you can even imagine," Dr. Djusky said. "She killed two of your own men before killing the Net's president."

"She had no idea she was killing them. No charges have been brought against her." Andrea looked from Dr. Djusky to Frank Dinde. "You both understand that."

"She knows now and expresses no regret at all. If she escapes your control, she will commit murder again. She has no moral values whatsoever," Dr. Djusky said.

"Whose fault is that?" snapped Andrea. "You said yourself that she was not human. She wasn't raised as a human, so why would she react like one?"

"The others adapted to our world." Frank Dinde shrugged.

Andrea stared at him. "They do not live in our world," she said finally. "They live in their own worlds. Let Madeline stay in the world she created for herself."

"We can't do that." Dr. Djusky shook his head. "She will find a way to escape and then every male on the Net will be in danger."

"You don't think you're exaggerating?"

"No. I'm sorry. If you'll just sign here, I'll take care of everything." Dr. Djusky pointed towards the paper with the tip of his pen.

Andrea frowned. "I'd like to ask Ms. Andrews about…"

"Your signature is just a formality," Dr. Djusky's voice held the faintest trace of a threat. "I am M-19's legal guardian."

"Fine. Then do without it. You told me what you were going to do. I'm against it. I would prefer to leave Madeline alone. I think we can keep her contained, without any danger to anyone else. Monkey gave me a report, explaining how it could be done. All he has to do is lock Madeline out of the Net, and he knows how to do that."

"How can you be so sure? M-18 is a mutant. His loyalties lie with them."

"She doesn't deserve to be punished; she's like a child who doesn't know any better. In my opinion, she's suffered enough. If Monkey can restrain her, she can invent her own worlds and be happy there. I see no reason to go beyond that."

"This whole fiasco has set us back weeks and countless millions." Frank Dinde shook his head. "You know the law is right in this case, Andrea. Just give us M-19 and we'll leave you alone. We won't try to prosecute."

"Prosecute me? Madeline? You couldn't win either case in a million years." Andrea pressed harder with her hands, whitening the skin around her nails.

"No, but we could make things very difficult for you," Frank Dinde said.

Andrea smiled. "Your threats don't work anymore. I gave up my share of Virtual Tours. If I were you, I'd be careful whom I threatened in the future. As it stands, I can make your lives miserable, not the other way around. It's true I don't have the power to protect Madeline from you, Dr. Djusky, because you are her legal guardian. But I have the power to close off large sections of the Center. If you don't want to find yourselves restricted to levels minus fifteen to minus ten for the rest of your tenure, I'd find another way to take care of this problem."

"All right." Dr. Djusky shrugged. He took his pen and scrawled on the document. Andrea looked at it. He'd deleted the sentence saying he intended to use shock treatment on the mutant. All they were going to do now was move the mutant into another room.

If she signed the paper, she gave up her responsibility. But she didn't like it at all. She'd always faced up to her responsibilities, and Madeline...Well, Madeline was part of the Center. By signing the paper she took Madeline off her list of mutants. By not signing, she would simply put off the inevitable by a few days. Dr. Djusky could easily get a court order. He didn't need her signature. In a way, he was being remarkably transparent by showing her the paper and everything he intended to do.

Andrea looked from one man to the other. Frank Dinde stood very straight, his face contorted in his usual frown. Dr. Djusky was another matter. His look of faint amusement never failed to set her teeth on edge. Their request to move Madeline from her case in the Center to another location didn't please Andrea at all, but at least she'd obtained a small measure of protection for the mutant. Taking a deep breath, she slid her hands towards the document. She read it carefully, making sure there was nothing in it that could possibly hurt the mutants or her new company. She found nothing, so, despite her trepidation she signed.

* * *

Professor Toutbon strode down the endless hallway. His long legs ate up the distance. He walked as fast as he could without actually breaking into a run. Laurel jogged at his heels, her face a thundercloud of pent-up anger. Lighting bolts sparked from her eyes. If she could, she would be screaming now, like a Valkyrie sweeping down from the heavens. Just behind her was Monkey. His face wore an expression of terrible worry. Now and then, he would stop and gasp for breath. His body still hadn't adapted to walking or running any great distance, and these hallways were interminable.

"Are we nearly there?" he asked.

Laurel couldn't hear him, but Professor Toutbon slowed a bit.

"We're almost there."

"Why was she taken so far away?" Monkey asked.

The door was locked. Professor Toutbon knocked once, twice, then nodded to Laurel. She reached into her pocket and pulled out a set of brand new keys. Her deft fingers separated them as she looked them over, then she nodded decisively. She slid one into the lock and turned it. The door swung inwards.

* * *

M-6—Mahler

There is something wrong in the Center today. We mutants are restless and pressing against the glass walls of our cases. Mutants who haven't moved in years are shifting now, lights flashing on their consoles as they search the Web for something, or someone. There are two empty cases now. M-18 and M-19 have been taken away. Monkey is living in the real world. Madeline is a prisoner in an empty room.

Not so empty, after all.

Dr. Djusky and Frank Dinde have decided to punish her.

* * *

"Wake up, Madeline! We're here to speak to you."

The voices are blurred, muffled by thick glass and clouds. I open my eyes. Where am I? These past weeks have been so strange. I was taken from my home in the dark vaults and transferred down endless corridors. The room I ended up in had so much light it blinded me for many days. My eyes took a long time to adjust. Dr. Djusky says it's part of learning to live in the real world. Soon he will let me out of my case and I will be able to live in that warm, sunny paradise I saw in my dreams.

Was it part of a dream? Some days I'm not sure. I'm anxious to leave my case and walk among men, like M-18 does. Is my sister there? Will I see her? My heart is pounding so hard it hurts. I want my sister.

I also want to see Monkey. What a funny name. I wonder if he will be here today.

"Is she awake?"

The voice is louder now. I smile.

Dr. Djusky and another man lift the top of my case off. Clouds escape, obscuring the harsh light. In the misty surroundings, I feel suddenly exhilarated. I want to move, to stand up and stretch my body, but I cannot. Perhaps all these years of inaction have stiffened my muscles. I will need to take it slowly at first.

A face appears in the mist. It is Dr. Djusky. "Hello, Madeline," *he says. Mr. Dinde, a man I've seen a few times before, is standing nearby.*

I want to reply, to use my voice, but again something is wrong. I move my lips, force air into my throat, but all that escapes is a strange croaking noise.

Mr. Dinde is staring at me. His hands creep up to his face and he grabs his mouth. How strange. How very strange. He is backing away, his eyes as round as marbles.

Dr. Djusky is talking to me. I try to listen, but my ears are not used to such clear sounds. There is no more mist now, cushioning me. He is saying something about how I was misguided by the Virtual World. He is saying something about not having any idea of reality. He says I need to understand.

I do, at least I think I do. My beauty killed the men. They couldn't handle my perfection. I will be careful from now on. I will choose my lovers with care and go gently, slowly, at first. I hope he understands what I am trying to say. I wish he would plug me into the console again. I would tell him in an instant all he needs to know. Where is my sister? When will she appear?

Dr. Djusky is shaking his head. Apparently, I don't understand. He will help me see. He nods wisely.

"You will see, Madeline," he says, "what the real world is really like."

I am confused now. I have seen the real world.

Something flashes. A light blinds me, then it flattens and turns to silver.

"A mirror," Dr. Djusky says.

He holds it over me so I can see. The lab assistant takes the other end and straightens it. An image appears.

* * *

Laurel didn't hear the screaming. She wasn't knocked backwards by the sheer agony of the cries. In the room, brightly lit with halogen spots, two men held a full-length mirror over a glass case.

Monkey's knees buckled, icy sweat popping out on his forehead. The sounds of anguish made him moan. He held his hands over his ears.

"What is going on?" cried Professor Toutbon.

Dr. Djusky nodded to his assistant. "That's enough. I think she understood." They lowered the mirror to the ground.

"Understood what?" Professor Toutbon flinched as another scream split the air. He hurried towards the glass case, his face tense.

"She is unhurt," Frank Dinde said stiffly. "We never touched her." The Net man wiped sweat off his forehead. For the first time, he appeared shaken.

"You didn't have to do that." Professor Toutbon knelt by the case and leaned his forehead against it. "Put the top back on and fill it with the clouds. Can't you see she's having trouble breathing?" His voice was filled with a terrible pity.

Monkey stood, frozen, in the doorway. His eyes showed their whites, like a spooked horse. Laurel stood near the glass case, her face twisted in horror and fear.

Inside the case, Madeline writhed and her mouth opened and closed, screams tearing her throat. Her face reflected all the terror she'd experienced as she suddenly came face to face with her own reality.

She was not a beautiful woman. Her face was nearly intact, except for the missing nose. But her body was a bloated sack where dark organs showed against transparent skin and blue veins traced squiggly paths. She had no arms, and only two twisted stumps instead of legs.

Her eyes were wide open, a deep, frosty plum color, and completely demented now.

"Why?" whispered Monkey, his hands pressed against his stomach. "How could you do such a thing?"

"I think we can take her back to the vault now." Dr. Djusky collected a sheaf of papers and nodded to his assistant.

Frank Dinde shook his hand. "It was an enlightening experience, Dr. Djusky." He nodded to Professor Toutbon, still rooted to his spot, and left the room. "I'm looking forward to seeing you again, M-18," he said as he passed.

Monkey swung his head around. His eyes were haunted. "Goodbye, Mr. Dinde," he said, Professor Toutbon's lessons coming automatically to his lips.

Afterwards no one spoke. The mutant was transported back to the vault and hidden once more behind thick clouds. She was plugged into her console again, but it did no good. She was never to communicate with anyone again. Three days later, she was dead. She managed to twist around and around in her case and strangle herself with thin wires.

Chapter Thirteen

It is time to explain myself—let us stand up.
What is known I strip away,
I launch all men and women forward with me into the
Unknown.
—Walt Whitman, *Song of Myself*

Mitch watched as Digby inserted the needle in his arm. The new program was ready; he was the first to test it. Monkey had worked for months developing it, another Virtual World. A Japanese client had ordered it, and it took place in the American West in the late 1800's. It was complete with wild horses, cowboys and campfires under a star-spangled sky. Coyotes howled at the moon, and Mitch returned after three days, swearing he was going to become a cowboy and live on a cow farm.

"They're called ranches." Sally handed him a cup of tea and checked his pulse for the third time. "Your heart rate is back to normal. It was a bit slow coming out of your sleep. I wonder if it was a physical reaction to part of the program."

"The program was incredible," Mitch said. "Monkey, you're a genius!"

Monkey ducked his head and blushed. "I would like someone besides you to go on a trip. I mean, someone who's never gone."

Dr. Djusky, present as an observer, cocked his head and peered at Monkey. "Do you mean someone like me?"

Monkey scratched his head and laughed childishly. "Well, maybe someone like you. Have you ever taken a virtual trip?"

"No. Perhaps I shall someday." He nodded curtly and strode off.

Mitch didn't think anything about it until Dr. Djusky went to see Andrea and booked himself a trip on her Virtual Tour.

* * *

Dr. Djusky smiled at Digby as he tapped the glass syringe. Digby didn't return the smile. He was concentrating on the yellow liquid. Nearby, lying next to Dr. Djusky, was Monkey. He was humming softly, looking out the window at the bright sky. In the distance, a lone cloud was slowly being shredded by the wind.

The voyage was to last three days. Monkey was taking the trip as a guide to show Dr. Djusky the tropical paradise Virtual Tours offered to their clients. He seemed pleased about his job, even joking with Mitch about it.

Digby could see Mitch and Sally leaning on their elbows on the ledge of the plate-glass window outside the sending room. It felt odd not seeing Mitch on the couch, but since Mitch had become his assistant, he didn't have time to be a guide.

Digby pressed electrodes against Dr. Djusky's skull. A thin, silver shunt ran from an electrode in his ear to the machine. He checked it in time to see Andrea come around the corner, her arms full of papers. She saw Mitch and Sally leaning against the glass. Andrea hesitated, then joined them at the window. Her eyes were on Monkey, though. Laurel drifted by. She signed hello to everyone. Digby waved at her. He liked Laurel and he, Laurel and Carlos often talked together until late at night. Now she looked worried for some reason. Digby took a light pen out of his pocket and wrote in the air so all could see. "Everything is fine. Houston, we are ready for lift off!" The words glowed bright blue in the air before fading, but Laurel's expression was still strained.

Digby was finished. He took his place at the console and smiled at Dr. Djusky. "Have a nice slip."

* * *

Monkey twitched a bit, then his eyes closed and he slipped into a deep slumber. On the console behind him, the lights blinked to life. He was in the virtual world, on the dock, waiting for his client.

The sun was hot. It burned his shoulders and sweat trickled down his temple and neck. Above him, the sky was like a blue porcelain bowl cupped over the islands. There were no clouds, only the blinding sun. Light sparkled off the waves, dazzling his eyes. It danced off the aluminum masts of the sailboats, reverberated off the pale, glittering sand, and reflected everywhere.

Monkey reached into his pocket and drew out a pair of sunglasses. He put them on and cocked his head. His fair skin would burn in this climate. He reached again into his shorts and came up with sunscreen, which he applied lavishly. All the while he kept an eye on the horizon, waiting for the boat.

While he waited, he searched the sky. Every now and then, a bird screeched and he craned his neck to see it. A pelican attracted his attention. He peered up as it flapped through the sky, but he couldn't see it well enough. He reached into his pocket, pulled out binoculars, and spent a while watching the bird, a smile across his wide mouth. It wasn't a pleasant smile.

If Mitch could see him now, he wouldn't recognize his friend Monkey. The hair was still a riot of bright, copper curls and his face had the same features, but they were put together differently, somehow. There was an assurance, an arrogance that came from being in his element. He was at home, here in the virtual world. Even his stance was different. He was standing with his legs apart, his arms crossed on his chest, a sword hanging from his belt.

The boat arrived on time. Dr. Djusky stepped off the plank onto the cement pier. The light blinded him. He screwed up his eyes like a mole and smiled. "Monkey! I made it!" He laughed like a child. "What an incredible experience. I should have done this years ago! Where do we go now?"

Monkey put out his hand. "Dr. Djusky, I presume? This way, please."

Dr. Djusky grasped Monkey's hand.

There was a shift in the scenery. The sun suddenly disappeared behind a dark cloud. The light faded as if someone had turned a switch. Beneath their feet, the cement gave away to rocks. Dr. Djusky tripped on a boulder and landed on his knees, skidding on slippery shale.

"What happened? I didn't think a tropical storm could..." he faltered, raising his head and looking around. "Hey, where are we? This isn't the Caribbean!"

Monkey was standing a ways away, his hand on his sword. He wasn't looking at Dr. Djusky; his eyes were searching the gloom in the distance. His sunglasses were on the ground. Deliberately, he stepped on them.

"Answer me, M-18. What is going on here?" Dr. Djusky got to his feet and brushed the dirt from his knees. "Look at this. I cut myself! When I get back to the Center, you'll hear about this."

Monkey glanced at him then smiled. "You won't be going back, doctor."

"What do you mean?" He snapped his head around. "What was that noise?"

"Did you ever hear the story of Prometheus, doctor?" Monkey hefted the sword in his hands and looked at it critically. "It's a story about a god who makes the king of gods angry. He is chained to a cliff where an eagle comes and rips his liver out each day. Of course, he's a god, so he doesn't die. He simply suffers."

"What are you babbling about?" Dr. Djusky sputtered. His eyes widened. "Look out behind you!"

Monkey pivoted gracefully, and with a smooth movement, cut the head off a six-meter cobra. "That was just a small one," he said, prodding the body with his toe. He cocked his head. "Where was I? Oh yes. Well, in this world, you are a god. You cannot die. You can suffer, though, and believe me, when you're eaten by an iggabit you suffer for years. It takes that long for your molecules to reconstitute themselves."

"An igga-what?"

"Iggabit. They are large man-eating plants. That gives you the advantage, you realize. They can't run after you. You'll have to learn how to avoid them and how to recognize their many forms. One looks so innocuous..." he chuckled. "Well, I must be going. I'd leave you this sword, but it's mine. I forged it myself. Maybe you will learn to do the same."

He paused and sniffed the wind. The air was heavy with an acrid, burnt smell. "It's not a bad world here, once you get used to the darkness. Cloud cover makes it very gloomy. Rather like being in a glass case somewhere—except for the monsters. Here, they are inside with you, not on the outside." Monkey cocked his head, listening. "And if I'm not mistaken, another one is coming up the hill. I'd take shelter, if I were you. Beware caves; you never know what lurks in the darkness." He smiled...then turned and vanished.

Dr. Djusky leapt after him, but there was just empty air. He slithered on the shale and nearly fell again. The sound of footsteps was getting louder. He turned towards the sound, his heart pounding. Coming over the crest of the hill, just behind him, was small shaggy pony.

His shoulders sagged in relief. "My God, it's a horse."

The pony opened its mouth. Needle-sharp teeth gleamed in the half-light. Its eyes glowed red.

Dr. Djusky started to scream.

* * *

Back in the sending room, all the lights suddenly went out above Dr. Djusky's head.

Laurel couldn't hear the shrieks coming from the doctor's throat, but she could see his body convulsing. She screamed hoarsely, her palms pressed against the glass. Then she started battering the window, drumming her hands upon it trying to get someone's attention. Why had they all left? Where had they gone? What was happening with Dr. Djusky?

Mitch and Sally came running. Andrea dropped her papers and sprinted towards the noise. Digby, who'd stepped out of the room for a quick cup of coffee, spilled it down his lab coat. He rushed into the sending room and started ripping the electrodes off Dr. Djusky's head.

Monkey sat up from the next couch and started peeling off his own electrodes. He carefully unhooked his IV, pulling it out of his arm and wincing a bit. He took his shunt and wound it around his fist before stuffing it in his pocket.

All the while, Dr. Djusky screamed, thrashing blindly, his eyes open and unseeing, his hands pushing, clutching. Then suddenly he was silent. His body became limp. His eyes rolled up in his skull and he slumped back onto the couch.

* * *

"What in the hell happened?" cried Andrea, sweeping into the room. She stopped suddenly, all color fading from her face. "What are you doing awake, Monkey?"

Digby's mouth opened then closed. "How did you wake up? Tell me what happened, Monkey."

"No." Monkey got up off the couch and rubbed his arm where the needle had been. Then he went to peer at Dr. Djusky.

Seemingly satisfied, he turned to Andrea. "You can put him in my old case. Or in M-19's case. He will never wake up. He'll need to be hooked up to intravenous and electrodes. Don't worry, though. He'll never die, unless it's from old age."

Andrea watched him walk out of the room. Laurel made as if to go after him, then stopped. Her eyes met Andrea's. The two women stared at each other. Then Laurel's hand dipped into her pocket and she pulled out her light pen. "It's over," she wrote.

Andrea closed her eyes. "Maybe not."

* * *

Carlos and Laurel walked through tall grass. It whispered all around them, but only Carlos could hear it.

They could both see the sand dunes and the pewter water. Dolphins rose and fell in the bay, water sliding off their shining black skin in sheets. A small wooden house stood near the shore. In front of it, a dock reached out into the water. Tied to it was a sailboat, its sails neatly reefed and a picnic lunch packed and waiting under the tarp.

Inside the house, there were bare hardwood floors, scrubbed nearly white and smooth as silk. It had a small kitchen, a living room, and a porch that overlooked the bay. Upstairs was a wide, white bed with linen sheets and mosquito netting hanging like a fog around it.

Gulls wheeled overhead, screaming. Carlos's fingers tightened on Laurel's arm and she looked at him, her eyes shadowed.

"Do you miss the Center?" Carlos asked her.

Laurel looked startled then shook her head.

"When do you think Andrea will be able to open it again? Damn Monkey. He's set us back decades."

Laurel wrote with her light pen. In the evening air, the words were pale lavender. "It's not his fault. It was Dr. Djusky's fault. He got what he deserved. I only wish I hadn't been there to see it, that's all." There was a spark of something in her eyes. Anger perhaps, or a sort of fierce joy. She turned her face to the setting sun. "He got what he deserved," she wrote on the sky, and then, inexplicably, she started laughing.

* * *

Andrea and Tony cuddled under the blankets, the fire casting a red glow on their faces. Cocotte was curled at their feet, her silken ears perked for noises in the desert night.

A coyote howled, and Cocotte answered with a little growl, sounding more like a kitten than a dog.

"Will you still be in charge there?" asked Tony, taking a lock of her auburn hair and twirling it gently around his fingers.

"I don't know." Andrea looked at him and he was glad to see her face had gotten some of its old arrogance back. "But I'm not worried. I'm perfectly happy here, in the desert with you," she answered. "I don't ever want to go back to the city."

"That's not what I meant."

"I know." Andrea gave a wry laugh. "I'm no longer Andrea Girt, president of Virtual Tours, or president of anything. I'm Andrea Girt, soon to be Mrs. Tony Perrini, and we're camping in the desert while the FBI and the CIA make a decision about the Mutant Center. But I'm not worried. Sonia Andrews is there, and she'll do her best to keep it open. I've decided to consider this an extended vacation. I'm happier now than I've ever been." On her hand, something sparkled. Her diamond.

"I'm glad." Tony kissed the tip of her nose. "I often wonder about Dr. Djusky."

"Shhh." Andrea put her hand over his mouth. "Let's talk of nice things. Did you hear what happened to Frank Dinde?"

"He was fired," Tony said. "The CIA is talking about prosecuting him."

Andrea kissed his mouth. "Let's drink a toast to the CIA."

"Shall I open the bottle of champagne?" Tony asked, nuzzling her neck.

Andrea felt a shiver of pleasure. "Of course," she whispered.

* * *

Mitch and Sally stared at the letter. They had been trying to decipher it, but the ink had faded as soon as light had touched the words and now they were looking at a blank piece of paper.

"Lemon juice?" Mitch murmured.

"Here's a candle." Sally held the flame with care and the words slowly reappeared.

Dearest Mitch and Sally.

I think of you every day. I hope you are both well and have found peace where you now live. I am very well, thank you, although I still have trouble sleeping. Perhaps this will pass. The people you sent me to visit were gentle and kind. Sally, I really appreciate your mother. She is a lovely, mysterious person. She has a friend named Deer, although I didn't get to meet him while I was there. Perhaps I will go back and visit again. You were right; they were just what I needed. How did you know that, Sally? They gave me back some of my self-esteem, not that I had very much to start with. Digby is still with me, still complaining when it rains. I love the rain. He has shown me how to make invisible ink, so I am writing with that now. Tomorrow we will get on a train and visit a place called Yellowstone. I am looking forward to seeing real bears and buffaloes. Our tent is very cozy and I am quite proficient at making fires. I will let Digby finish this letter. As your mother would say, Sally, Nirvana to you guys.

Monkey

Dear Mitch and Sally.

Monkey told you most of the news. I always wanted to travel, and the world is vast. After Yellowstone, we will head north towards Alaska. Monkey wants to pan for gold and I want to see the Arctic. We will keep in touch. Someday, perhaps, I will find a room and plug myself into the Net once more. Perhaps I will try to talk Monkey into coming with me, to show me his wonderful world. For now, though, he won't let me even speak about it. Perhaps it is too soon. Don't worry about him. I will keep my promise to you, Mitch. I will never leave him alone. When he's better—you know what I mean—I will try to bring him back to you. Andrea writes often. She's still waiting for the verdict. She seems to have confidence in Ms. Andrews. I guess I will wait and see what happens. I'll have to think about taking my old job back, although I really loved working in the Mutant Center. I suppose it will all depend on Monkey. He's still hypersensitive, but I think that will fade in time. Until then, take care.

Digby.

They stared at the letter a moment, then the flame strayed too close and it caught fire. Sally gave a small cry, but Mitch just held the paper until it had almost entirely consumed itself. Then he let the black ashes drift to the ground.

"Will we ever see him again?" she asked.

"I think so. With each day that goes by it gets easier to think about. Someday I might even be able to call Professor Toutbon and ask how Dr. Djusky..."

Sally clapped her hand over his mouth. "Hush. Don't even say his name, I beg you."

* * *

M-6—Mahler

The Mother Tree shimmers and sparkles in the lustrous moon. At her roots, the dark sea is as smooth as obsidian. I sit here for longer and longer periods now. There are no more commands; the scientists leave us alone. Only Professor Toutbon is left. He and I talk. I enjoy his conversations.

We wander as we like in our own worlds now. The outside world has been cut off from us. There is not the slightest whisper of regret from any of us.

Perhaps I will end up taking root like the tree and grow branches. The wind will whistle among them, waving them, and I will sway at the will of the wind. I do not know what will happen. My world is vast, but since Monkey came and left, it seems empty. I wonder if I will one day receive a visitor. Will one of my own kind grow lonely and seek me out? I hope so. There, I said it. Monkey, will you please come home?

There has not been a sign of him since Dr. Djusky disappeared.

Epilogue

There was a child went forth every day,
And the first object he looked upon and received with
wonder or pity or love or dread, that object he became,
And that object became part of him for the day or a certain
part of the day...or for many years or stretching cycles of years.
...Failing to fetch me at first keep encouraged,
Missing me one place search another,
I stop some where waiting for you.
—Walt Whitman, *Song of Myself*

Professor Toutbon sat at his desk in minus fifteen. He'd moved his desk to that room after the Center closed. All around him was dimness. In their cases, the mutants floated within thick clouds. There were still nineteen cases. Dr. Djusky had been put into Monkey's old case, wires attached, feeding tubes and shunts put into place. He wouldn't have survived in a hospital bed. He was in a virtual world now, a world that existed only in his mind, but paradoxically, was controlled by the computer in the Center. Professor Toutbon went to see him sometimes, but there were never any signs that Dr. Djusky would ever come out of his coma.

Professor Toutbon's eyes strayed back to the circle of light on his desk and the white paper it illuminated. He wanted to finish his report and get some sleep. He reread what he'd written, nibbling on the tip of his pen. Sonia Andrews wanted a full report from him, and he was agonizing over it. It didn't help his nerves that the FBI and the CIA both had agents in the Center. The men and women were polite, seemed capable, and so far, had remained open minded about the whole thing. What bothered them the most—what bothered everyone—was the fact that no one could wake up Dr. Djusky.

Professor Toutbon sighed and went back to his report, but before he could put pen to paper, the elevator door opened and Sonia Andrews strode out. Her pale hair glittered in the halogen light. "How is Dr. Djusky?" she asked.

"Dr. Djusky is in perfect health. However, unlike the mutants, he cannot or will not communicate through the console."

"Ah." She nodded. "And the others?"

"M-1 through M-17 are cut off from the outside world. They create their own worlds, from what Mahler tells me. They don't seem to mind, but then again, I have no way of confirming this. I have noticed, however, that once in a while the clouds around the mutants take on a faint hue, sometimes blue or green, and once or twice I have seen small flashes like electric sparks."

"Oh? What can that be?"

"I have no idea, but Mahler says it is of no importance. He says that as the mutants' worlds become more complex, small exterior signs escape."

"How can virtual worlds let anything physical escape?"

Professor Toutbon shrugged. "Good question. Mahler says the brain is the most powerful computer in the world, and if we didn't exist, the universe would not exist. He and I discuss philosophy. Our favorite theme right now is the tree falling in the woods where no one can see it." He paused and rubbed his chin nervously. "Excuse me, I digress."

"You digress." Ms. Andrews smiled and perched on the edge of his desk. It was so out of character for her that Dr. Toutbon felt his mouth fall open. He snapped it shut.

"I've been reading your reports," she began, her hands crossed on her lap. "They all start with M-20. Do you know what really happened that day?"

He shook his head. "Not really. For a long time, I puzzled over three things: what M-20 had wanted to say the day she was freed from her cage, who killed her, and why the men watching her became so aroused by her presence."

"Having accessed some of the CIA and FBI records of the event while sorting everything out, I believe I can answer at least two of those questions," Sonia said.

Professor Toutbon gaped. "They showed you their records?" He hoped his voice sounded normal.

"Of course. The first question is impossible to answer, but the second question is easy. One of the FBI agents shot M-20. Her orders had been to protect Dr. Tergiversates. When the mutant threw the doctor against the wall, she opened fire."

"She?"

"Yes, she. Women can be bodyguards too, you know."

He felt his face get warm. "I didn't mean that. It confirms my theory, that's all."

"Which was?"

Professor Toutbon hoped he wasn't blushing "That no man could have fired a shot at M-20."

Sonia nodded slowly, her pale eyes thoughtful. "You're probably right, but we don't know why. The third question pertaining to the men's reactions upon seeing M-20 is hardest to answer. I have a hypothesis that will have to suffice for now. The mutants evolved in a vacuum. Their emotional needs were never addressed, so they developed their own ways of meeting these needs. M-20 needed love. As you quoted Mahler, it was the human being trying to overcome the machine. Monkey inspires a strong, protective instinct in all who come in contact with him. They feel the need to look after him. This, I believe, will fade after a while, through contact with the outside world. Madeline was desperate to find her sister or someone to replace her loss. Failing that, she mistook physical pleasure for emotional fulfillment. In the virtual worlds, she was as strong and as beautiful as she could make herself. The mutants have nothing to compare themselves to except their own imagination. No limits. None of the laws of physics apply in the virtual world. We learned that too late."

Professor Toutbon looked at his paper. The writing seemed to mock him. "And the result of all this?"

"The result is that we have to cut off all communication between the mutants and the outside world permanently. As you know, Monkey helped. It was his punishment, and his redemption. It was his freedom in exchange for the imprisonment of all the others. They are now locked in their own worlds while he is free to go wherever he likes."

"Yes, as Mike Palo. The FBI gave him a new identity. Will the Center open for business again? Will Ms. Girt come back? And what about you? What will you do?"

Sonia raised her eyebrows. "Of course the Center will open again. Ms. Girt will have to decide if she wants to take the responsibility, but I think she will." Here she paused and smiled. "As for me, I'm to be the new Net president. You're the first person I've told."

"Why me?" He couldn't suppress a sudden surge of pleasure.

"Because I like you, professor." Sonia Andrews leaned over and kissed the professor on the cheek. She rose gracefully and smoothed her skirt. "I'm going to the cafeteria. Would you like to join me for dinner?"

"Of course. Of course I would." Toutbon stood, knocked his chair over, grabbed at his desk, scattered his papers and dropped his pen. By the time he'd picked everything up, Sonia had gone.

Professor Toutbon grinned and scratched his head with the tip of the pen. Dinner with Sonia? How amazing. Humming, he went to the elevator. In the reflection of the mirror-bright doors, he straightened his tie and rubbed at a spot of ink on his temple.

Behind him, pinpricks of halogen light illuminated his desk and the mutant's glass cases. He glanced at the silent cases where they floated. What worlds were they creating now? What were they like? What rules governed them? A surprising longing tugged at his mind. Wouldn't he love to be able to see them?

A WORLD BETWEEN

Sunlight sparkled on water the color of aquamarines. Overhead, pelicans flew in a 'V' formation, their wings held stiff as they glided in the steady breeze. The pelicans banked and came around, aiming for a school of fish swimming near surface. They surfed in, not breaking formation even when they landed, their feet jutting out like skis. Heads bobbing, beaks clacking in satisfaction, the pelicans jabbed their heads into the water, then lifted their great bills and gulped fish as they paddled into the smooth bay. In the distance, in open sea, whitecaps curled over indigo waves.

In the deepest part of the bay was a small marina, quiet, except for the pelicans' raucous cries and the dry rustle of wind in the palm trees. Boats were all docked, their sails reefed, their anchors weighed. The air shimmered with heat, but no radios played. The place could have been empty, almost. With a bump, a wooden dinghy came to rest at one of the docks. Inside it, someone bent over, rummaging in the bottom of the little boat. Without looking up, he tossed a rope up onto the dock, followed a second later by a pair of shorts, a diving mask, and an empty beer can.

A brilliant flash of blue light came from behind the marina, but the figure in the boat didn't notice. Right after the flash of light, a lanky, broad-shouldered young woman stepped out of the shadows behind the marina and strode to the end of a dock. The wind immediately tangled her hair into a riot of ash-brown curls. She had a pale, freckled face, and she repeatedly glanced at a heavy watch on her thin wrist.

The figure in the dinghy stood up and revealed itself to be a young man wearing cut-off shorts so low on his narrow hips that it seemed they would slide right off. His shirt flapped in the breeze, its buttons all undone, revealing a sleek midriff and a flat, tanned chest. He climbed out of the boat onto the dock and deftly tied the boat to a cleat. Then he took off his baseball cap and ran his hand through his short, blond hair. He was barefoot, and kept hopping lightly from one foot to the other on the blistering wood. When he noticed the girl, he nodded in greeting.

"Are you Jack Winter?" the girl asked, coming right up to him and pushing curly hair out of her eyes.

"That's my name. Just call me Jack," he added, with a grin.

"Jack, I want to save the world," the girl said seriously.

A spark of amusement danced within his deep blue eyes. "You do? First, what's your name?"

"Maggie." Maggie stared at him, bit her lip, and then blurted, "Is that the only shirt you have?"

He looked down, and a frown creased his clear features. "Why? What's wrong with this one?"

"It's a Hawaiian print. Is that anything a secret agent would wear?"

"Secret agent?" Jack looked up, his eyes suddenly as round as blue marbles.

"Why do you think I'm here?" Maggie tapped her foot on the dock. Impatience clipped her words. The sun was hot, and it didn't help her temper to feel a trickle of sweat running down her back. She squinted against the glaring light, and wished she'd asked for sunglasses. The man in front of her was staring at her as if *she* were the one who'd lost her mind. "Well?" she insisted.

"Do you want to go fishing?"

Maggie stomped her foot. "I can't believe this! You're supposed to answer, '*I don't know if I can save the world, but I can give it a try.*' You're a secret agent!"

Jack paused. "This is the second strange thing to happen today. Earlier, a pelican dropped a beer can on my head. Luckily it was empty." He rubbed his head and grinned. "Eddy has been training that damn bird for months to carry beer to him when he's out fishing."

"I summoned you!" cried Maggie.

"I didn't realize I'd been summoned. When you came over, I thought that you wanted to go fishing," he said, hopping nimbly. "Hold on a sec." He reached down and snagged a bucket from the dock, then sluiced seawater onto the wood. It steamed. He smiled, wriggling his toes. "Ahhh. That's better."

"I...want...to...save...the...world," said Maggie, biting each word off.

"Save the world?" Jack raised his eyebrows. He glanced at the marina where boats bobbed and water sparkled. "It looks fine to me."

"This is not working," Maggie said, speaking into her watch.

Jack shrugged. "That's all right, tell Eddy it was a great joke, and that I nearly fell for it. It was the best he's thought of so far, honestly."

"Joke?" Maggie raised her face, her mouth open.

"That Eddy's such a crazy guy I nearly believed him this time." He laughed and shook his head. "Actually, it was pretty lame. I didn't believe it for a second—well, maybe when the pelican dropped the beer can on me, but don't tell Eddy; his feelings might be hurt." He looked up at the sky. "Still a couple hours of fishing time left, if you'll excuse me now." He touched his fingers to his forelock in an echo of a scout's salute, turned, and trotted lightly down the dock. He lifted his bare feet quickly, because the wood was as hot as the sun could possibly scorch it.

Maggie watched him go, a mixture of emotions flitting across her face. Then she turned and spoke into her watch. "Get me out of here; we have to talk."

If anyone had been watching, and nobody was except a brown pelican sitting on a tarred post, they would have seen Maggie step back into the cool shade of the cinderblock marina and fade from sight. Another flash of blue light, and she was gone. The pelican only fluffed its feathers and went back to scanning the clear water of the bay.

* * *

"He's not programmed correctly," were Maggie's first words as she emerged in a large, bright, air-conditioned room where eight men and women sat at a long, marble-topped table. She took off the glasses hiding her eyes and peeled off silvery gloves, setting them on the table in front of her with a slap. On the arm of her reclining chair was a large button. She pushed it, and the chair raised itself back to a sitting position. The young woman spoke into the microphone on her lapel. "Shut it off now; it was a bust." Then she looked around with a pugnacious expression at all the men and women in the room.

One of the men, dressed in beige chinos and a blue Oxford shirt with the sleeves rolled up, started to speak. "Maggie, in my opinion…"

"When I want your opinion, Ryan, I'll ask for it," she snapped. Her head had started to hurt, and she thought she'd like to give a nice, loud scream right about now. Three years! Three years of work, and the game hadn't even started.

She glared at Ryan. She didn't want to glare at him. She didn't want to appear churlish and bad-tempered, but that's what he thought of her anyway. So why did that sharp pain stab her every time he looked at her with that half-mocking way of his? A lock of his straight, brown hair fell over his eyes, making him toss his head like a nervous colt, and she always wanted to reach out and brush it back. One day she'd done that, and he'd caught her wrist and told her to keep her hands to herself.

She dug her fingernails into the palms of her hand. Ryan had made it very clear from the start that he was not the least bit interested in her. The only thing she had left was her pride; she would never let him see how much she'd been hurt by his words.

Ryan put his pen down on the notepad in front of him and placed his hands flat on the table. "Fine, tell us what happened, Maggie, if you can remember everything that happened."

At the head of the table, a woman with gold-rimmed glasses waved impatiently. "Enough, you two! Maggie, your report." In front of this woman, a small sign discreetly proclaimed her Ms. Lucille Wrain, President of Carver Games, Inc.

"He thought it was a joke," Maggie sputtered.

Stunned silence greeted her words. Then the young man with the notepad raised his pen.

"Ryan?" President Wrain's voice was dry. Her glasses glittered as she leaned forward.

"What were your exact words when you met him?" Ryan asked her.

Maggie clenched her fists beneath the table. "I told him that I wanted to save the world. That should have triggered a definite response. Instead, he asked me if it was a joke that some chump named Eddy thought up! Then he turned his back on me and went fishing. Fishing!" Her voice rose to a shriek. "Fishing, after we spent three years creating this program!"

Ryan stopped jotting notes and looked up, puzzled. "Eddy? There's no Eddy in the program. Sam, what do you think of this?"

The man on Ryan's right rubbed his forehead. "It's worse than I thought," he said. "Obviously the program is totally insecure, parasites have infiltrated from God knows where, wrecking circuits. Who knows what damage has been done?"

"Not much, I don't think." A slender woman on the opposite side of the table stood up. A pen was tucked behind her ear; coppery hair fell forward, obscuring her face. She brushed it back with a white, narrow hand. "From what I can tell, Eddy could very well come from a minor problem. Eddy could mean eddy, a slight ripple, if you prefer. Jack, being ultra sensitive, picked it up and translated ripple into eddy, capital 'E'."

"Abridge, Houston," Maggie said in an icy voice. She had taken an instant dislike to the woman. She was lovely, had a soft, sweet voice, and her clothes never looked too tight or rumpled. In the three days since Miss Houston had arrived, she'd managed to charm everyone on the team. Including Ryan, who couldn't seem to tear his gaze from her.

The woman flushed, but held her ground. "One moment, please. We suspected a glitch; obviously the system has been tampered with, and we need to assess the damage to flush out the invading parasite or find out whether this problem stems from something else."

Groans sounded from around the table. Ms. Wrain picked up a tiny wooden hammer and hit the table with it, hard. "It won't hurt anyone if Miss Houston rehashes the problem we're facing. I have the feeling most of you have already forgotten exactly why we're here. Each of you is involved in several different projects. It's easy to get muddled." She smiled, and most of the people around the table winced. It wasn't a friendly smile. "Miss Houston, please continue."

"All right, it's simple. Carver Systems developed this program, a fairly straightforward spy game. You enter and become one of several protagonists in the script; the only invariable is the character known as 'Jack,' who is sent to help you. He is the part of the game designed to gather information, to physically touch and hold the clues you find, and to interact in a physical way in the virtual world surrounding you. Enough factors are included in the program to make it extremely flexible, and from twenty different paths in the beginning fan out a myriad of interconnected choices that make this game unique in its complexity."

Maggie had to bite her lower lip to keep from snarling that she knew that—that everyone knew it, and could she please get to the point? Miss Houston paused and looked around the room. The men all nodded at her with ovine, besotted expressions on their faces. Maggie ground her teeth together and wished Miss Houston had been a dumpy, gray-haired matron instead of a slim, cinnamon-haired pin-up girl. Damn it!

"The problem is threefold." Miss Houston plucked the pen from behind her ear and stabbed the air with it. "First, the problem getting the game started. Apparently the visual and tactile simulation is nearly perfect; the glitch starts as soon as the main character receives his prompt. In fact, he doesn't respond to it at all. Second, the main character speaks about a certain Eddy, but there is no such character in the game. The closest name to Eddy is Ted, and I doubt that Jack meant to say Ted. Third, we have to decide if the problem is from an outside source, or if there is someone in this program sabotaging it." She smiled, put the pen down on the table, and sat down.

Silence. Maggie felt a little whisper of disquiet run down her spine. The silence was broken by a loud snort.

"We don't mention that word here," snapped an elderly man sitting to the right of the president. He didn't need a plaque in front of his seat. Everyone knew who he was. His profile was incorporated on every Carver logo in the building and around the world. Maxwell Santiago Carver, founder of Carver Toys, Inc., had a very prominent forehead, making his profile a very easy one to memorize. His strange eyes flashed angrily from behind thick lenses. Maxwell Santiago Carver was an albino, with fine, white hair and skin that looked perpetually powdered with talc. Maggie didn't care for him, but today she felt like patting his back. Ha! That put Miss Houston in her place; sabotage indeed!

Miss Houston flinched, but didn't lower her gaze. "I don't know any other way to phrase that possibility."

"You don't even envision the possibility," he replied. "Everyone here is part of my family, we're all together in a wonderful adventure, and we stick together like..." He paused and raised a palsied finger.

"Birds of a feather," chanted the group around the table. Maggie chimed in, although his clichés usually irked her.

"That's right!" he crowed. "No one would ever dream of sabotaging me, because I pay the best salaries, I have the best office buildings, the most advanced research teams, the most liberal work schedules with infant care and psychological counseling freely available to every employee. Even my lawyers can be consulted free of charge! Who else can beat that? Why bother with...the 's' word?" He wriggled his shoulders and waggled his hand. "I think we must concentrate on a glitch in the program, my dear Miss Houston. I forgive you this time, as you're new to our family. But don't do it again!"

Miss Houston nodded faintly at the president. "I'd like to take a look at the game myself, if that's all right with you."

"It won't do any good," said Maggie. She glared at the slender redhead. "I'm the expert and I couldn't get it working. It's back to the old drawing board, I'm afraid." She smiled and shrugged.

"My goodness, so many clichés in this company," Miss Houston said with a bright smile. Maggie felt her smile slip. That was her line.

Miss Houston gathered her papers into a leather briefcase and turned to the president. "I will be ready to check the game out tomorrow. I'll be here at eight a.m. Do you have any problems with that?"

"No, of course not." Mrs. Wrain smiled and this time it was warm. "I'm sure you'll do just fine. Thank you, Miss Houston."

Deep silence filled the room as she walked across the thick, plush carpet and let herself out the mahogany door. Then everyone began to speak.

The hammer hit the table again. "Ryan, do you want to say anything?"

He stood up and placed his hands on the desk, leaning over it and staring hard at Maggie. "You stupid…"

"Ryan!" Mrs. Wrain's voice cracked like a whip.

The young man straightened, but his furious gaze didn't budge from Maggie's face. "All right. We have a problem with the game. Fine. But a simple test expert can't possibly tell the difference between a problem with the programming, a virus, or fabrication. For that we need a programmer, and Miss Houston is the best. We asked her to come," Ryan said angrily. "You have no right throwing a temper tantrum simply because you couldn't get the game started." He nodded at Mrs. Wrain. "That's all I wanted to say," he said, before sitting down again.

Maggie sat, too stunned to leave. How could he? How could Ryan take that woman's side like that when she, Maggie, had worked on this program since the beginning? Her hands shook as she pushed her files into her briefcase.

The president whacked the table again with her hammer. "Back to work. Everyone be here at eight a.m., tomorrow." She stood, unfolding her tall, bony frame from her chair. She leaned over and said to Maxwell, "This program had better work."

"It will, it will!" Maxwell Santiago spoke in a loud voice to compensate a slight deafness.

"How much did you invest in this one?"

"Oh, about the same as the others." He shrugged. "Don't worry, don't worry. The company is healthy and the stocks are selling like hotcakes. The public is holding its breath in anticipation of another Carver game, and this one will really knock their socks off!"

"If we can get it working," murmured Mrs. Wrain. When she heard this, Maggie raised her eyebrows in surprise. Mrs. Wrain was never pessimistic.

"Worry-wart," said Maxwell, and left the room, leaning heavily on his ebony cane.

Mrs. Wrain bit her lip. "I'm supposed to worry, I'm the president. Maggie, what are you still doing here? Get back to work!"

* * *

"Miss Houston!" Ryan sprinted down the hallway and just managed to slip his hand in the elevator's sliding door. "Going down?" he asked, flashing a wide grin.

"It looks that way." She didn't return the smile as he settled himself in the elevator next to her and punched the button for the lobby.

"Look, don't mind Maggie, she's always like that. She's so self-absorbed she thinks the sun rises simply so that she can get a tan." He peered at her face. "You're not mad, are you?"

"Mad?" She frowned. "No," she continued slowly. "I think horrified is the word I would use."

Ryan was taken aback. "Excuse me?"

"How long have you been working at Carver Enterprises?"

"Six years, since I got out of college," he replied, cocking his head.

"I see."

"You see what? By the way, what is your first name, if you don't mind me asking."

"I don't mind. Why should I? It's June."

"June. June Houston?"

"My mother was not a particularly imaginative woman."

"You were born in June?"

She nodded, the first trace of a smile crinkling the corners of her mouth. Encouraged, Ryan cleared his throat. "Would you like to have a drink with me?" he asked.

She hesitated, then nodded. "I suppose I could spare a few minutes. I'd like to ask you a few questions about the program, anyway."

Ryan nodded. "Fair enough. Here we are. Turn left out of the lobby and go south two blocks. There's a nice pub called Paddy's on the corner. I'll be right there."

She quirked a smile. "Have to go to the men's room?"

"No, I left my wallet in my desk." Ryan shrugged. "I couldn't see myself inviting you for a drink, then asking you to pay."

"That's very gallant," she agreed, turned, and walked gracefully out of the lobby.

Ryan counted five male heads swiveling around to follow her out of the building. He watched as she disappeared around the corner, then headed towards the men's room. Once in front of the mirror, he gave a loud groan. His wallet showed very clearly through his shirt pocket. He braced his hands on the sink and leaned towards his reflection. "You are no Don Juan," he said sternly. "So just give up. Don't even try to act sophisticated. Be yourself."

"I wouldn't, if I was you," came a deep voice from one of the stalls.

"Harry?" Ryan spun around.

"What's the pep talk for? Finally get up the balls to ask Maggie for dinner?"

Ryan gave a short bark of laughter. "Are you nuts? I'd rather ask my aunt's chimpanzee for a date."

Harry flushed the toilet and came out, straightening his pants. As he washed his hands he asked, "So, what is it? Why the grim look?"

"Did you see the programming expert we asked to take a look at our new program?"

"No." Harry shook his head and stuck his hands beneath a dryer.

"I asked her to have a drink with me, and now I'm getting cold feet all of a sudden. I don't know, it's weird, I'm afraid that every time she looks at me she thinks I'm an ass."

"One of those superior women who looks down her nose at us poor men, huh? A real ball-breaker on heels?"

"No, I don't think so." Ryan washed his hands, and ran them through his hair.

"Nice, the surfer look." Harry tilted his head and made a face. "Why don't you unbutton a few buttons, show some of that massive, hairy chest."

Ryan plucked his shirt out and looked down. "No hair," he said despondently. Then he glanced at his watch, swore, rushed out of the men's room, dashed through the lobby, spun out the revolving doors, and pounded down the pavement towards Paddy's Pub on the corner.

Harry picked up a wallet that had fallen on the floor and riffled through it. "Seventeen dollars and three credit cards. Ryan, my boy, you're about to make quite an impression on the woman."

* * *

"It wasn't that bad," Ryan said to his aunt, later that evening. He lay on the sofa, his head in the lap of a very large female chimpanzee. The animal was gently plucking at his scalp, running her dexterous fingers through his hair looking for imaginary nits.

"I'm sure she didn't mind paying for the drinks. Women these days are very independent, and don't want men to think that they're a financial handicap." Ryan's aunt finished watering her plants and sat down on a chair facing the sofa. "She sounds like a perfectly lovely young woman. Why don't you invite her to have dinner with you?"

Ryan shuddered. "No, thanks. I'm trying to figure out a way to sneak into the office tomorrow without her seeing me."

"Nonsense, I'm sure she'll have forgotten all about it," said his aunt with airy certainty.

"Aunt Ree?"

"Yes, dear?"

"Do you think that I'm…I mean, do I look…uh, would you be interested in me if you weren't my aunt?" he finished in a rush, his cheeks a bright crimson.

The old woman put her hands on her lap and leaned over the coffee table. "My dear Ryan. If you weren't my nephew I'd be ravishing you right this second." She peered at him from behind her bifocals. "Look at Sissy, she loves you."

"Sissy is a chimpanzee."

"She is very discerning. She won't let Dr. Grady near her; she'll only go with Dr. Thomas, the nicest vet in the group. He doesn't hurt a bit when he gives his shots, and Sissy saw it right away."

"I don't believe that June has the same criteria Sissy does," said Ryan.[kww1]

"Don't be so sure." His aunt stood up and clapped her hands. "Sissy!" she cried, and spoke to her in sign language. *Please go wash up and get ready for bed,* she motioned. The big chimp tilted her head, nodded, and gave Ryan a smacking kiss on the cheek before hustling away in her swinging walk towards her pen.

"Sissy is getting very gray," remarked Ryan.

Ree nodded. "She's quite old, for a chimpanzee. She'll be forty-three in August. It seems like it was only yesterday the lab brought her in, a tiny baby, clutching that wire dummy they'd rigged up." She shook her head. "She was the sweetest one of the lot. The others all turned vicious, not that I blame them."

"I can't imagine life without her."

"You grew up with her," said his aunt fondly. "When you were born, she thought you were her baby. She used to…"

"Carry me around clutched to her chest. I know. And when I was big enough, I rode on her back."

"You are still her little baby. You'll see, before she goes to bed she'll come in and check on you, just to make sure you're all right before she goes to sleep."

Ryan sighed. "I don't remember my mother at all."

"It's been a long time since you've spoken about her." Ree looked at him closely. "This June must have stirred up something."

Ryan blushed again. "It's not that, it's just all this talk about Sissy and, well, and, oh hell. You're right. I can't believe it, Aunt Ree, but I saw her and my heart just sort of jumped out of my chest."

She smiled and gave a sigh. "She must be a special lady, sweetheart, because you're a very special man."

"Aunt Ree!"

"Shall we eat?" she asked, with a bright smile.

* * *

The next day Ryan tried to stroll nonchalantly into his office, but he collided with Harry, who hollered, "Hey, how was your date, Casanova?"

"Fine," he said softly, between clenched teeth.

"Aren't you going to thank me for taking your wallet to the lost and found?" he continued loudly.

"You could have brought it to Paddy's." Ryan seethed.

"What, and ruin the atmosphere? No, my boy, that would have been very—" he broke off with a low whistle. "Will you look at that vision? Who is that foxy lady?"

Ryan stiffened and turned his head, ever so slightly. June was walking down the hallway. Her skirt had a slit in the front that opened slightly, revealing a creamy white leg each time she took a step. Ryan felt his chest tighten and his tongue suddenly felt too big for his mouth. Muttering something about work to do, he dashed into his office and closed the door, leaning against it as if he was being pursued.

"What's the matter? Mrs. Wrain find out what a rotten programmer you are?" Maggie's voice was dry. She was sitting in his chair, her legs on his desk.

"What the...?"

"Surprised?" Maggie frowned. "I wasn't about to let the bimbo, oh, excuse me, computer expert, flail around in our program without proper surveillance."

Ryan stared at her feet and said, "I'm going to count to three, and if your feet aren't off my desk, I'll knock them off."

"Sweet." Maggie swung her legs down and glared at him. "Aren't you worried about the program?"

"No." His voice was steely. "I have a feeling it's just a simple glitch to be worked out. It shouldn't take more than an hour or so, and then we'll be able to start test-driving."

Maggie smiled, showing all her teeth. "That's my domain, sugar."

"Sugar?" Ryan winced.

June poked her head in the office without knocking. "Oh, hello, Ryan, Miss Verano. I'm ready to get started. If you'll accompany me to the shop, we'll get this program running."

Ryan found his teeth were locked together. He smiled weakly and walked out the door, passing so close to June he caught a whiff of her perfume. Why did his feet suddenly feel leaden? He tripped over a speck of dust, tried to ignore Maggie's muffled snort of laughter, and took a deep breath to steady himself. He had no feeling in his extremities. His hands were icy and his legs were numb. He couldn't tell if he was smiling or if his mouth was simply hanging open and drooling. He felt as if everyone was staring straight at him, especially June.

Was this what it felt like to be in love? If so, he wanted nothing to do with it.

* * *

June put the headset on and slipped her hands into the silvery silk gloves. There were no wires. Those were passé. The headset was as simple and light as technology could make it. It was like wearing a pair of gossamer sunglasses with tiny pads pressed into each ear and onto each temple. She turned her head side to side, testing the field of vision. Satisfied, she nodded to the technician standing near the console and said, "I'm all set. Whenever you're ready, switch it on."

She settled deeper into the comfortable reclining chair and waited.

A chill washed over her entire body. It was akin to diving into cool water. The feeling was not unpleasant, but it was disconcerting the first time. This was not the first time June had experienced the rush, so she didn't quiver. Then her fingers started to tingle as the sensory devices started to take effect. Her eyes were wide open, but all she saw was a velvety blackness. As she watched, though, a pinprick of light appeared and grew. It grew until it resembled a sun shining in the depths of a starless night. It glowed while growing larger and larger until it revealed a world just behind it. It was as if June was looking through a doorway set in space. The doorway gaped and space disappeared as June was suddenly swallowed by the light, the sky arching above her head and the land slipping beneath her feet. The sea, the palm trees and the marina appeared so quickly, it was as if a magician had whipped a satin cover off the world. June smiled. It was perfect.

* * *

Back in the room, the technicians saw the smile and slapped each other's palms.

Ryan gnawed on his lip and wished he were on the receiving end of that smile.

Maggie scraped a nail across the wall and grinned as Ryan winced. "Back to the old drawing board," she whispered loudly.

* * *

June stood for a moment, then looked around. Smoothly, the scene followed her glance. No feeling of motion sickness, no slight jerk, nothing awkward happened to indicate that she was not actually standing on a cement pier. A seagull screamed, and she tipped her face up to watch it soar across the sky. Wisps of cirrus cloud showed high overhead. She turned back to the marina and scanned the three wooden docks sticking into the water like the letter 'E' from the cement pier. Boats lined the docks, small sailboats and powerboats berthed side by side. The bigger boats were anchored in the bay. One sailboat caught her eye. It was a schooner, with clean, swooping lines. As she looked, a man appeared on deck and sloshed a bucket of water across the deck. Then he took a mop and swabbed energetically. No one else was around. The marina was deserted, except for a large, brown pelican sitting on a tarred post. The bird looked at her and ruffled its feathers in an exaggerated shrug.

June raised an eyebrow. Was part of the game getting out to that boat then? She pursed her lips. She hadn't thought the game started with a puzzle. After yesterday's report, she hadn't gotten that impression. With a sigh she walked to the end of the wooden dock on her right and shouted to the man on the boat.

"Ahoy there!" she called, feeling a bit foolish.

The man raised his head and waved. "Be right there!" he called back. His voice floated easily across the water.

June waited, wilting in the heat, wishing she had a pair of sunglasses to ease the dazzle of the sunlight on the water.

"You should have waited in the shade," were the man's first words to her, as he leapt off the dinghy and onto the dock.

"Why do you say that?" June asked.

He tied up his boat and glanced up at her. "You look pale," he said, a note of worry in his voice. "Come on, I'll get you something cool to drink."

"No, I have no time for that." June stood up a little straighter, fixed him right in the eyes and said with authority, "I have to save the world."

He blinked. Then a wide grin spread across his face. "I'm sure you do," he said soothingly. "My, isn't the sun hot today? You're new down here, aren't you? I bet you didn't even think to bring a hat." He shook his head. "Tourists." He chuckled. "Why don't we go to the bar?" He led the way down the dock towards the cinderblock marina.

He held the door open for her and waited until she stepped inside. "It's not very luxurious, but we're not a very big operation." He nodded at the small bar.

June was thankful to get out of the heat. Perhaps that was part of the problem, she thought. If the program was generating too much heat, it could be interfering with the circuits. She raised her wrist to her mouth and spoke into the watch. "Too much heat," she said succinctly.

The man watched her, a spark of humor dancing in his blue eyes. The corners of his mouth were turned up in a perpetual smile. His short, yellow hair was spiky and rough, and he wore a green and white tee shirt with the words "The First Mandahl Festival" printed on the front. On the back was a large, skinny, Canadian maple leaf. "I'm Jack Winter," he said.

"My name's June." She frowned. "I want to save the world."

"You said that already. You want to hear something strange? You're the second woman to say that to me."

June sat up straighter. He wasn't supposed to register that, unless Maggie had pressed "game save." "Are you talking about yesterday?"

"No, it happened last week, I think." He shrugged and pounded on the bar. "Hey, anyone here? I'd like some drinks!"

June felt completely lost. "Last week? But Maggie was here yesterday."

"Maggie, yeah, that was her name, a tall, skinny girl with wild hair and freckles. She had this scowl on her face at all times that made her look about five years old." He made a gesture with his hand. "She was always muttering into her watch, just like you did there. She told me she wanted to save the world, then she just left." He snapped his fingers. "Like that."

June opened her mouth, then closed it. Her mind was racing. He'd just described Maggie. How could he have seen her? When you entered the game, you entered as one of the pre-registered protagonists. You could use your own name, of course, but physically you were supposed to resemble the computer image the programmers had built. Without looking down at herself, she knew she was a medium sized woman, with straight, red hair and almond-shaped hazel eyes. She had chosen a figure that most resembled her real body. Maggie had chosen a willowy blonde persona. June was quite sure of that because the icon had been glowing in the air in front of Maggie as she entered the program. Moreover, Maggie had been here yesterday, not a week ago.

Jack sighed loudly and slapped the counter. "Well, seems the barman's abandoned his post yet again. Luckily, I know where the key to the fridge is hidden." He vaulted lightly over the bar. "What would you like? A piña colada?"

June just nodded. She was trying to work out how he'd been able to see Maggie as she really was, and how he even remembered her. She watched as he busied himself chopping up pineapple and putting ice into the blender. He glanced at her and grinned. "The bartender is an old pal of mine, but he's usually gone fishing 'round about now." He reached up to the shelf and took a bottle of Mount Gay rum.

June nodded again. Of course, there was no bartender. The bartender wouldn't appear until the game was launched. Then the character that had been programmed into the game would appear. The bartender was a directional player; that is, he gave hints such as "why don't you go to slip thirteen?" That meant you would go check out the boat docked in that berth for another clue. He would also make a drink, if you wanted, although you couldn't actually drink it.

Jack set a tall glass in front of her and poured a frothy, pale yellow mixture into it from the blender. He fished in a narrow jar and took out a maraschino cherry. "Tada!" he said, setting it gently in the piña colada.

June smiled, but made no move to pick up the drink. She knew that the game wasn't that refined. No one could make a game where you could eat and drink yet. She could touch things, but not pick them up or really feel them. She could interact verbally with certain characters, but she wouldn't be able to do anything that wasn't already programmed into the game. Drinking a piña colada wasn't part of the game.

"What's the matter, don't you like it?" Jack frowned at her.

"No, it's not that." June sighed. "Jack, I really want to save the world." She watched him closely, hopefully.

He raised his eyebrows. "Save the world?" he echoed.

June smiled.

He reached over and touched her forehead. His hand was firm and cool. "You're burning up. Too much sun. You'd better..."

June jerked away from him as if she'd been burnt. "You touched me!" she gasped.

"I'm sorry!" Jack drew back. "I didn't mean to offend you, honest. I just wanted to feel your forehead, really. I'm sorry!"

"It's not that, I mean, you shouldn't be able to touch me. How did you do that?" June held her watch to her lips and said, "He touched my head. How could he touch my head? He's only supposed to be able to touch my hand where the gloves are!"

Jack took both of her hands and led her to a couch in the back of the bar. "Lie down here," he said softly. "I'll go get the doctor. I won't be long. Just rest here."

June was about to sink to the couch when she glanced at the mirror hanging on the wall behind it. Her pale face stared back at her. Not the face of a computer-generated character. Her own face—her green eyes, her copper hair; she was even wearing the thin gold chain and locket that her mother had given her around her slender neck. She reached up and fingered it. "How is it possible?" she whispered. Her heart suddenly started to hammer in her chest. "Excuse me," she said to Jack, disengaging her arm. She lifted her watch to her lips and said, "I see myself in the mirror."

Jack spoke up, his voice gentle. "That's right, you see yourself in the mirror. That's what they're for, you know. Now you lie here, nice and quiet, and I'll be back in ten minutes. I'll just get into my boat and I'll go right around that spit of land you see there. I'll get Doc Haybert, and I'll be right back. Don't worry, I won't leave you alone too long."

June gaped at him. She tried to think of something to say, but the only sound that came out of her throat was "Ack."

"Jack. That's right. I'm Jack." His face was creased with worry. "Are you sure you'll be all right here? I'd use the phone, but it's quicker to just go by boat. Doc lives on an island right across the bay."

"I'll be fine." June drew a shaky breath. "I'm fine. Don't bother the doctor. There's no need, and besides, you won't be able to fetch him if the game hasn't started."

"Heatstroke." Jake spoke firmly. "Pale, clammy skin, delirium, feverish." He nodded. "Heatstroke for sure. I'll be back in a flash." He touched her face softly, drawing his finger lightly down her cheek. His eyes grew cloudy, and he looked troubled. "Please don't move. Stay here in the shade, I'll be right back." He left, padding silently across the floor on bare feet. At the doorway, he paused again, looking over his shoulder. His face had lost its puckish good humor and two deep lines dove from his narrow, high-bridged nose to his mouth. Then he shook his head. "No, I can't leave you here. I'll take you with me; it'll be quicker. But wear this hat; it'll keep the sun off your head." He plucked a wide-brimmed straw hat from its hook on the wall and placed it on her head, smoothing her hair from her neck. Then he leaned down and hefted her into his arms. "Oof! You're heavier than you look." His grin reappeared.

June was too astonished at first to struggle, but as soon as he passed the threshold, she wriggled out of his arms. "That's enough. I'll be glad to walk. He carried me," she added into her watch. "There is certainly a physical glitch that enabled that."

She decided she would accompany him to the boat. As soon as he saw that he couldn't get out of this frame until the game had started, maybe the character would respond to the code words. She let him help her into the dinghy and settle her on the seat. He took his place at the back, near the outboard motor, and pulled the cord. The motor sputtered to life, and Jack eased the boat away from the dock. The water slapped against the hull, and June leaned back to enjoy the scenery.

The boat couldn't go past the bay. If the game hadn't started, and the correct clues weren't picked up, the marina was the only frame a player could visit. The frame was limited to the marina, the bar, the docks and most all the boats, and the mouth of the bay.

Jack steered the dinghy past the schooner, out into the bay, and around the spit of black, volcanic rocks keeping the waves tamed.

"It'll be a bit rough here, hang on," he shouted.

June clutched the seat, her mouth open. She finally gathered herself together to sputter into her watch, "He's gone around the spit; we're heading for the island just off shore."

Jack heard her and nodded. "Doc Haybert lives in the white bungalow you see there. Don't worry, he'll take care of you."

June didn't answer. She was too busy trying to figure out what kind of a glitch would permit the program to jump its tracks and run without prompts. The only thing that she could imagine was a virus, probably introduced by an industrial sabotage expert. She spoke into the watch. "I suspect sabotage; look in the mother-gel-crystal and see if you can spot any signs of tampering. I am starting to suspect a whole new program has been grafted onto this one."

Jack slowed the motor, and asked her, "Do you mind telling me what you meant by those last two statements?"

June sighed. "It's unimportant for you to know."

"Maybe I can help. What's going on?"

"This is a computer program." She shrugged. No sense hiding it from him. The character wouldn't respond anyway.

"What's that? Your watch is some sort of game?"

"No, not my watch. All this. The boat, the sea, you, even the seagull. It's all part of a program that the Carver company has been working on for three years now." June pointed to her watch. "This is the link to the people who made the game; my comments are recorded and sent through a microphone back in the center."

"Really?" Jack looked stunned. "You must have gotten more sun than I thought. Hold on, we'll be there in a minute."

June waited until the boat was tied, and then she leapt lightly onto the dock. Jack took her arm and led her up the steep steps towards a bungalow perched on the hill. The path to the house was lined with spiky aloe plants and red and white flowered hibiscus bushes. Two magnificent, flamboyant trees spread shade over the picture-book house, and its welcoming veranda was comfortable with deep wicker furniture and hanging pots of air-fern. Banana trees and fig trees were planted in the garden, and several rare turpentine trees rose majestically above them. A g'nip tree stood by the mailbox, and next to that a tamarind tree waved feathery leaves. Mock orange trees, miniature lemon, and lime trees were planted in antique pots and placed on the veranda steps. The wooden house was painted pink, with white gingerbread trim on the tin roof. The veranda was white, and the floorboards were gray with age and smooth as silk.

June admired the effect of the program, bending down reflexively to sniff a hibiscus.

"They don't have any smell," Jack apologized.

"Of course they don't, the program isn't that complex."

"The mock oranges smell nice though," he offered, plucking a waxy white bloom from a small bush and handing it to her.

June smiled. "You don't believe me, do you?"

"I think you had better sit down. I'll go see if the doctor is here."

"Of course he won't be here, the program hasn't started yet."

Jack stared at her, indecision on his face, and then he nodded curtly and stepped into the dark doorway.

June sat on one of the chairs overlooking the bay and leaned back. The view was magnificent. The ocean was dotted with little white caps. Deep water was indigo, turning to turquoise near the shore. The marina wasn't visible from here; the doctor's house overlooked the open sea. To the left she could see the garden and the narrow red dirt road leading from the house towards the interior of the island.

June twirled the orange blossom in her hand and stared at the scene. Something was bothering her. Something was niggling the back of her mind. She lifted the blossom to her nose and breathed in its delicate scent. Her hand started to shake. She sniffed again, fearfully. The orange blossom smelled divine. That was not right. She raised her watch to her lips and said, "The flower has scent." Her voice wavered and she turned to see Jack staring at her with concern. "It shouldn't smell at all," she wailed.

"Miss, why don't you come in now. The doctor is just coming up the drive. Everything will be just fine." Jack took her arm with extreme delicacy and led her into the cool, shady house. He plucked the blossom from her unfeeling hand, and pointed to the door where an elderly man was just walking into the front hallway. "There's Doc."

June felt her head spin and the room went suddenly dark.

It was just a faint. The sharp bite of smelling salts woke her and she sat up coughing.

"There now, Miss. I'm Doctor Haybert, but you can call me Doc. Maybe you can tell us your name, and how you came to the marina." The doctor was tall and thin, and had a smooth, deep voice that made June think of thick honey.

She was sitting on an examining table in the doctor's office. She felt the crisp paper beneath her with her hand. "My name is June Houston," she said. "I'm an engineer in a special program that designs virtual games."

"Hmm, sounds fascinating." The doctor put his stethoscope on her back. "Breathe deeply."

The stethoscope was cold. Her heart began to pound. She took a deep breath. Then another, at his urging.

"Heart seems perfect." He took off his stethoscope. "Say 'Ah'."

"We are in the middle of testing a new game. That's how I came here." June paused and said "Ahhhh" as the doctor peered down her throat.

"There's no sign of heatstroke, no fever, no inflammation at all. You seem perfectly healthy."

June looked down at her hands, clutching the white paper beneath her. "Perfectly healthy." She raised her head and gave him a crooked smile. "I have breast cancer. That's not so healthy, is it?"

"When do you start treatment?" Doctor Haybert looked sufficiently shocked.

"In three days."

"Where is it?"

June shrugged and lifted her blouse, pointing to her left breast. "I found a lump here last month. My mother died of breast cancer, so I didn't wait. They did a biopsy, and found it malignant. They took more out, and..." Her voice trailed away as her fingers felt her breast. There was no tenderness where the stitches had been. She had no mark at all. She looked down and yanked her bra off, staring at her breast. It was perfect.

"It looks fine to me." The doctor frowned at her. "Are you sure it was this one?"

She nodded, but looked at the right breast just the same. It was fine. She prodded at them, searching for the telltale lump that had iced her blood just four weeks ago. Nothing. She could see nothing at all. She raised her head and stared at the doctor.

"I don't understand," she whispered. She stood up, her bra dangling, her blouse open, her face haggard. "I just don't understand."

"You seem to be fine," said the doctor soothingly. "If you want, I can do a quick scan."

She shook her head. She cupped her breasts in her hands. "I had a scar here, and the doctors told me that the treatment would make me lose my hair. They say that to everyone, so we're prepared. I was going to cut my hair short, so that when it started to fall out, it would be easier to shave off. I was even planning to buy a blond wig, just for the fun of it." Tears dripped off her chin; her hands were still pressed to her bosom. She took a huge, shaky breath. "I wanted my mother to live forever. I thought that we'd always be together. When she died, I thought the whole world should be in mourning. I couldn't believe the sun still shone, that the sky could still be blue, or that flowers should bloom when she was gone."

"How old were you?" The doctor took her hands and gently pulled them from her breasts. He eased her bra back on, slipped the straps over her shoulders and buttoned her blouse. Then he took a handkerchief from his pocket and wiped her face.

"Twelve." June blew her nose into the handkerchief and sat on the chair the doctor pulled out for her.

"Do you have your purse with you?"

She shook her head. "This is just a virtual world, it's just a game. I don't need a purse. Why?"

"How will you pay me?" he asked, a faint twinkle in his eyes.

June blinked. "Pay you?"

"Thirty dollars for the first visit, twenty dollars for all the rest. House calls are twenty-five for long-time patients, thirty-five for new ones." He leaned over his desk and smiled at her. "I'm sure Mr. Winter will lend you the money, if need be. I wanted to check your identification papers as well. Your hotel should be notified if you're ill. Your insurance should cover this visit."

"This is just a game!"

"Do you have a psychologist back home?" The doctor sounded worried.

"I'll prove it to you." June pushed a small button on her watch, held it to her lips and said, "Bring me back now. There's a problem."

The room became darker and instinctively she turned and walked towards the doorway, where light spilled through the screen. Her breathing got louder until it was all she could hear. The colors slipped away, the doctor's house dissolved, and she found herself sitting in a comfortable chair in the shop. The lights blinded her for a minute, and she sat there blinking. Then she peeled off her gloves, took the frail headset off her head, and looked at Ryan.

"Can I see you alone a minute?" she asked, before anyone could speak. She heard muttering, and an attractive girl with a sulky, freckled face, Maggie Verano, the test expert, made an audible, disagreeable comment. June stood up and touched her face. It was dry. No signs of weeping. Her hands were steady. She nodded to herself and strode into Ryan's office. When the door shut behind them, she whirled around and said, "All right. What is going on?" Her voice came out remarkably steady although she felt as if she was about to fly to pieces.

Ryan looked puzzled. "What do you mean?"

"I mean that program is amazing! The flowers smell! I looked into a mirror and saw my own locket around my neck!" She realized she was sounding strident so she took a deep breath. "There are no frames. I got into the boat before the game even started and visited the doctor's house. I even had a check up."

Ryan gave a start. "The doctor's house? He doesn't have a house. I mean, he does, but we never went beyond the façade. The clues are hidden on his porch. All he does is come to the door and talk."

"No. I went inside. He has an office. He even…" She paused. "Excuse me a minute." She pulled her blouse out and peered down at her chest.

Ryan cleared his throat. "What are you doing?"

"Checking something." She sounded sad.

"What?"

June looked at him. He stared back at her, his eyes wide. She recognized that look. Puppies got it when you reached through the bars of their cages in dog pounds and tickled their tummies. Suddenly she turned away. She couldn't get involved with anyone now. Her hand strayed to her breast unconsciously. It was swollen and sore. Her last visit to the hospital had frightened her. The surgeon had tacked the X-rays on the wall and pointed out little clouds in her chest. One here, one here, and one here. His voice had been so calm, so very far away. His eyes had been wary. He was trying to tell her something. She understood. Sometimes intelligence was a curse.

"Miss Houston? June?" Ryan got up and knelt in front of her.

She tried to smile but it wobbled across her face. "You don't even know how you did it, do you?"

"I don't know what?"

"How you created such a program. It's perfect. It's a whole new world."

"I don't understand."

"We'll go back and I'll show you."

"Together? We play a multi-player game?"

"Yes. Right now. And Ryan?"

"Yes?"

"Not a single word to anyone about this yet."

They went back into the shop and sat on matching reclining chairs. Both put on head-sets and gloves. June felt the familiar electrical current running through her, then the darkness came. Pinpoints of light, the doorway, and the rush of scenery as it engulfed her. She was standing at the marina, in the shade near the doorway to the bar. The sunlight sparkled on the water and the heat washed over her as before. She stepped out of the shade and looked for Ryan. He was nowhere in sight. Sighing, she wandered to the end of the dock and looked for a sign of life. A pelican sitting on a tarred post fluffed its feathers and clacked its beak at her. Otherwise, all was quiet. She went to the bar and pushed the door open. Sitting at the bar, his back to her, was Jack.

"Hi," she said, a bit shyly.

He spun around, nearly falling off the stool. "You!"

June hesitated, then walked over to him. "Thank you for taking me to the doctor's office this morning. I'm sorry I was such a trouble-maker."

"That wasn't this morning, that was three days ago." Jack plucked at the label on his beer. "Look, miss, I don't want to pry in your private life, but, what exactly is it you want from us? The doc was pretty shook up when you left his office."

"He said I left?"

"He said you got up, walked to the front door, and disappeared."

"I went back to my world," June said. "This is nothing but a virtual computer game."

"I'm sorry, but I can't take your word for that." Jack shrugged. "You owe me thirty dollars."

"I don't have any money."

"Where are you staying?"

"I'm not staying anywhere. I don't live here!" June was getting impatient. "Look, someone will be joining me soon, any second now. We want to save the world."

Jack stood up so suddenly his barstool fell over. He looked down at June, and she realized he was very tall. "Listen to me, miss. I do not like being jerked around. I think we'd better call it quits right now. You forget all about me, all right? And I'll try and forget about you." He started to leave.

"Wait." June caught his arm. "I'm sorry if you don't believe me. I don't know how to convince you, though. Just wait for my friend."

"No." Jack was standing very close. Her hand was still on his arm. She could feel the heat of his body through her blouse, and as she watched, a trickle of sweat beaded on his temple and ran down the side of his face and down his neck. It disappeared into his shirt.

A tremor ran through her. Her hand tightened convulsively on his arm. Without knowing why, or even thinking about it, she pulled him closer and kissed him. He was taller than she was, and he had to bend his head down. Their lips met with a shock that was palpable. June felt like a drowning person. She threw her arms around his neck and held on for dear life. His body pressed hard against hers; she felt his hands clasping her tightly, drawing her into him. They kissed for what seemed like hours, until her head swam and her legs suddenly gave out beneath her.

"Why did you do that?" he gasped, as he lowered her onto the plush bench beneath the mirror.

"I needed to," she replied. She was panting.

He was breathing heavily. Sweat glistened along his temples and jaw. A muscle twitched there. He ran his finger along her face, down her neck, across her collarbone. When he drew it back, it was wet with sweat. Staring at her intently, he licked it off.

She moaned as a pang of desire so sharp it was painful stabbed her low in her belly. Her eyelids felt too heavy.

"Let's go." He pulled her to her feet and led her outside. The sun's heat nearly flattened her, and she let him half carry, half lead her to his dinghy. They didn't speak as they crossed the harbor, heading towards the schooner moored in the bay. He tied the dinghy to the stern line, and helped her up the ladder. His hands were sure; hers were shaking.

Without pausing to look around the deck, he opened the hatch door and handed her down the steep ladder. Then he climbed down after her. They were in a spacious room, half galley-half dining room, with the navigational center in a tiny office on their left.

"Down there." Jack pushed her through a narrow hallway. Two doors on her right, two on her left, and a door in front of her. She opened that one, and found herself standing in a stateroom. She had time to see two round port windows, sunlight streaming on a white cotton bedspread, and a bouquet of red hibiscus. Then her clothes were flying across the room and Jack's hands were running over her ribs, her hips, and her shoulders. Her breath came in deep gulps. Her body, his body, the bed: all were shaking.

"Take off your clothes," she told Jack.

He did, dropping his pants and shirt to the floor in a heap, and stood in front of her, naked. For a minute she just looked at him. Tall, and lean, he had a small scar on his side, and his muscles were all drawn finely, as if an artist had outlined them in pencil. His eyes were dark blue, like the sea, and his mouth quirked in a smile that was both tender and assured.

"You're beautiful." He tilted his head.

"So are you." She'd never called a man beautiful before, but Jack was gorgeous. Heat that had nothing to do with the tropics surged into her belly. Her heart pounded.

He slid onto the bed with her and took her in his arms. They kissed. Jack held her so tightly she could hardly breathe. But she clung to him, her arms wrapped around his broad shoulders, her legs around his hips. She could feel his erection pressed against her thigh, and the heat in her belly grew even more intense.

Sunlight streamed in a narrow ribbon through the open window, burning where it touched, and when the breeze blew in, its coolness was a shock. The room was so hot. Jack's skin burned hers, and his mouth was a firebrand. Where they touched, they sizzled.

Sweat stung their lips, made their bodies slippery. Skin, slick and wet, pressed upon skin, and where Jack's body left off and hers began, she could not tell. She didn't care. Then he entered her, and a sharp pain made her gasp. The salt from the sweat, she thought. The heat made her feel as if she were covered in warm honey. Then she couldn't think at all,. She could only cry out and pull him into her deeper, harder. She wanted him completely. She'd never felt like this before. It made her bones shake.

She[kww2] couldn't stop shaking, even afterwards. He raised himself on his elbow and stared at her. He stared at the sheets, her body, drew a deep breath, and then his face shattered. "Why didn't you tell me?" he asked. He looked as if he wanted to cry.

She lay on the bed and trembled. He gathered her in his arms and crooned soft words and meaningless phrases into her ear. He smoothed her hair back, held her gently. Finally, her breathing evened out. She looked at him and smiled. "I didn't know."

"You didn't know you were a virgin?"

"In my world, I wasn't." She wanted to laugh. She felt like crying or laughing, she wasn't sure which. Tentatively she moved her hips. An ache answered her. There were dust motes in the sunlight that sparkled like diamonds. She felt as light and bright as one of those motes.

"Let me tell you everything from the beginning," she said to Jack, and she did.

* * *

Ryan waited for June. The marina was empty. He strode around the docks getting hotter and more bewildered. Nobody was around. Finally, he went into the cinderblock building that doubled as an office and a bar. It was cooler inside. The bar was empty, a stool was knocked over and a warm bottle of beer stood on the counter. Its label was half off. Ryan smoothed it back on, then unthinkingly, and because he was hot and thirsty, he tilted the bottle to his lips and drank.

The bottle fell from his fingers and smashed on the floor. He took a step backwards, tripped over the barstool, and went sprawling. Gaping, he stared at the broken bottle, the barstool, and at his knee, skinned and bleeding.

"Shit!" Then he pushed the button on his watch and said, "Get me out of here."

He woke up in the reclining chair and the first thing he did was glance at his leg. Nothing. Then he looked over at June, lying peacefully in her chair. As he watched, a red light illuminated above her head and the technician hovering over her said, "She's coming back; hit the wake-up switch."

June opened her eyes and seemed to shrink a bit. After a minute, she sat up and swung her legs over the side of the chair. Ryan couldn't help admiring her legs, even as he tried to figure out what had happened to him in the game. A wry voice interrupted his reverie. "So, what's the verdict, Sherlock?" Maggie leaned over him, anger making her face tight.

Ryan ignored her. "June?" he asked. "Are you all right?"

She shook her head at him. "Not here. Let's go back to your office."

Ryan very desperately wanted to smirk at Maggie, but he was feeling too confused. He trailed after June, his throat dry, no trace of beer in his mouth anymore.

When they reached the office, June sat down heavily and stared at Ryan. He couldn't help noticing that her eyes were the color of emeralds in the sun. His chest ached, and he wished he were braver, or handsomer, or just crazy enough to grab her around the waist and...

"Where were you?" she asked.

"Looking for you. I found no one in the marina, at the bar, or in the office."

"I was on the schooner."

"The what?"

"The large white boat moored in the harbor."

"That's not possible." Ryan pulled a chair out and sat down, facing June. She didn't answer him. After a minute, he bit his lip. "I drank beer."

She closed her eyes. It was like the sun going out. He reached across his desk and took her hand gingerly. "I don't understand it any more than you do," he said.

"Whatever you do," she said, keeping her eyes firmly shut, "do not change this program. For now, keep it exactly as it is. I am going to be absent until Thursday. When I get back, we'll discuss what can be done. Until then, no one goes back. No one touches the gel crystal. No one. Do you hear me?" Her eyes opened and she looked at him.

His heart flipped over in his chest. "You're going away?"

She smiled. It was a sad smile, and Ryan had the absurd urge to kiss her. Actually, the urge had been there since he'd met her, but he didn't think he could ever act upon it until she smiled at him so sadly. He took a quick breath and took her face in his hands, kissing her on the lips before he chickened out. He broke off and stared at her.

"Don't look at me like that," she said. The sorrow was still there, tugging at the corners of her mouth.

"Can you tell me about it?"

She gazed at him levelly. "I have cancer."

Ryan felt as if someone had just punched him. He thought his grin must appear stupid, frozen on his face, but he couldn't move it. He managed to speak. "Is the prognosis good?" he asked, searching for lines to say, anything, something he'd heard in a film or read in a book to help him out in a situation like this one.

June shook her head. "No, I'm afraid not. It's in my chest, and my breast." Her hand pointed, moving slowly through what seemed like horribly thick air. "It's reached my lymph nodes, and now it seems to have migrated all through me. I guess it likes me." Her voice was steady.

Goosebumps rose on the back of his neck. "That's no reason not to kiss someone," he said hopelessly.

"It's the best reason," she replied softly. "I don't want to leave any holes behind me. No empty spaces."

"It's too late," said Ryan, and he felt his heart crack like marble breaking.

* * *

June dressed in a hospital gown and lay down on a table. The machine swallowed her whole. She thought of Jonah and the whale as she watched the machine inching over her body. Invisible rays poured over her, seeping into her cells, searching out the hiding places of those that had mutated and were wreaking havoc in her body. Behind a dark glass wall technicians were moving levers, watching screens, but she knew it was futile. The machine swallowed her and then spit her out. She emerged once more into the brightness of the white-walled room and waited until the nurse came to lift her off the table. An odd, queasy feeling and a memory as old and blurry as a sepia photograph came to her. She was lying in bed with a vinegar-soaked sheet covering her body. Sunburn, her grandmother was clucking, as she spread the sheet. June had the same feeling that she'd had that day. Only the sunburn was inside of her now, and her grandmother was long gone.

She dressed, signed a sheet of paper on a clipboard, and took the bus back to her apartment. Once she got home, she lay on her bed in utter darkness and waited until her head stopped spinning. Then she listened to her messages. Ryan had called twice.

She wanted to call him back. She wanted to hear the doctors say that she was cured. She looked out the window at the night lit by a million city lights and thought about a white boat floating in a tranquil harbor. She put Beethoven's Ninth Symphony on her stereo, settled back into the couch, and curled her legs beneath her. Somewhere around the third movement, she started to cry.

* * *

Small waves clapped gently against the white schooner. Jack sat on the deck and watched the sunset. Soft jazz music came from a small radio, and a fishing pole was propped up next to him, its line dipping into the water although it had no hook on it. Lights were on at the marina. The sounds of laughter floated over the calm water. It was Friday night, and the boat owners were getting ready for the weekend to take their crafts out to sea.

Jack tipped his chair back until he could see the empty rigging above his head. When June had vanished before his eyes, he had been successively horrified, frightened, shocked, and finally angry. Someone, he decided, was fooling with things he had no business fooling with—namely, Jack and Jack's world. He looked over the black water and frowned. The sunset cut an orange swath across the bay. Just around the spit, he could see Doc in his little outboard heading towards town. He dined there every Friday with his long-standing lady friend.

They had talked, Doc and he, about the possibility that their world could be a figment of their imagination. It was a philosophical discussion, spiked with liberal amounts of lime wedges, sea-salt, and tequila. The two men had each seen a lovely young woman disappear, literally vanish like a hologram fading out. The hologram theory had been touched upon, but Jack still had a sheet with her blood upon it. Holograms don't bleed, he reasoned. They don't do any of the things June and Jack had done that afternoon on his boat, things that made his heart race just to think about them.

He took a long swallow from his soda can. The sweet, bubbly stuff made him wince, but he was still recovering from his philosophical discussion with Doc.

Of all the theories they'd bandied about, the parallel universe was the one Jack preferred. Somehow, Carver Games had opened a breach from June's world to his. He only hoped that she would return. Waiting for her was the hardest thing he'd ever done in his life.

Doc had called it puppy love.

"It's not puppy love," said Jack aloud, tossing his empty soda can into the plastic cooler at his feet. He looked up at the starry sky. "Since my family died I haven't asked anything of you, have

I?" he asked, a note of anger in his voice. "I lost my sister, my father and my mother in an earthquake. Everyone, including the insurance agents, called it an act of God, but I never blamed you, did I? I just kept on going with life, trying to keep everything together. I tried, God knows how I tried." His voice broke with a sort of sob, and he stopped speaking and glanced over at the brightly-lit marina. The sun had sunk below the horizon and the darkness was like black velvet. He lit the gasoline lamp hanging from the yardarm and sat back down. The boat rocked softly, tiny waves slapping ever so quietly against the hull. Jack sat in silence for a while. Then he looked at the sky again. "I never asked for anything but I'm asking now. I just want to see June again. I want another chance."

Receiving no reply from the empty heavens, he sighed once, then got up and made his way down the ladder to his dinghy. He didn't start the engine. Instead, he began rowing steadily towards the marina where the smell of barbecued chicken was starting to make his mouth water.

* * *

Maggie slipped the glasses on her face and pulled the gloves on. Her movements were furtive; she didn't want to be discovered. It was dark, the offices were empty, and the whole building was still. Only Patch, the night watchman, sometimes broke the silence with a little song as he made his rounds. She sat in the reclining chair and switched on the machine. It started up with a low hum, prompting her to take her glasses off and look around nervously. There seemed to be nobody about, so she relaxed and put the glasses back on. Her hands waved in the air as she chose her game, and then she selected her player. As before, she chose a tall, willowy blond with wide blue eyes and a sexy pout on luscious red lips. She settled deeper into the chair and pushed the button, launching the game.

When she was in, a light in the console above her head turned green. As soon as that happened, a figure limped out of the darkness and looked down at Maggie's motionless body. Maxwell Santiago Carver watched for a few minutes, making sure Maggie was in the game before he settled onto another chair nearby and selected a pair of gloves and glasses. His movements were rapid and sure. Within moments, he was lying still, a green light glowing above his head.

Maggie found herself near the marina. This time, however, it was night and there were lights and music coming from the cinderblock building. She paused, puzzled. The story line had never started at night. Obviously, the problem with the program went much deeper than she had feared. She raised her watch to her lips and spoke quietly. "The scene is taking place at night. On my right is the marina's main building. Colored lights are strung up from the doorway to the docks, and there are people in some of the boats docked in slips. The odor of barbecued chicken in the air, I can smell it. That's not right at all. I don't remember programming anything like that. The lights look cheap, like old Christmas decorations, and some of the bulbs are burned out. It looks very tacky. Steel drum music is coming from inside, someone is playing the guitar too, but not very well. Where did we get this terrible background music? Out in the bay someone is rowing a boat. He's coming close to the dock now. I recognize Jack, the main character. He must have been activated by my presence here so something is going right, after all." She clicked her recorder off and strode out of the shadow into a halo cast by the naked bulbs strung along the cement walkway.

Jack looked up and recognized Maggie. His face creased in a frown. Then he saw another figure behind her, a tall man. He straightened up, trying to get a better look, but the two figures were too far away. Maggie's eyes were locked on his; obviously she'd recognized him. She almost waved. Then suddenly she pitched forward onto her face and lay still. Behind her, the figure of a tall man whirled around and dashed back into the darkness. Jack only had time to catch sight of a glint of glasses and a strange, high, round forehead.

By the time he reached the spot Maggie had been, she had vanished, and he saw no sign of the other person. He scanned the ground, but all he found was an earring. He looked at it carefully, but he had no way of telling to whom it belonged. He put it in his pocket and continued his search. After fifteen minutes, he gave up. His stomach was growling. He was hungry.

* * *

Maggie's eyes snapped open and she flailed her arms. She was blind! *No, idiot,* she said to herself. *Your glasses are on.* She removed them, then peeled off her gloves. The light above her head blinked red. She had somehow disconnected herself from the game. Her last memory was of waving to Jack. Then everything had gone black. Another virus to be ironed out, she thought in fury. What in hell was going on with this game? All the others had gone so smoothly. It would have to happen now that she was chief tester. Her lips pinched together tightly. Everything was wrong: the music, the smell of chicken, and the night scene. She rubbed the back of her neck. Her hand brushed against her ear and she froze. She clapped her hands to her head. No mistake about it; one of her earrings had disappeared. She sat up and searched the chair, the floor beneath her, and carefully combed her fingers through her curls. Still no sign of her earring. Swearing, she forgot about discretion and turned on the overhead lights. On her hands and knees, she looked for her earring. Nearly in tears after a half an hour, she gave up and turned the lights back off. Glaring at the game console, she picked up her purse from her desk and let herself out of the shop. For some reason, her head ached.

Maxwell Santiago Carver watched her go. He didn't know what she had been searching for, but a frown of worry creased his face. He couldn't fail now, now that he was so close to success.

* * *

Ryan glared at the girl perched on the edge of his desk.

She glared back at him. Sparks flew from her eyes. "I want to know what is going on," she hissed, leaning so close her nose almost touched his.

"I don't know what you're talking about." He tried to keep his voice level. It didn't work. It cracked at the worst possible moment.

"All right, I'll tell you." Maggie drew a deep breath. She seemed suddenly unsure of herself. "Last night, I went into the new game."

"You did what?"

"I wanted to see what you and the bimbo…"

Ryan's hand slapped so hard on the desk they both jumped. "If you say another word about Miss Houston, I'll pick you up and throw you out my window."

"You wouldn't dare."

"Just try me. You are way out of line, Maggie."

Maggie bit her lip. "Sorry."

A little silence settled between them. Then Ryan said, "Why did you go into the game when I expressly asked you not to touch it?" He held up his hand. "No, don't even try to explain. I know. You couldn't bear to be kept out of any part of it. I admire your professional tenacity. As your direct superior, though, I can ask President Wrain to take you off this game. Can you give me any reason why I shouldn't do that?"

"For the same reason you won't really throw me out the window?" Maggie asked in a small voice. "Because it would kill me?"

Ryan sighed. "Is this project that important to you?"

Maggie nodded, her face turning bright red. She blinked hard, trying unsuccessfully to compose herself. "I love my work, I loved this game—the whole idea was so fun, so incredibly complex—and when I was chosen to be chief tester, it was wonderful. Can you understand that? It was better than wonderful; it was the best thing that had ever happened to me."

"Tell me what happened in the game," Ryan said. His voice was still sharp.

"I want to tell you what happened. I can't explain it, no matter how hard I try."

"Go ahead." Ryan glanced at the door, making sure it was firmly shut. He thought he knew what was coming.

"I went into the game wearing a pair of earrings I inherited from my grandmother. I am positive I was wearing them; I remember putting them on just before I left my apartment." Maggie's hand strayed up to her ear and she had a frightened look on her face. "Ryan, when I got back, one of the earrings was gone."

"You must have lost it on the chair, or on your way to the office. That doesn't mean anything."

"No, that's not all." Maggie stopped and actually wrung her hands. "My ear isn't pierced anymore! I got back, and my earring was gone and so was the hole. It's impossible, but that's what happened."

Ryan stopped breathing. He felt as if someone had just given him a jolt of electricity. "Say that again?"

"It was night. I arrived at night. I heard music, and smelled barbecued chicken. I saw Jack getting out of his boat, and then everything went black. I found myself back in the shop, sitting in the recliner, and when I took my headset off, I discovered my earring was missing." Maggie stopped and looked sharply at Ryan. "You know something about this. You and Miss Houston know something you're not telling me."

Ryan didn't answer right away. He was trying desperately to think of all the reasons he should lie to Maggie. Finally he looked at Maggie and said, "One second, please." He picked up the phone.

Ryan kept his eyes on Maggie while he spoke. "Hello, June? How are you feeling? How was your appointment yesterday? Oh, I see." He listened for a long while, then he said, "What you're saying is that there is no change? All right. No, I'll tell you later. Will you be here Thursday? Good. See you then." He hung up with a frown, setting the receiver down carefully. He ran his hands over his head, making his hair stick up, then he smoothed it down.

"Can you tell me about it?" Maggie asked.

"It's hard to explain."

"As hard as my earring?"

"When June went into the game she discovered that there were no frames. The characters didn't respond, and she went places that we never developed. She fainted, and when she woke up, she was in a doctor's office. When he examined her, he said that she was perfectly healthy, and she was." Ryan broke off and stared at Maggie. "Here, in this world, June has cancer. It's spread all through her chest, and she has a scar on her breast where they removed a tumor. In that world, she had nothing wrong with her at all. Here, she can hardly climb a fight of stairs."

"But that's normal, it wasn't her body! She chose a player!"

"No. It was her body. She saw herself in the mirror and she had her own necklace on."

"I don't get it." Maggie looked stunned. "What happened?"

Ryan shook his head tiredly. "Whatever happened, it only happens there. I just spoke to June. She went to the hospital yesterday. Everything is the same. She didn't come back cured."

Maggie fingered her ear. "I'm sorry I was so mean to her," she said softly.

For a minute, Ryan almost liked her. Then his expression hardened. "Whatever you do, don't talk about this to anyone. Do you understand me?"

"Sure, whatever." Maggie hesitated, then she said, "On one condition. You don't take me off this project. I want to go back there."

"I don't think so," said Ryan steadily. "I don't think anyone is going back, ever. I want to scrap the project; it's starting to frighten me."

* * *

Ryan finished his work in time for lunch. He was just backing up his files when Harry poked his head in his office and winked.

"Shall we eat at Paddy's?" Harry asked.

"No, thanks, you go on. I have some more work to do here."

"All work and no play make Jack a dull boy," said Harry.[kww3]

"What did you say?" Ryan's head jerked up and he frowned at his friend.

"Shit, you know that saying! Carver is always spouting it."

"Along with a million other clichés," muttered Ryan.

"Huh?"

"Nothing. Listen, if I finish early I'll join you, OK?"

"Sure." Harry shrugged and gave a little wave as he left. "Later, alligator."

Ryan waited until his footsteps had faded before peeking out. The hallway was empty. Quickly, before he could change his mind, he walked to the fire-escape door and climbed two floors to the tenth floor where the accounting records were kept. He still had the key to the record room that an ex-girlfriend had left at his office one day. There was something to be said of office romance after all, he thought, as he opened the locked cabinet where the cost records were kept.

"Cyber Jack, Super Spy," Ryan whispered to himself, as he pulled a thick file from the cabinet and flicked through it. Then he was silent, except for a barely audible, "What the hell?"

An hour later, when the secretaries and accountants started filing back into their offices after lunch, Ryan slipped back downstairs.

For a half an hour, he sat behind his desk with his head in his hands, just thinking.

The file for "Cyber Jack, Super Spy" was confusing. According to the numbers on the very bottom of the last page, the game hadn't cost much more than the preceding action game; thirteen million dollars had been spent so far developing the game. Nothing odd there. The odd thing was the consulting firm. Instead of Dream Weavers Inc, the company that built visuals for the last game, Cyber Jack had been developed primarily by a company called Specu-Ace. Now who were they? Ryan had never worked with anyone from there that he could recall. As far as he knew, the visuals came from Dream Weavers, and he'd spent at least three weeks with Yves Rousset, in charge of frames. Yet in the files, he found no mention of Yves at all. Instead, a certain Professor English's name appeared in front of two headings. One read "Barrier Reef." The other was "Doorway to Javonka." Something was not right. Reaching for the phone almost as if in a trance, he called June.

"Hi. It's Ryan. Something has come up. I have to see you tonight. Is that possible? Seven p.m. will be fine. Thanks." He hung up and then took a deep breath. What was he going to tell Maggie?

* * *

"There is no Javonka in the game. No reef either." Ryan finished telling June about his discovery and looked at her worriedly. The woman in front of him seemed paler, thinner than before. He wondered how three days could have made such a difference.

As if reading his mind, June picked a folder up off her coffee table. "I won't be around to help you figure this one out," she said. "The doctors say it's spreading faster than they can control. I told them I was finished with my treatments anyway."

"I'm sorry," Ryan said inanely.

"I agreed to see you tonight because I've been thinking," June said. "I've been looking at it from all angles, and I'm sure now how to do what I want to do, which is why I need you."

"What do you want to do?"

"I want to go back into the game and stay there." June looked at him as she said this, her eyes never wavering. Then she told him how it had to be done.

Ryan felt the bottom drop out of his world.

* * *

The sunrise made the whole sky look as if it was bleeding. Buildings were dipped in scarlet; it dripped from the bridges and treetops, reflecting in shiny puddles. All night it had rained. All night long, water had poured from the sky. Then sunrise came, the clouds moved away, and the world turned red.

Ryan walked for hours. He was drenched. His feet were numb. His legs hardly kept him upright. As he stepped off a curb, he slipped, staggered, and a taxi-driver nearly hit him. Slamming on his brakes, the driver managed to avoid Ryan.

He leaned out the window. "Can't you look where you're going? Stupid kid, look at yourself! You're filthy drunk!"

Ryan raised his eyes and peered at the man in the yellow cab. He had thought he'd heard it all that night. "My heart is broken," he said evenly. "I'm not the least bit drunk."

The cab driver snorted, and then sighed. "Get in," he said, reaching back and opening the door.

Ryan stared at the opened door. He shrugged and got in.

"Where to?" the driver asked.

"Any high bridge." Ryan leaned his head back on the seat and closed his eyes. His face felt fragile, as if the bones were made of glass.

"What's she like?" the cab driver asked, after they had been driving aimlessly for fifteen minutes in silence.

Ryan smiled into the rear-view mirror. "She has long legs, and small hands. You think she's shy, because her hair sweeps in front of her face, but she looks at everything head-on. She has green eyes that sparkle even when she's sad, and she knows how to make you feel as if you're stronger and wiser than she is, even if you're not, really." He stared out the window and watched dawn breaking over the river. The park was waterlogged. Swings and teeter-totters stood knee-deep in puddles. Trees were shiny with wet, and as he watched, a couple of ducks lifted off the grass, flapping their wings, heading back towards the river. When he closed his eyes tears rolled down his cheeks. "I hardly know her at all."

The two men were silent a while. The taxi driver took the winding road through the park, the one that ran next to the river. Spring flowers, revived by the rain and watery sunrise, poked yellow and white blossoms out of carpets made of soggy leaves. A woman in a pink raincoat walked a Dalmatian. Two joggers in bright raingear trotted along the pavement, sneakers splashing in puddles. The sun sparkled off everything now, dewdrops looking like diamonds. Ryan blinked. The dazzle hurt his eyes.

"Where to, son?" The cab driver's voice was kind.

"Eighty-seventh Street and First." Ryan rubbed his face. Maybe Sissy could cheer him up.

The cab driver refused his offer to pay, and drove off before Ryan could insist. The sun flashed off the rear window, a bright farewell, and Ryan greeted Stanley, the doorman.

"Going up to see your aunt?" Stanley asked. He asked that every time.

Ryan always said yes, but sometimes he wondered what would happen if he said no. Today he just nodded, waved faintly, and took the elevator up to his aunt's floor, noticing as he did that he was dripping onto the carpet.

His shoes sloshed as he walked, and when he reached out to buzz the door, he saw that his hands were wrinkled from the wet. He stood there, looking at his feet, until strong hands took his arms and pulled him inside, and a warm voice spoke to him, but he didn't hear anything.

"Ryan!" His aunt's voice woke him from a sound sleep. He found himself on her sofa, tucked in a warm, flannel blanket, with Sissy sitting near his head. The chimpanzee's fingers were tickling[kww4] his ears, and he smelled toast and oranges.

He sat up, discovered he was naked, and frowned. He looked at his aunt. "Where are my clothes?"

"In the dryer, dear." His aunt put a tray down on the low table in front of the sofa. "Why don't you eat something?"

He yawned. "What time is it?"

"Eleven-thirty." His aunt sat down on the sofa facing him. "Ryan, are you all right?"

"No." He smiled faintly at his aunt, then reached for some toast and crunched it, sharing with Sissy automatically, one bite for him, one bite for her, as he'd done since he was a child. The orange was divided up the same way. He sipped coffee, while Sissy drank a glass of milk. They both had napkins on their laps. Sissy picked up every single crumb that fell, though; she didn't really need the napkin.

His aunt didn't press him. She poured herself a cup of coffee and waited.

"That was wonderful." Ryan tried to smile, but it wobbled across his face and he ended up looking forlorn.

"Is it the young lady you told me about?" Aunt Ree spoke quietly.

Ryan trusted few people as much as he trusted his aunt. Even so, he hesitated. He took Sissy's hand and held it tightly. The grizzled chimpanzee patted his shoulder and then hugged him. In Sissy's arms, Ryan felt suddenly peaceful. He snuggled into her chest, letting her rest her chin on the top of his head as when he was little. He took a deep breath.

"June is dying." He stopped for a second, letting the words echo a bit. He didn't look at Ree's face. He stared at Sissy's furry arm, noticing all the gray hair now mixed with the black. "She has cancer in its terminal stage. Nothing can be done; they can postpone it for a while, but that would mean she would suffer. For now, she hardly realizes she's ill."

Now he glanced at his aunt. Her face was still, but there were tears in her eyes. "I'm sorry."

He nodded. "Me too." He drew a shaky breath. "There's something else. Right now, we're developing a new game at Carver Corporation. It's called—well, it's not important. What's important is the fact that we seem to have opened a doorway into another world. It sounds mad, but I swear it's true. Somehow, there's a breach and we went through it."

"A breach?" Ree's hand reached to her throat. At that moment, the doorbell rang. "I'll get it," she said faintly, and stood up. She looked at Ryan and frowned. "Were you expecting anyone?"

He shook his head, as the bell rang again.

"Who is it?" asked Ree, looking through the peephole. She turned to Ryan. "It's a young woman!"

Ryan's heart leapt, only to crash to splinters as Aunt Ree opened the door and let Maggie step in. "What are you doing here?" he asked harshly.

Maggie stood hesitantly in the doorway, then looked at Ree. "Come in," said Ree, looking sharply at Ryan.

"My name's Maggie Verano." Maggie stuck her hand out awkwardly and shook Ree's hand. She looked flustered, and then she saw Sissy. She froze. Her whole face seemed to contract, and to Ryan and Ree's astonishment, she burst into tears.

"Now, now," Ree said, patting her back and leading her to the couch. "What is it, dear? Can I get you some coffee? Ryan, where are your manners?"

Ryan rose off the couch, then suddenly remembered he was nude and dove back under the blanket. Sissy seemed to think this was hilarious, and gave a shrieking chimp laugh, which only made Maggie cry harder. She buried her face in her hands and sobbed.

Ryan looked at Ree and mimed confusion. He shrugged and shook his head, all the while shooting irritated glances at Maggie's heaving shoulders. His aunt threw up her hands and said, "Your clothes are in the laundry room, they should be dry by now. Just open the dryer, it will stop automatically."

Ryan wrapped the blanket around his hips and stood up. He hesitated a moment in front of Maggie, but she wouldn't look at him; she kept her face buried in her hands, and he went to get his clothes.

"Women!" he said, his voice breaking in the middle of the word. He took his warm clothes and put them on, holding his shirt next to his cheek for a moment, eyes closed, with the smell and warmth reminding him of his childhood. Visions of himself as a child flashed in his mind. Sitting in the laundry room in the plastic basket while Ree ironed, putting the basket over his head and hiding under it, pretending he was an animal in a cage. He always stopped when he thought of Sissy in her cage, though. When he was little, his aunt often took him to her laboratory and he would sit on a high stool and watch as the chimpanzees were tested. Sissy was always his favorite because Sissy had carried him around the lab and around Aunt Ree's apartment when he was a baby. Even now, he could remember the strong arms holding him tightly. Aunt Ree had told one horrified woman, "Chimps are stronger and more agile than humans. Sissy won't drop Ryan." In his mind he saw his aunt Ree sitting at her desk, not even looking up as the woman protested about the chimp holding him.

It was funny, but he'd never realized before that Maggie reminded him of his aunt Ree. Seeing them together had made him realize they shared a lot of the same qualities. Both were single-minded career women, both had freckles and crooked smiles. He gave another sigh. Maggie had taken his mind off June; that was another point in her favor.

Ryan pulled on his shirt, pants, and sweater, and walked over to Maggie. She was sitting on the couch, sipping coffee, looking as if she was just about to have another crying fit.

"What was that about?" he asked her.

She turned red-rimmed eyes in his direction and said, "I heard what you always say to Harry."

"To Harry?"

"You said you'd rather date your aunt's chimpanzee than take me out!" Her voice was raw, her eyes wet and furious.

Ryan was too wise to answer that one. Besides, he was a bit embarrassed. He'd said that each time Harry (or anyone else) jokingly asked him if he was interested in Maggie. Not a surprising question—they were the only two single people on the team. Instead, he leaned over and snagged his cup of coffee. He sipped it, and then said, "Why are you here, Maggie?"

"I didn't think you were serious. I thought it was just a joke. But no, your aunt really does have a chimpanzee, and you were quite serious, weren't you? You really do detest me. Why? What did I ever do to you?" She tried to keep her voice level, but it wavered, and then broke. More tears flew out of her eyes.

Ryan watched, fascinated. He'd never seen tears pop out so quickly. Usually they seeped, or trickled. Maggie's tears hardly seemed to touch her freckled cheeks; they shot out of the corners of her eyes like raindrops. "I don't want to discuss that," he said, handing her a napkin. "I want to know what you're doing here." He supposed shock was keeping his own voice so calm. Shock, grief, whatever. He sounded as bloodless as a robot. "Blow your nose."

"Ryan!" Aunt Ree, on the other hand, sounded angry. "You owe Maggie an apology!"

"That's not why I'm here." Maggie sniffed furiously and wiped her face.

"I'm sorry." To Ryan's surprise, he meant it. He'd never meant to hurt Maggie.

Sissy, bored with the scene, climbed over Ryan's lap and went to investigate Maggie. She pulled a bit on Maggie's curls, and sniffed at her legs.

Ryan waited for the inevitable protests, flinching, squeaking, or gasping that usually accompanied Sissy's investigations. However, Maggie simply waited until Sissy finished examining her. Then she reached down and tickled Sissy behind her ear. Sissy gave a little grunt of delight, and clambered onto the couch next to Maggie, laying her head on her lap and raising her arms in an invitation to tickle.

Ryan felt oddly annoyed. Sissy was supposed to be on his side, wasn't she? There she was with her arms held over her head, her chin raised, while Maggie stroked her chest and dripped tears onto her fur. He folded his arms across his chest. "Well?" he snapped. Immediately feeling churlish, he cleared his throat and softened his tone. "I mean, what did you want to tell me?"

Maggie rubbed her face dry. She did it like a child, smearing tears across hot cheeks, pushing tangled hair behind her ears. She folded her arms across her chest and said, "There is something strange going on with the program."

Ryan snorted. "Oh, you mean, more strange than a door into another dimension suddenly opening up and a whole new world appearing?"

"I'm sorry about June," said Maggie. "I wish I could do something for her."

"You can't," Ryan replied, but he was touched by her sincerity.

Maggie sighed. "Maxwell Santiago Carver has put a seal on the door."

"What?"

"He won't let anyone in."

Ryan frowned. "Did you ask anyone what was happening?"

"I asked President Wrain what was going on, and she replied that she didn't know. She also said," Maggie's voice broke. "She also said…"

"Said what?"

"That I was fired." She leaned over Sissy and sobbed.

"Fired?"

"Fired!" Maggie looked at him furiously. "Why did you have to go and report me? Why?"

Ryan shook his head. "I didn't have anything to do with this. I made no complaints, wrote no report…" His voice trailed off and he tapped a finger against his coffee cup. A deep silence grew in the room while he thought of the repercussions of Maggie's words. "Did anyone see you go into the building?" he asked.

"No. I swear, no one was there when I arrived, and I left all the lights off to make sure nobody saw me."

"I'll call President Wrain and see if I can straighten this out." Ryan stood up and bent to kiss his aunt Ree. "I'm going back to my apartment. Thanks for breakfast." He hesitated, then touched Maggie lightly on the cheek and let himself out. When he glanced back, he saw his aunt sit next to Maggie. Maggie was crying again, and Sissy had fallen asleep.

* * *

Ryan took the downtown bus and got off in front of his building. Instead of going inside, he turned and walked the ten blocks uptown to the Carver Industry office building where Maxwell Santiago Carver's profile seemed to be staring at a cheeky blonde on a billboard advertising soda.

Milton, the doorman, let him in.

"Hi Milt," said Ryan.

"Busy morning," Milton replied, keys jangling as he locked the door again.

Ryan stopped and turned. "Who else is here?" he asked.

"Mr. Carver himself, I let him in two hours ago, and President Wrain just left."

Ryan thought about this. He glanced at the elevator, then at the front desk. "Can I use the desk phone a second?" he asked.

"Local call?"

"Of course."

"Go ahead." Milton shrugged. "Be my guest. I'll just sit down if you don't mind now."

"Sure." Ryan dialed June's number. When she answered he said, "Something has come up. It's now or never."

"You must be at the office." June's voice was faint.

"Are you all right?"

"Now or never sounds like something Carver would spout, not you, Ryan."

"June, you know what I mean."

"I know." She paused. Her breathing slowed. "Thank you, Ryan."

He hung up, bit his lip, then dialed again. "Aunt Ree? I need you." He paused. "It's got to happen as soon as possible. Right now. Will you come?" He nodded at her response and replaced the receiver as slowly as if it were made of fine crystal.

"Everything all right?" called Milton from his post at the door.

"Yeah. Everything." He rubbed his face. It felt numb. "Oh Milton—I'm expecting two visitors. Ms. Houston, you remember her, don't you, and Ms. Ree, my aunt. When they get here would you please show them straight to my office?"

Milton gave a salute. "Sure thing, Ryan."

The elevator seemed to take forever. The hallway was suddenly five miles long. He pushed his office door open, and sat down in his chair. After a minute, he stood up again and took off his coat. He could do nothing now except wait. He slumped over his desk, his face in his hands. Then he looked up at his ceiling and frowned. Milton said Santiago Carver was in the building. What was he doing?

He gazed upwards, his brows drawn together in thought. Santiago Carver had been ill for several months last year. Rumors flew about, some said he was dying. Mr. Carver had denied everything. He'd given a dinner for his employees. He'd stood up and addressed them all. What had he said? He'd spoken about the new game they would be developing; the one called "Cyber Jack to the Rescue." The name had changed, of course. That had just been a working title. Now it was "Cyber Jack, Super Spy." But he'd said something else. Ryan put his head in his hands. He could picture the old man standing behind the lectern, cane in hand, his strange, globular eyes staring at his employees. What were his exact words?

"We're creating a new world, and I want it to be perfect. I want it to be something you would like to escape into and stay forever."

At the time, the speech didn't seem too different from those he'd used for his other games. However, he'd never used the words "escaped into and stay forever" before, at least not while Ryan had been listening.

He glanced at the clock. Time. There was no stopping it, was there? You were born, you lived, and then you died. The way it was supposed to be. Where was Santiago Carver planning on going? He had to find out. He picked up his telephone. "I'd like to make a person to person call to Switzerland," he said, glancing at a note he'd scrawled on a yellow paper. "Professor English, please. Specu-Ace, yes, that's right." His conversation was short, yet when he hung up, he had to lean very hard on his desk before he could stand up.

He left a note on his desk. "June - Ree - I'm in the Game Room. M." Then he shut the door quietly behind him.

The walk down the hallway seemed endless. Each door was sinister, somehow. He imagined opening them one after another and seeing something besides empty offices. He imagined a tropical paradise behind one door, a winter wonderland behind the next. What would happen if man created worlds into which you could step in and out? What laws would govern them? Were the people living there real, or were they creations? What would happen to the world if the game cube were destroyed? Ryan walked faster.

In front of the Game Room, he hesitated. A new sign hung on the door. It was bright red and had a large exclamation point in the end. It said "Access Strictly Denied!" However, the door was slightly ajar, as if someone had entered in a hurry and neglected to close it. Using his index finger, he opened the door and peered in. Behind the glass wall separating the controller's desk from the sending room were two chairs. In one, lying as still as an alabaster statue, was Maxwell Santiago Carver.

Ryan's feet made no noise on the thick carpet. Quietly, he padded over and stood next to the man supine on the leather chair. A small, black silk mask hid his eyes and bright filaments of wire glittered, connecting him to the Machine. It hummed faintly, and green lines humped up and down on the screen. His hands clutched the arms of the chair; they were gloved in the silvery, fine-mesh gloves and looked alien, as if they didn't belong to the old man's body.

Ryan examined him for a minute. Usually you weren't connected physically with the wires. They were hidden in the gloves. Maxwell had pulled them out, though, and attached them to the console. Now his heartbeat and breathing showed up on a screen. According to the console, he hadn't entered the game yet. He must have just pressed the switch. He still had time.

"Just what do you think you're doing?"

The voice behind him made Ryan jump. He whirled around, finding himself face to face with the president of the company.

"Mrs. Wrain!" he stammered. "I thought you'd left. I mean, hello, how are you?"

"I asked you what you were doing."

Ryan shrugged. "I left a folder here, and came to get it. On my way down the hall, I noticed the door was open." He feigned confusion. "Why is Mr. Carver plugged into the new game? He knows it hasn't been de-bugged."

Lucille Wrain didn't answer. She had her eyes riveted on the green lines. They were flashing now.

"Ms. Wrain?" Ryan prompted.

"I think you had better leave, now." She said. She wrenched her gaze from the screen. "I'll take care of this."

"What did he ask you to do?" Ryan asked. He sat down on the free chair. He got no response, only a perceptive tightening in Ms. Wrain's posture. Her hand crept towards her purse. She dipped it in, and came out with her wooden hammer. Ryan's heart stopped beating.

"You can't destroy the gel-cube until he's completely out of the game, you know that." Ryan managed to keep his voice level. "Whatever he told you, if you smash the cube while he's still connected, he'll be trapped somewhere in-between. He won't be in that world, and he won't be here. You'll leave him in a vegetable state if that happens."

Lucille Wrain turned to him, her mouth open in a soundless 'O.'

Ryan heard footsteps in the hallway. "What is he suffering from?" he asked gently.

"Only arthritis and advanced old age," she answered. Her voice was a whisper. "I didn't believe him. I was going to break the cube, and then take him out to lunch. We could have laughed about it later."

"What did he tell you? Hurry!"

"He said he'd created another world. He said he'd found a way to live forever. I thought it was just one of his stories. He has so many, you know."

"They are not stories," hissed Ryan. "They're clichés. He didn't create anything. It was an accident."

"I don't know what you're talking about."

"I'm talking about Professor English of Specu-Ace, a physics company based in Switzerland. Did you know they were working on something called molecular distances? Did you know that this game cube," he motioned towards the gel-crystal set in the console, "holds the key to a different world than ours, in a different time-scale?"

Lucile Wrain shook her head. "Specu-Ace? It's not possible."

"I called Professor English this morning. He confirmed my theory. He's been working on creating a world within a world. He thought that if he could adjust the space between the molecules he would be able to place a whole new program in that space that would run on a slightly different time-scale than ours."

"He succeeded!"

"No," Ryan said tiredly. "What happened was a fluke. He didn't create anything, he simply discovered a passageway. It's not the same thing. The rules of physics explain it better than I can. Matter cannot be created or destroyed. The world this game leads to is simply a parallel world. The only thing separating it from ours is time - molecular time. Professor English was very precise. He said something else. Mass will even itself out. If a certain mass goes there and tries to stay, the same amount of mass must come back here. Do you understand what I'm saying?"

Ms. Wrain shook her head. "I'm not a scientist, or even a computer expert. I'm simply a business woman, and Maxwell is an old, decidedly foolish friend. Wake him up, Ryan, then we'll smash the cube."

"I can't." Ryan sat down in a chair and put his face in his hands. "It's not that simple anymore."

"Why not?"

"Look at him. He's plugged himself into the machine. My guess is that he thought that it would help keep him there when you broke the cube. We have to wait until he comes back himself."

Lucille Wrain went to Maxwell and shook him. He didn't move, so she shook harder. "Maxwell, wake up! This has gone on long enough. You're making a spectacle of yourself. Get up now!" Her last words were shouted into his ear. The man didn't move. She looked at Ryan. "Do something."

Ryan pretended to think. "If I sent someone in after him, perhaps we could convince him to return."

"I'm the one who agreed to his folly, I'll go." Lucille Wrain put her purse down and smoothed her skirt.

"It would be better if a programming expert did that."

"Maggie?"

"I was thinking more of Miss Houston."

"Can you reach her?"

"If I call her, she'll be here in minutes," promised Ryan.

"Well, what are you waiting for?"

He dialed June's number. When the recording device clicked on, he said, "Miss Houston, this is Ryan from Carver Toys. Something important has come up. Come right away." He hung up, hoping June wouldn't step in the door too quickly. Now his biggest problem was getting rid of Ms. Wrain.

"I need the records for this program. They are kept on the tenth floor, and I don't have access. It will be quicker if you go get them. You know all the codes." Ryan tried to look occupied with a useless bit of wire. "I'll be busy getting the sending chair ready for Miss Houston."

The president of Carver Toys looked undecided. She wasn't used to receiving any type of order, no matter how politely it was couched. A faint moan from Maxwell seemed to jar her, though. "I'll go right away," she declared. She opened the door and collided with June.

Stunned, Ms. Wrain turned to Ryan, her mouth gaping.

He gave a crooked grin. "It was good of you to come so promptly, Miss Houston."

June was very pale. She was dressed in an antique lace dress. It was faded yellow, and fold lines still showed clearly, as if it had just been lifted out of a trunk. Her hair was pulled into a loose chignon with a white rose tucked into the side. She wore two necklaces, there were rings on almost all her fingers, and a heavy gold bracelet made her wrist look ridiculously thin. She stepped past Ms. Wrain, hardly glancing at her. "I came as quickly as I could."

"You were in a taxi, right? Just in front of the building. On your way to a party?" Lucille Wrain's voice rose. She looked from Ryan back to June. "Was that what happened?"

June didn't look at her. "Yes," she said. "I'm ready." Her voice was as colorless as her face.

"Before you go..." Ryan stopped and cleared his throat. He frowned. "Before you go, I have to tell you that I spoke to the man who created this program."

June stiffened. "And?"

"Whatever mass goes to stay will come back here. Not necessarily the same matter, but the same mass. That's important. Are you following me?"

June was silent for a moment. Then she nodded once. "I understand."

"You must get it exactly right. Will someone there be able to help you?"

"What's this all about?" Ms. Wrain's voice was strident.

"I need the records," said Ryan. "Please go get them now."

"What about Maxwell?" she asked.

"Miss Houston will go after him now."

Ms. Wrain raised her hands in a gesture of surrender. "All right, I'm leaving. Don't do anything until I get back. That's an order. Your job is on the line, Ryan."

Ryan's eyes bore into June's. "My whole life is on the line," he said evenly.

There came an exasperated sigh from the president, then the sound of the door shutting.

"I'm sorry," whispered June.

Ryan drew a shaky breath. "I want to kiss you good-bye."

June shook her head. "Don't make it harder still."

"It can't get any worse." Ryan took her arm and drew her to him. He held her gently, feeling the tremors running through her body. "I can't believe you're leaving," he said. "I saw you, and…"

"Shhh." June tilted her head back. He saw tears in her eyes. "I'm so scared," she said.

"I promise, you won't feel a thing." He kissed her then, letting his lips rest on hers, the soft curve of her mouth imprinting on his. He closed his eyes, concentrating his whole being on the feeling of her lips on his.

She kissed him back, for a minute she relaxed in his arms. Then she gently broke loose, stepped back and looked at the empty chair. "When is your aunt coming?"

"She'll be here any second."

They waited in silence. Ryan held June, and she rested her head against his chest. He felt as if he were holding a butterfly, or something else incredibly fragile. Her bones moved beneath his hands, he felt her skin quivering and he kissed her temple. The door opened.

Ree was carrying a small, black case. Maggie stood behind her, a defiant expression on her face.

"We came as quickly as possible."

Ryan shivered. Ree was using the same voice she used to use when he was small, and very ill. Once, he'd nearly died of pneumonia. Between bouts of delirium and fever, he'd held onto Ree's hand and begged for stories. She'd rubbed his aching back and talked to him in the softest voice imaginable.

"Lock the door," Ryan said to Maggie. "And don't let anyone in, not even if it's the president of Carver Company herself, do you understand?" He spoke with his chin on June's shoulder, holding her tightly. His voice cracked.

"I understand. I won't let anyone in, I promise." Maggie bit her bottom lip and nodded. Tears started running down her cheeks. "I'm so sorry," she said.

Ryan didn't know if she was speaking to him or to June, but he didn't care. His heart was breaking. He let her go slowly, stepping back, finally, breathing hard, as if he had just run.

June turned to his aunt. "You must be Mrs. Ree," she said. "Thank you for coming."

Ree opened her black bag. "Are you sure this is what you want?"

June nodded.

"Lie down, push your sleeve up." Ree's voice was still soft. Chills ran up and down Ryan's back.

"Do you want me to hold your hand?" he asked.

"No. Don't make it harder on yourself." June looked at him and her smile was very sad. "I didn't want to hurt anyone, Ryan. I'm sorry, I hope you understand."

Ryan understood. But he stood rooted and watched while she slipped the small mask over her eyes and pulled the gloves on. Then she lay back and reached for the game switch. Her mouth trembled. "Good-bye," she whispered.

Ree waited for Ryan's signal. Then she inserted a needle into June's arm.

Outside, there came the sound of someone pounding on the door.

* * *

June watched the glowing pinprick grow brighter. It was like being reborn, she thought. The world appeared in a rush, swallowing her and casting her into the light.

A soft breeze tugged at her hair. Copper-colored tendrils escaped from her chignon and blew around her cheeks. June picked up the skirt of her great-grandmother's wedding dress and stepped into the sunshine. On the dock, as if waiting for her, was Jack wearing a Hawaiian print shirt and cut-off denim shorts sitting so low on slim hips they looked as if they would slide right off. He saw her, and his whole face broke into a wide smile. He waved, and leapt over a mooring rope. In five strides he was at her side, and he took her hands. He looked her up and down. "What kind of a dress is that?" he asked, cocking his head.

"My swim suit," said June.

"Are you here to stay?" He grinned like a child, shaking his head, holding her hands so tightly it was almost painful.

"I think so. We have a problem, though." He listened while she told him about Maxwell Santiago Carver, and Maggie's earring.

"The earring is easy; I have it in my pocket. Finding the albino won't be hard. He wants to go fishing with Eddy, so he'll be on his boat." Jack pulled her into his arms and hugged her. "When will it happen?"

"As soon as we send him back."

"How can we do that?"

June lifted her arm and showed him the heavy gold bracelet. "It's not jewelry," she said. "It's a control panel. The game comes equipped with this bracelet or a watch. You can wear whichever one you want. When we find Mr. Carver, I push this little button, and it opens the com-link. I say, "Beam him up, Scotty," or something silly like that, and off he goes."

"And what about you?"

"We have to calculate my exact mass. Do you think you can do that?"

Jack looked at her and grinned. "Do you mind getting wet?"

"Let's go find Eddy first." June laughed then, and shook her head. "Eddy—that's a good one."

The boat was moored on the far dock, at the tip of the top of the letter 'E'. On deck, a brown-skinned man was busy pouring a foul-smelling mixture of rotten fish and blood from a jar into a plastic bucket. There were fishing poles lined up along one side of the boat, and the scent of kerosene was as overpowering as the bait smell. The brown-skinned man glanced at June, and nearly dropped the jar.

"You must be Eddy." She smiled.

"Hello." He straightened up and put the jar at his feet. He took a towel from a deck chair and wiped his hands. "What kind of a dress is that? Are you going on a fishing trip in that outfit?" he asked, not taking his eyes from her.

Jack gave a delighted laugh. "No, she's going swimming. Now, where is your client?"

"Down below smearing sun-block on his skin. I told him to get a hat and sunglasses too, and he'd better wear some protective clothing." He lowered his voice and said to Jack and June, "I ain't never seen someone with such fairy-white skin. Sheesh, it looks like he crawled out of a cave."

"He's not going fishing with you, I'm afraid." Jack pointed to the stairs. "Is he down there?"

Eddy nodded. "Something I should know about going on?"

June looked at Jack. She held her breath. His grin was wide and carefree. "No," he said, "he has business elsewhere, that's all."

Eddy shrugged. "All this chum bait going to waste. Seems a pity."

"Freeze it." Jack was practical. He leapt lightly on board and held his hands out to June. "My lady," he said, giving a bow.

She stepped carefully on deck, holding her skirts well out of the way of the bucket. With a shy wave at Eddy, she stepped into the dark cabin, and bending over so as not to knock her head, went down the small flight of stairs leading below deck. Jack followed her.

She knocked on the heavy door, then when bid to, opened it. She thought perhaps Maxwell wouldn't recognize her, but she was mistaken. Sun-block spilled as he backed up against the wall.

"What are you doing here?" he asked. His voice was high-pitched.

"I'm sorry, Mr. Carver. You have to go back." June spoke firmly, and started to raise the heavy gold bracelet to her lips.

"No!" he screeched. "I won't go back! Look at me! Look! I can stand up straight here! I can move without pain. There's no arthritis here at all, in this world! I can live another ten, fifteen years!"

"I know you," said Jack, frowning at the memory. "You were here a few days ago at night with Maggie. I saw you, but you disappeared."

Maxwell stared at Jack. He licked his lips. "Stay away from me, both of you. I won't go back, and you can't make me." He stooped and grabbed something off the floor. It was his cane. Brandishing it, he said, "Get back, go away. I'm staying here."

June spoke into the bracelet. "Take him back now, Ryan. All you have to do is unplug the electrode on his right temple. Leave the mask and the gloves on."

Maxwell gave a strangled scream and leapt at her, bringing the walking-cane down with wicked force.

"No!" Jack grabbed at the ebony stick just as June dodged. It struck Jack on the forearm, and bone crunched horribly. Jack gave a hoarse cry, but tried gamely to hold onto the cane. He wrestled for a moment with Maxwell but the older man was strong, and Jack's arm was shattered. In a flash, he wrested the cane from Jack and struck him across the shoulders twice, knocking him to the floor.

"I won't go!" he screamed, and lunged at June. He crushed her against the wall and pried her bracelet off her wrist. "Give that to me!" he said. She struggled but was no match for the heavier man. He shoved her roughly and she fell to the side, hitting her head on the wall. She was stunned, and watched helplessly as Maxwell raise his cane to hit her. She tried to roll aside, but the cane came down upon her back. The pain blinded her; she thought she would faint. It hurt too much to scream even, she could hardly take a breath.

Galvanized by rage, Jack stood up and grabbed the cane. "Leave her alone."

Maxwell whirled around and leapt at him. "You're the ones going back!" he cried in triumph, and he pressed the button on the bracelet.

Jack lunged at him, grabbing at the bracelet. Then he gave a sharp cry as his hands suddenly slid into Maxwell Santiago Carver as if into butter. He let go, his face turning chalk-white, as the walking cane flew halfway through Maxwell's rapidly fading image. An explosion of scarlet seemed to freeze in the air. Maxwell screamed but the sound was chopped off as if someone punched the volume.

Horrified, Jack and June watched as the man disappeared completely. A blue flash blinded them, and there came a loud whoosh, then the air seemed to go all quiet.

"The cane," whispered June. She thought she was going to be ill. Then her whole body stiffened. "The bracelet. Jack! Did you get it?"

He didn't answer. He opened his hand and the bracelet fell to the floor. Then he leaned over and was sick. He trembled violently, holding his broken arm cradled next to his chest He rested on his knees, hardly daring to breathe. Each movement rubbed the broken ends of his bones together. He raised his head and tried to grin. "You'll have to ask Eddy to help you. He has a tub on deck, we'll use that."

"What will we send back?" June knelt by Jack and gently took his arm. "Here, let me help." She tore her dress and bound his arm as tightly as he could bear to his chest.

"Eddy did say he hated to waste his bait, didn't he? Hey, don't tear your swim suit."

June bit her lip. "Don't worry about it. Let's get you to the hospital first."

"No, we have no time. You'll be pulled back when the door closes, as soon as they destroy the cube. We have to hurry." He looked at her and with his good hand, shakily smoothed her hair back. "Are you dead yet, there?"

She hesitated. A shiver ran up her spine. "Not yet, I don't think. They have to wait until…"

"Until what?"

"I'm not sure; all this talk about matter doesn't make sense. My body is here, and yet, it is there at the same time."

"It's not exactly you, though, is it?"

"It's me separated from myself by a few nanoseconds." June closed her eyes. "We have to hurry; I feel my bones starting to ache."

He shuddered. "You can't go back," he said. "I won't let you go."

"I won't leave you." She felt a great weight lift from her. At once she felt both incredibly light and fragile, and terribly strong. "I want to stay. I love you, Jack."

He smiled then, his beautiful, wide smile, and said, "I'm glad." Then he tried to stand up and nearly fainted.

"Lean on me." June held him upright, and they made their way onto the top deck. Eddy was standing on the pier, coiling a rope in hands, whistling. Without looking at them, he called out, "Where's the white guy?"

"Gone," said Jack succinctly. "You must have just missed him."

Eddy took his dark glasses off and looked at Jack. "What the... What happened, man?" He tossed the rope away and jumped on board. Taking Jack ever so gently by the shoulder he lowered him onto a seat. "Shit, it looks bad," he said, examining the arm in the makeshift sling. "Hold on, I've got my portable. I'm calling Doc."

"Wait. First, we have to fill your bait tub." Eddy wanted to argue, but Jack's eyes were pleading. "Please?" he said.

The tub was filled with water. June sat in it, slipping all the way under the water, and Eddy carefully drew a line level at the top of the water. "What the hell is this about?" he kept on asking.

June stepped out of the tub and stood next to Jack. Her heart was thumping so hard she thought it would break through her chest. She kept glancing at her hands; she expected to see them turning transparent. Despite the heat, she shivered.

"How many buckets does that make?" she asked Eddy, who was busy adding water to make up the difference.

"Hold on. Eight, nine, ten, eleven, twelve." He put the bucket down and wiped his forehead. "Now what?"

"Where should we put it?" Jack asked June.

"Anywhere, I guess. All I have to do is put the bracelet into it, and hope for the best. Oh, and don't forget the earring."

"Are you scared?"

June looked at him, her eyes immense. "God, yes," she whispered.

June watched while Eddy poured the rest of his chum bait into the tub, filling it to the line he'd drawn. Then she took the bracelet and carefully pressed the button. "I'm ready. Good-bye, Ryan, and thank you." Then she tossed the bracelet into the tub.

She waited. A strange feeling grew in her bones, as if they were vibrating subtly. She sat down, resting her head on Jack's knee. "Hold me."

With his good arm, he encircled her slender shoulders. Her copper hair was wet and dripped down his bare leg. She was shivering violently.

Eddy peered at them, then frowned at the tub. "So, what's supposed to happen?"

"I'm supposed to die, and the tub should empty," she whispered.

"You're nuts, girl." Eddy's voice ended on a high note. "Look, my bait is disappearing!" he shrieked.

They looked. A sort of mist formed inside the tub as everything seemed to whirl into nothing. Then June gave a strangled cry.

"What is it?" asked Jack, panicked.

She put her hands to her head and then started to laugh. "My hair, my hair is shorter. We must have been off by a few grams. It was probably the scrap of cloth around your arm." Jack slumped over her, his face in the back of her neck. She felt hot tears on her skin, and she twisted around. Taking his face in her hands, she kissed him. "It's over, Jack. I'm here to stay." With her thumbs, she wiped his tears away. "Don't cry, please."

"I'm so glad." He tried to stop crying, but couldn't. "Can you call Doc now? I could use a shot of something strong. Eddy? Eddy, can you call him?"

"He fainted," said June, reaching for the portable phone. "Give me his number, I'll call him."

While she waited for Doc, June sat between Jack's legs, her head resting in his lap. His hand tangled in her hair, they didn't speak. She just wanted to feel him next to her, feel his hands on her head, hear his soft breathing. She ran her hand up his calf. Suddenly, she felt very shy.

"I love you," said Jack. His voice was very low.

June faced him. Her eyes were very bright. "I know," she said. "That's why I came back. I didn't come back just to save myself, I want you to know that."

"I do know it," he said. "I feel as if I've known you forever, as if you were meant to be with me."

She reached up and traced a line from his forehead to his jaw with one finger. "I was meant to be with you," she echoed. "Otherwise all the bait in the world, and all the control bracelets invented, wouldn't have left me here. It's not matter that matters; it's what's in the heart. That's what really matters." She paused. "This is my wedding dress, you know."

Jack's smile was blinding. "I was hoping you'd say that."

* * *

Maggie screamed once when the body on the chair suddenly jerked, then seemed to implode. With the sound of ripping cloth, Maxwell's ribs shot out of his skin, opening like the jaws of some monstrous creature. With a whir, the cane lying on the floor flew through the air, narrowly missing Ryan's head, and sank into Maxwell's stomach. Blood rose in a fountain. It made a horrible noise, like someone sucking on a straw, and the scarlet stream reversed itself, falling with a resounding splash on the supine figure while the rib bones clamped shut around the ebony cane, locking it in place.

Ryan stood transfixed, holding a thin wire. One end was still attached to the console. The other end was connected to an electrode he'd removed from Maxwell's temple. Finally, he said, "Jesus."

Harsh noises came from the doorway. Maggie stood there, her hands pressed to her mouth, little gasps and screams bursting from between her fingers.

"It's all right." Ryan took a step towards Maggie, then turned. June was still lying peacefully on her chair. He licked dry lips. "Aunt Ree? What do you think happened?"

The older woman shook her head. "I don't want to know." She turned away from the sight. Her face was gray, but her hands, holding the syringe and a bottle of clear liquid, were steady. "Try to calm Maggie, will you?"

Ryan didn't want to leave June, but he nodded and went to Maggie, crouching at her side. "Are you all right?" he asked softly.

Behind them came the sounds of fists banging on the door. Ms. Wrain shrieked. "I'm going to get the security guard to let me in. I want you to know that you're all fired! I'll be right back!" They heard her heels tapping a furious staccato on the marble floor as she went to fetch someone with a key.

"Maggie, it's all right," said Ryan, although he knew, and she knew, that nothing was right.

Her hands reached for him, clutched him, and wouldn't let him go. He gathered her in his arms. She sobbed like a baby.

Part of him was thinking about the blood, and the dead man lying in the room behind the glass wall. Another part of him was drifting—surprised—along another path of thought. Maggie smelled like sun on fresh clover and like lavender-scented powder, and the tang of fright that he could practically taste. Her hair, so fine, ash-brown and curly, tickled his face. Her body shook in his arms, but it wasn't an unpleasant sensation. He rocked slowly, holding her tight, crooning soft nonsense in her ear until she stopped hiccupping, and sniffed once or twice, loudly, then relaxed against his chest.

"Ryan," called his aunt.

He got to his feet, and led Maggie to the console where June lay.

A faint buzz sounded, then June's voice came over the intercom. "I'm ready. Good-bye Ryan, and thank you." Her mouth didn't move. It wasn't this body talking. This was already a wax figure. June was gone. His aunt pressed the plunger, then drew the needle from the still arm. The form on the chair let out a faint sigh, then she wavered and was still. Slowly, the face beneath the silken mask turned grayish blue. Ree looked up at Ryan and Maggie. "She's gone."

Ryan swallowed very hard, hardly daring to breathe. A knot drew tight around his heart. He stared at June's face, until Maggie tugged at his arm and led him away.

"What is going on?" The door burst open, Lucille Wrain marched in, stopped, and screamed. A hole suddenly opened in the air above her head and a shower of fish guts, rotten fish, blood and sea-water fell on her. A heavy gold bracelet thumped to the floor beside her.

A horrible odor filled the room.

"My earring!" cried Maggie, and she stooped to pick up something that glittered from the floor.

Ryan took his aunt's arm, and the three of them picked their way cautiously past the sputtering president and gaping security guard.

"There are two bodies in the game room," said Ryan, pausing by the doorway. "The president had an accident while returning to this world. I think Professor English can explain to the police how it happened. Miss Houston died of a heart attack. We could do nothing to save her. I'll be back tomorrow to clear out my office, and if you need to reach me this evening, I'll be at my aunt's apartment with Miss Verano."

Maggie gave a start at that, but said nothing until they were outside the building. "Are you still angry with me?" she asked in a small voice.

"Of course." Ryan found he was holding Maggie's hand, and it felt extremely comforting for some reason. "You have the ability to make me lose my temper faster than anyone I've ever met, but I'm starting to appreciate you, Miss Verano." He looked at her and smiled. "I wish you'd stop crying."

Aunt Ree gave a little snort. "That's very romantic, Ryan."

"What do you expect?" he asked, with a ghost of a grin. "I was brought up by a chimpanzee."

"One you'd rather date than me," said Maggie, but it was said with no anger, only resignation. She looked at their hands, entwined, and frowned. "Why are you holding my hand?"

"I'm not sure," said Ryan, lifting it up and studying it. "It feels right." She stared at him and he felt the knot in his chest start to loosen.

To make sure, he drew her nearer and kissed her lips. The knot unwound, leaving him with an empty space that needed filling. He kissed harder, and felt her arms creeping around his neck. With a muffled sob he took her in his arms, holding on to her, clutching Maggie, his mouth fastened to hers, filling the empty spaces.

"Here's a taxi!" cried Ree, waving until the car came to a stop at the curb. "Let's go, Romeo. You can ravish your Juliet when you're alone together. In the street it attracts too many stares."

Ryan let go of Maggie long enough to get into the cab. Then he pulled her close again. She gave no resistance; she lay her head on his chest and sighed deeply.

"You're fired, you know," he said, wiping tears out of his eyes with the back of his hand. He fished in his pocket for a handkerchief and blew his nose.

"So are you," she replied.

"Don't you mind?"

"No. I was more upset at the thought of not working with you or seeing you anymore than the thought of leaving Carver Toys. I had such a crush on you. Now we can work together, maybe make our own company. Would you like that?"

Ryan gaped. "You had a crush on me?"

"Why did you think I was so obnoxious?" Maggie shook her head. "You know nothing about women, Ryan, nothing."

"I know lots about chimps," said Ryan. "Tell her, Aunt Ree."

"Ryan is an expert on chimps," said Ree, smiling suddenly.

The cab driver twisted around in the seat, looking from one to the other. His eyes widened and he grinned. "Hey, you're the heartbroken guy! Is this the gal you were crying about?"

Ryan shook his head. "No." He felt a pang, but it wasn't as sharp as before. He could picture June sitting on a white sailboat, the wind in her hair. "She left me for someone else," he said, giving a shrug.

"Left ya for someone else?" the cab driver asked, pulling into traffic.

Ryan leaned back, hugging Maggie. "That's exactly what happened," he said.

"Ah well, you can't win 'em all. Looks to me like you got things in hand though! So, where to, pal?"

Ryan wanted to answer, but Maggie's lips were on his, and he closed his eyes, settling deeper into her embrace.

"Eighty-seventh Street and First—and hurry" said Ree, looking out the window, a smile on her face.

Jennifer Macaire

Jennifer Macaire also writes books under the name of Samantha Winston. She has always been an iconoclast of sorts, willing to break everything and start anew. Rules are no exception. For her, rules in art and literature are limits, and limits can't be set on things like love, passion and imagination. Leonardo daVinci knew the human body perfectly, yet he would change the shape, and even the number of muscles in a torso or arms, to make his paintings seem more lifelike and vital.

She uses the rules of writing in order to break them, stretching the boundaries of imagination to create characters and worlds that don't fit into any mold. She takes preconceived notions about genres and shatters them. She hopes that her books will be part of your life, good friends you reach for when you need a smile, a sigh, or even a tear.

Find out more about Jennifer by visiting her website at http://www.jennifermacaire.com. You can also reach her via email at jennifermacaire@wanadoo.fr

Check out these other titles in print from Loose Id®

WHY ME?
Treva Harte

THE PRENDARIAN CHRONICLES
Doreen DeSalvo

SHE BLINDED ME WITH SCIENCE FICTION
Kally Jo Surbeck

FOR THE LOVE OF...
Kally Jo Surbeck

THE SYNDICATE: VOLUMES 1 AND 2
Jules Jones & Alex Woolgrave

STRENGTH IN NUMBERS
Rachel Bo

REBEL ANGELS 1: BORN OF THE SHADOWS
Cyndi Friberg

AVAILABLE FROM YOUR FAVORITE BOOKSELLER!
Publisher's Note: All titles published in print by Loose Id® have been previously released in e-book format.

Printed in the United States
53653LVS00002B/4-93